BanGk!

A crime caper with a slap of betrayal, the smack of
a con, and a spank of revenge.

Mark Wesley

Second Edition

For Pierrette

Acknowledgements

A few heart-felt words of thanks to my friend, mentor, and fellow author, Brian Cook who took the trouble to give the early draft a full read through. This book benefited enormously from his incisive contribution.

I troubled three other trusted and knowledgeable friends to check for typos and other errors that would otherwise have littered the pages of this work. So, thanks for reading with such enthusiasm: Bob Eastham, Barrie Mckay, and Jezz Leckenby. I'm grateful that they all spotted the spell-checked correction – 'bank suppository'!

Thanks also to our dear friend Hillary Wright. Being steeped in the mysteries of English grammar, Hillary's kind encouragement and gentle advice was a welcome and generous gift.

Any errors that remain, are, of course, entirely my own.

JAMES STACK: Ex-captain Special Forces, a tough, intelligent, risk taker, figured out that if you want to rob the Bank of England you don't go through the front door, guns blazing. You don't tunnel up through the floor either. You don't climb through windows, lower yourself on a harness, screw around with the computers, fix the security cameras, or play Twister with invisible Laser beams. You don't do any of that stuff because it won't work. That's why gold has never been stolen from the vaults of the Bank of England. They've got every angle covered.

Except one.

A Few Golden Nuggets

4,600 tonnes of gold in the Bank of England (BoE)
Value: £187 billion / $315 billion
A 24 carat bar weighs 400 fine ounces (13.4kg) 28lbs
Each bar is worth approx. £350,000 (June 2013)
80 bars per pallet
1 tonne per pallet
4 pallets to a rack
368 tonnes belong to the UK
Oldest gold bar in the vault is nearly 100 years old, deposited in 1916

Foreign Custodial Gold Held in BoE.

(By country)
Germany
Holland
Mexico
Austria
Australia
Ireland
Greece
Cyprus
India
Venezuela
Most of the old Commonwealth Countries
Many Middle East and Asian countries

Prologue

James Stack balanced precariously on the narrow wooden handrail, near the bow of the tourist boat. Only his one-handed grip on the rust encrusted steel-work of the deck above prevented him from falling overboard as the muzzle of a hand gun pushed hard into his back. The man with the gun wanted him to jump – now! Jim hesitated, but he knew he didn't have a choice.

Above him a brilliant display of fireworks lit up the night sky. In the background, the iconic shape of Tower Bridge framed the scene with its two granite towers and ornate, cast-iron superstructure – the scattered reflection of several thousand watts of floodlit illumination dancing on the surface of the dark waters of the Thames.

Inside the boat, unaware of the drama being played out on deck, a wild crowd were partying noisily to the sound of a DJ playing an old Gloria Gaynor disco classic from the seventies.

Just audible above the noise, Jim heard the distinctive metallic *snick-click* of a round being chambered. Got another mean shove of the gun into his ribs and another menacing demand to jump.

A warm evening breeze had sprung up, carrying a wisp of acrid blue exhaust from the boats engines that caught in Jim's throat. He looked around. He couldn't see Charlie, so there was no way he could delay any longer.

He'd been in the risk business all his life, but if a bookie offered odds on who would survive, he'd put his money on Gloria.

This wasn't how the plan was supposed to go. Which left just one question – how the hell did he get himself into this mess?

Take the Money and Run

Eight months earlier

The driver in the parked car was getting rattled.

His elbow rested on the sill of the open window, a half smoked cigarette hung from his mouth, lit from the cigarette butt he'd flicked onto the road outside a few moments before. He took another nervous look at his watch.

The robbery was running late and the old Volvo had been parked up on the double yellows outside the bank way too long. Only people with disabilities who display the distinctive Blue Badge Permit on their vehicles are allowed to park on double yellow lines.

In this small town, mid-day, mid-week, and late summer, the high street resembled a ghost town. Only a handful made it in: mothers driving SUVs, pensioners using the rare bus service and those whose mobility was restricted, but were still able to drive – the ones with the Blue Badge parking permits.

While he waited, one had arrived and parked in front. Shortly after, another had parked up behind him.

Only a moment ago, a female traffic warden had strolled over and signalled for him to move on. He pleaded with her that his heavily pregnant wife was in the bank and wouldn't be more than another minute.

Fortunately, in small market towns such as this, traffic wardens enlisted from the local population occasionally take a sympathetic view of such things, so she allowed him the extra time. He knew the good will was very time-limited. She could be on her way back now.

He checked in the mirror one more time. The beard worked if you didn't look too closely. The sun had finally come out and the day was warming up nicely, so the sun glasses didn't look out of place. What remained of the early morning shower, could be seen in the rapidly evaporating puddles lying here and there along the high street.

'Come on for Christ's sake,' he hissed through clenched teeth, banging his gloved hands on the wheel in frustration.

At that moment, a dark shadow engulfed the Volvo as an enormous five-axle bulk tipper truck drew noisily alongside, eclipsing the sun as it double parked next to him. Its driver, jumped down and ran across the road to a newsagent. The getaway car was now stuck between two parked cars and the DAF truck, the driver's door unable to open against a large, mud caked nearside wheel.

'What the hell...?'

He heaved himself across the seats and climbed out through the passenger door, ran out into the road and round to the driver's side of the truck. He checked the cab and up and down the main street, but the driver had vanished. His agitation increased when he looked at his watch and then at the bank. Still no sign of the other gang members, James Stack and Toni 'Zero' Zeterio.

After a moment's hesitation, he climbed up into the cab, at the same time keeping an eye out for the pain in the arse truck driver. He looked around the filth strewn cab and tentatively jiggled the gear stick while giving the other unfamiliar controls a cursory once over. The keys were still in the ignition and the engine was turning over noisily with the uneven clatter of an arthritic castanet player.

He looked up as two men rushed out of the bank. They ran straight to the getaway car but stopped dead when they noticed the huge red truck.

Hard to miss!

The driver leaned over and shouted down to them through the passenger window.

'Guys...change of bleeding plan!'

They rushed forward, clambered over the hood of their own car, pulled the cab door open, and squeezed into the passenger seat.

'Well, don't hang around. Let's go,' Jim Stack said with a profound sense of urgency.

The driver yanked and stirred the stick, before finally crunching it into first gear, causing the truck to kangaroo off, very nearly stalling. Eventually, with the knackered gear box whining and complaining, it picked up speed – lurching down the high street.

Across the road the truck driver was just leaving the newsagent with his newspaper, cigarettes, and a Snickers bar, when his pride and joy lumbered past, gears crunching and engine clattering. He made a half-hearted attempt to run after it before coming to a standstill in the middle of the road waving his newspaper and hurling bitter abuse – shocked at seeing the cause of his large bank overdraft weaving dangerously down the high street and vanishing from sight. He stomped angrily back to the pavement, took out his phone and called the police.

On the edge of town, a compact Hyundai i10 police 'Panda' car was parked up outside a parade of shops. Inside, PC Evans was enjoying a late packed lunch. Small drops of grease slid off his chin to join the other canteen medals staining his tunic as he stuffed his mouth full of his favourite savoury snack. That's when the radio crackled into life with an urgent all units shout from police HQ about the bank robbery and a stolen truck.

PC Evans threw his lunch onto the passenger seat, swallowed a mouthful of unchewed food in a painful gulp and grabbed the radio handset.

'Papa one–two. I'm in the neighbourhood. Nothing suspicious to report.'

As the words left his lips, the truck barrelled noisily past: old plastic bags and newspaper pages billowing after it in the gust of its wake.

PC Evans was a careful man, not one of life's risk takers, which made the rigors of policing an odd career choice. Now, though, his face a study of fierce determination, he jammed the accelerator hard down to the floor – the Hyundai's tiny engine at first responded with insolent indifference then grudgingly picked up speed. He gave chase while providing a running commentary to Police Control.

'Proceeding down the high street. The truck's 100 yards ahead of me,' PC Evans said, all gung-ho and dogged resolve.

He wiped his sleeve across his greasy mouth and leaned forward into the chase.

Back in the truck, Toni 'Zero' Zeterio was giving the driver, Charlie 'Hollywood' Dawson, a hard time.

'Jesus Hollywood, couldn't you find something slower?' Zero shouted in panic above the noise of the engine. He rocked back and forth, eyes wide, mentally willing the truck to go faster. Hollywood took a quick drag on his cigarette before replying.

'What was I supposed to do, call the police and complain that some sod's double parked on the high street?'

'Leave him alone Toni,' Jim commanded. 'Just drive Charlie, there's a cop following us.'

'Yeah, it's only a little panda car. What's he going to do?' Hollywood said.

'Well right now he's telling the general police population of the UK where we are,' Jim explained patronisingly.

More crunching and lurching as Hollywood tried to find a higher gear.

Back in the panda, PC Evans attempted to keep up with the lorry, seen fleetingly ahead as it charged precariously down the narrow, winding country road.

'Just passing the cemetery, heading out of town towards Mrs. Lumsden's boarding house and kennels.'

Police Control. 'I have no idea who or what that is.'

PC Evans. 'It's where we put Mavis when we go on holiday.'

'Mavis?'

'Our Cocker Spaniel.'

'Just tell us stuff we can recognise.' *Click - buzz.* Then in a slow, patient voice. 'Listen, is there a sign for a town they're heading towards?'

'They might be heading towards the M1, so they could be heading towards London.'

'London is over fifty bloody miles away.' Then in a sarcastically posh voice. 'Look, if you find a road sign that gives a clue as to where they might be going, do be sure to let us know, won't you?'

'Check. Will do,' PC Evans replied with renewed purpose as he reached for his discarded sandwich.

Back in the truck, Hollywood was pushing his driving skills to the limits.

'Yeah, the best car chase was in the French Connection. Did you see that? Bloody brilliant.

Course, it wouldn't have worked with a truck would it? Mind you, Steve McQueen was great in Bullitt. You gotta love that Ford Mustang, I mean it's bloody marvellous ain't it. But all that 'Fast and Furious' stuff, well it's all been done before hasn't it?'

His enthusiasm for the subject was endless – once he got started, Charlie 'Hollywood' Dawson could bore for Britain.

'For Christ sake, Hollywood,' Jim pleaded. 'Give it a rest and just drive.'

***

They'd set out with what seemed a novel, if perhaps simplistic, plan.

No guns. Definitely not. But the threat of violence couldn't be avoided to ensure compliance.

Jim had made an appointment to see the bank manager of a suitably remote regional bank, under the pretence of raising a business loan for a local commercial venture. For this scheme to work it was important that the manager's office was a separate private room, so some research had to be discretely undertaken.

Jim arrived at the appointed time. The manager introduced herself and invited him into her office, closed the door, and offered Jim a chair. She took her seat behind a small but stylish, glass and aluminium desk, upon which she laid out some printed material.

Jim went through the motions of raising a loan – at least to start with.

Outside, in the main bank area, Toni Zeterio was posing as just another customer waiting in line. Timing was important.

By the time he arrived at the window, the bank was empty apart from him and another customer further along the counter. The robbery began by holding a printed note flat against the glass partition for the clerk to see.

'DO NOT ACTIVATE THE ALARM. *Your manager is being held in her office. Use the phone, she will confirm this. DO IT NOW.*'

In the office, Jim steered the meeting away from the subject of temporary borrowing to a more permanent arrangement whereby the bank gives large quantities of cash to his accomplice. He told the manager to expect a phone call from one of the clerks outside and to provide the correct responses if she didn't want the clerk to come to harm. Jim's scheme relied on her choosing to play it safe rather than risk the health of her co-workers.

Meanwhile, in the front office, Toni waited for a reaction from the clerk.

Apart from a definite paling of skin colour as the blood drained from her face, she just sat there, frozen in place with her mouth open.

Toni gave her his most aggressive, threatening glare and an emphatic nudge of his head towards the phone on the shelves behind her.

That did the trick. She de-frosted, slid off her stool, went over to the phone, and did as the message directed. Her fingers trembling, she tapped out, 1...0...1, the manager's office number. Turning back to face Toni, she placed the handset to her ear and waited for her boss to answer.

It was just as the message said. The manager was being held under duress. She must not take any risks. Do exactly what they ask. She nodded her compliance to Toni and replaced the receiver.

He signalled for her to return to her place at the counter, pushed some cloth bags through the gap between the glass shield and the counter and held a second instruction against the glass.

It was a simple and rather obvious next step: *'Fill the bags with cash, QUICKLY.'*

It was then that things started to fall apart. Seeing the unusual behaviour of his colleague, the other clerk left the customer he was serving and came over to find out what was going on. The woman, stopped stuffing cash into the bag and looked up in panic, first at Toni and then at her colleague.

'Tell him,' Toni said in a threatening voice, disguised, he hoped, with a Liverpudlian accent.

He raised the first message to the glass again and gestured for the other clerk to read it, but the man just shook his head slowly and didn't move. Toni tried the threatening voice and reminded him of the danger his boss was in. But the man just stood there stubbornly and folded his arms.

Toni didn't have time to screw around. He'd already got one bag full of cash, but the clerk, stuck in a loop of conflicting messages, had stopped filling the second bag.

'Don't just stand there, keep filling the bloody bag,' he growled at her with more than a hint of John Lennon.

She started doing just that, but superhero came over, grabbed hold of the bag, pulling on it. The woman clung on, desperately trying to stuff another handful of cash into it. The man gave it another hard tug and snatched it out of her hand, loose notes floating to the floor. Stalemate. Or more truthfully, checkmate!

Time to execute the next part of the plan: Exit the building and smartish.

'Time to go, Alpha,' he shouted in the direction of the manager's office.

Jim burst out of the office, following behind Toni who was already on his way through the automatic doors to the street.

They both ran towards the getaway car – and stopped dead when they saw the truck.

***

While Charlie struggled to get more speed out of the old diesel engine, Toni Zeterio reached over and fiddled with another lever.

'What does this do, make it go faster? Is it another gear or something?' Toni asked.

'Don't know, let's give it a jiggle.'

Glancing down momentarily, he missed the road sign, warning Low Bridge Ahead and yanked the lever back.

'Nothing seems to be happening.'

'Yeah, strange. Perhaps it's broken,' agreed Zero.

In the Panda, PC Evans noticed from a distance, that the shape of the truck seemed to be changing. It was getting taller!

Unseen by the three occupants in the cab as the truck careered along, swinging wildly from side to side, the tipper body had started to rise, shredding branches from trees as it passed.

As they rounded a sharp left hand bend, Hollywood saw the old brick railway bridge, half hidden by trees, its narrow arch already far too close.

Seconds later, as the large tipper body reached its highest point, the lorry rushed through the tunnel at high speed. The elevated bodywork smashed against the side of the bridge. The impact tore the tipper body away from its hydraulic mountings, leaving it teetering up-right on the road behind them.

Perhaps not surprisingly, with all the noise the old engine was making, and the shaking and rattling of the old chassis, the truck continued through the bridge and out the other side with only a small shudder marking the end of what for some years had been a productive relationship between the truck and its cavernous load bearing partner, an event noticed inside the cab as a sudden jolt that knocked Hollywood's fag out of his mouth. He did a cursory feel around his seat and on the cab floor between his legs for the burning remnant, but found nothing.

'What the hell was that?' Zero asked.

'Don't ask me mate,' Charlie replied, adding, 'Could've been the drive shaft or something. Look at the mileage. It's already done over 245,000. It's knackered.'

'Well, something must have happened 'cause we've picked up a bit of speed for some reason.'

Jim looked through the side mirror.

'OK, I've got some good news and bad news. The bad news is we've lost the tipper bit at the back.'

'Where the hell did that go?' Charlie asked as he checked the door mirror.

And the good news?' asked Zero.

'That copper isn't following us anymore.'

Behind them, teetering precariously on its back end, the tipper body rocked tentatively for a moment before coming to rest, light as a feather, against the tunnel brickwork, the open space of its metallic void facing back down the road. A gaping mouth waiting for a victim. It didn't have long to wait.

Just seconds behind, hurtling round the sharp left hand bend, PC Evans spotted the obstruction just in time to slam on the brakes.

The vast rectangular box of the tipper body quickly filled his windscreen. PC Evans gripped the steering wheel in terror and pushed down on the brake so hard his buttock clenching backside lifted off the seat. Somehow, he managed to slow the car enough that only the last faint dregs of forward momentum were left to push the front wheels slowly up, and come to rest on the raised lip of the tipper body. PC Evans just sat there in shocked silence – barely able to breathe – his hands still holding the wheel in a white knuckled death grip.

'Jesus!' he whispered somewhat prematurely. 'That was close!'

With the bulk of the engine sitting over the front axle, the weight of the car was just enough to cause the finely balanced tipper body to straighten up and begin an arc of travel that had just one inevitable conclusion.

It slowly started to keel over – several tonnes of tortured steel, moaning mournfully down towards the little Hyundai i10.

Horrified, PC Evans instinctively raised his hands to protect himself. He ducked down into his seat, looking up wide eyed into the darkening void that was falling down upon him.

Gravity finally won the argument as, with an enormous crash of metal on tarmac, the cavernous tipper body slammed down and engulfed the police car like a clam shell – clouds of dust, dirt, and leaves billowing up.

Inside, the Panda all was dark and quiet except for static from the police radio. The dramatic change of circumstances left him stunned for a moment. His hand shook uncontrollably as he turned the headlight switch. Only one came on, its light reflected back through the fractured glass of the windscreen. He took a breath to bring his pounding heart rate under control, slowly reached for his radio handset, and clicked the transmit button.

'Hello control, this is Papa one-two, can you hear me? *Static*...Hello control, can you hear me? *Static*. I'm no longer following the lorry. *Static*... Hello?...*Static*...Hello?...*Static*..'

***

The lorry had to be dumped as soon as possible.

They'd buried it deep in a thicket just off the road, having spotted farm buildings a short way off, half hidden amongst the trees in their own small island of uncultivated meadow in the middle of rolling fields of late summer corn.

It didn't take them long to make their furtive way to the nearest barn and commandeer a handy rusting Ford Sierra. If it was insured, the owner could reclaim its value and buy a packet of fags.

The Boys are Back in Town

Later that afternoon

An hour or so later, having abandoned the Sierra in a multi storey car park, they were safely gathered in the grubby splendour of Charlie Dawson's north London residence – a grimy, two room council flat in Finsbury Park, the contents of which represented the leftovers of the bitter final settlement of his divorce from a much neglected Scottish wife a few years ago.

Charlie flicked a switch and a single 60 watt bulb fitted into a cheap flower patterned shade hanging from the centre of the ceiling, lit up to provide stark, unflattering illumination. Nothing could have flattered the contents of this room.

Threadbare carpets. A couple of shabby sofas, the longer of which had two collapsed seat cushions permanently flattened into the shape of every arse that had ever sat in them. Remotes for the TV and DVD player lay abandoned amongst the debris of newspapers and cheese snacks partially hidden under curry stained cushions.

An empty beer can and an overflowing ashtray sat on a small coffee table. The permanent rings left by tea and coffee cups adding to the patina of cigarette burns and dimples on its chipped varnish surface.

The sofa faced a wide screen HD TV that sat on a chrome and glass stand pushed into a corner of the room. To the right of that, six rows of MDF shelving fixed to the wall held the source of Hollywood's extensive cinematic knowledge. Hundreds of DVDs, some clumped together in rows of vertical soldiers while others were simply laying on top of each other in small stacks.

If there was any methodology to the order of it, it would have been beyond the labours of code breaker Alan Turing to crack it. But of course Charlie knew precisely where everything was.

Name a movie and his fingers would trace a path swiftly and confidently along a small section of shelving, pausing briefly to peck out the requested title.

A table was pushed against a radiator under a window which looked out to the north London street. Framing the window were two 1970s flower print curtains which Charlie wandered over and drew against the sodium glow of the city skyline.

Apart from the curtains, which were coming back into fashion in a kind of retro 70's chic, if he put the whole lot up for auction on eBay he'd be lucky to get the price of a pizza, which, if he did, he'd have nowhere to sit down to eat it. Jim always thought Charlie should do a Tracey Emin – call it art and give the whole lot to the Tate Modern gallery.

'Hey Charlie, I like what you've done to the place,' Toni quipped breezily as he strolled in. It was supposed to be droll, but he'd repeated it too often to be funny. Charlie ignored it, took the bag from Toni and poured the contents onto the table.

'For Christ sake, Hollywood, are you still peeing into the wind?' Jim shouted out to Charlie from the bathroom after spotting the yellow stains on the filthy carpet to the left of the toilet bowl. One of Charlie's many endearing habits.

***

A few years before, Charlie had worked as a maintenance man on North Sea oil rigs. Because he spent most of his time outside on the rig platform, rather than make his torturous way to the nearest toilet in the accommodation block, Charlie found it much more convenient to pee over the side. Thanks to the prevailing north easterly wind, he developed a habit of over compensating to the left so that the wind carried the stream to the sea below rather than back onto the platform. Something of a hit and miss skill depending on which side of the rig he was on.

He'd been unable to break the habit since returning to dry land. Finding himself possessed by an uncontrollable urge to fire off to the left of the toilet bowl before retargeting and swinging right and centre into the bowl itself.

The result? Yellow stains on his carpet.

***

The bathroom was a small messy space with a filthy sink crammed in a corner. Jim only had to turn a little from the toilet bowl to be able to peer into the mirror above the sink. It was a stranger that looked back through the age-stained glass. He began removing his disguise.

***

Robbing a bank is not like shopping at Tesco's. You don't want old friends, enemies, or the public in general helping the police with their enquiries by recognising you in CCTV footage that gets shown on some trashy, 'Catch the Crook' TV cop show.

So, a change of names: Jim was 'Alpha' and Toni was 'Beta'. They wore wigs. Jim grew a moustache, wore designer glasses and sported a flat cap. Toni had grown some patchy stubble by the day of the robbery. Smoke tinted glasses hid his eyes. The finishing touch was a small but recognisable scar above Toni's right eye. Jim inked a temporary tattoo on his wrist deliberately visible below his sleeve. Only Charlie's beard was fake.

The disguises did a pretty good job. Jim adopted a slight limp and Toni pushed some cotton balls inside his cheeks to fatten his face, a nod to The Godfather that pleased Charlie. It made speaking a bit tricky. If he tried to say anything he risked spitting one or both of them out. The plan didn't rely on much chit-chat so they reckoned he'd get away with it. If he had to speak, Toni thought he could manage a Liverpool accent.

**

Jim peeled off the wig, revealing his own short dark hair underneath. He ruffled it with his fingers. It felt good to be free of the uncomfortable rug.

He shaved off his moustache and side burns and bent down into the basin to wash off the remains of the shaving cream. He stood back up and stared into what remained of the reflective surface of the mirror.

Many women would describe the face that looked back as moderately handsome. Attractive even, in a tanned, weathered sort of way. Not bad for a thirty-six year old, he thought.

Strong confident features sculpted by years of command in treacherous war zones, but unexpectedly softened by intelligent brown eyes set wide apart. The wrinkles of laugh lines told of a compassionate soul not far below the surface.

James Stack was, by general consent, the boss of the fledgling outfit. It was, after all, his clever idea – a novel scam involving distraction and an understanding of human nature – that they'd just put into play for the first time. James had a hang-up about being called Jim, so naturally, everyone did.

***

He re-joined the other two in the living room.

'OK, guys, your turn one of you.'

Charlie went next.

Jim sat at the table with Toni and looked at the pathetic piles of bank notes.

'So that's it is it?' He took a despondent breath. 'Hardly seems worth it does it?'

'Yeah, it didn't take long to count,' Toni said as he removed his wig and smoothed his thinning hair.

'Well, for our first bank robbery, it's hard to judge whether it's good or not,' he added attempting an optimistic tone.

Charlie returned looking much more like Charlie with his pale, clean shaven, round face and dark, collar-length hair. An average height, wiry, bean pole of a thirty-five year old man with an eager to please personality. Probably the result of being a Golden Retriever in an earlier life.

Toni was next.

Toni 'Zero' Zeterio, as his name suggested, had some Italian blood in him but his English father, Lionel Pendergrass, brought him up in Luton and blessed him with the very English moniker – Anthony Pendergrass. Not surprisingly, he preferred his mother's more exotic Neapolitan connection and her equally glamorous maiden name.

Friends called him Zero because it was easier than Zeterio.

He returned after a short while transformed into the trim, olive skinned, thirty-eight year old with brushed back hair, black, but flecked with hints of grey now. It had been receding since he was in his twenties in the way of most Italian men, but unlike many Italians, Toni Zeterio was quite tall at six foot, a genetic gift from his English father. With his aquiline features set in a narrow face, you might even call him elegant, if it wasn't for the pockmarks left over from an acne plagued youth.

Settled now around the table, the three gang members considered their next move. Jim was the first to speak.

'Can anyone think of a way to improve the plan?'

'It was always going to be risky,' Toni said.

'It's the nature of your bank robbery ain't it?' observed Charlie.

Toni urged just one more go, perhaps a really big one. Get enough to retire on. The usual post-felony small talk.

Hollywood got up and ambled over to his movie collection, hands stuffed in pockets.

'Well, if you want a real big bank robbery plot they don't come much bigger than...,' pausing until he found what he's looking for. He plucked out a DVD and held it out victoriously for the others to see.

'This!'

'What, 'Goldfinger?' asked Toni.

'Yeah. Well, more specifically the Goldfinger plot.'

'The what?' Jim asked resignedly. 'I know I'm going to regret asking.'

28

Hollywood returned to the table with the DVD, leaned back in his chair, and switched into 'movie-fan' mode.

'It's a clever plot. Auric Goldfinger gets this atomic device containing cobalt and iodine. I think Bond says, "It's a particularly dirty device".' Hollywood attempted the Connery accent. 'Goldfinger wants to explode it in Fort Knox, which is where all of America's gold is. Now, this would make the gold unusable for fifty-eight years and make the value of Goldfinger's gold worth quite a bit more. And definitely the best Bond film.'

'Good god, Hollywood,' Jim said irritably. 'If you put all the gold we've got between us, doubling the value would take it to about a hundred quid! And that's before you find an atomic device. I can't believe I'm bothering to explain this to you. Meanwhile, back on planet Earth...'

'Well, I don't mean doing Fort Knox. What about the Bank of England. Plenty of gold there.'

'Toni, for Christ's sake! Explain it to him someone.'

'He was in your unit, Jim. Too many loud explosions.'

'Yeah. Too many crappy movies,' Jim said with a laugh. 'Maybe he should get another hobby.'

'Hey guys, I'm still here.'

It was the kind of light banter they were sorely in need of at that moment – a welcome distraction– until Jim steered the conversation back to cold reality.

'Talking of bank jobs. Are you guys up for one more?'

'Yea, we've gotta do one more,' Charlie said eagerly.

'Looks like we got away with it this time, so why not?' He turned for a quick glance at the TV behind him.

'And there's still nothing about it on the news.'

'If you think it's worth it, I'm up for it,' Zero said.

James looked at the other two and shook his head.

'You crazy bastards. We *barely* got away with it.'

'I nearly crapped myself when I saw the truck, didn't I?' Toni joked.

'Yeah, you should have seen your faces,' Charlie said. 'I mean, using a lorry for a getaway – gotta be a first.'

Toni wondered what had happened to the police car that was chasing them. The other two shrugged.

'Yeah, strange that wasn't it?' Charlie said. 'Just vanished.'

James Stack, Charlie Dawson, and Toni Zeterio spent the rest of the evening picking over the ruins of their first bank heist. As the evening wore on – with the help of frequently replenished whisky and wine glasses sitting amongst the handfuls of cash spread across the table, life started to feel good – nobody had got hurt and they'd made some money – not much, but it was a start.

In the corner of the room the TV flickered silently with images from a 24 hour news channel that was rotating old news from the morning. If the news editor got a whiff of something fresh in the offing, it would be gratefully spun into a story. Such as the one appearing now on the ticker tape caption crawling slowly across the bottom of the screen: *Breaking News: Bank robbery in market town. Large sum stolen. Police car damaged during chase with stolen getaway truck.*

The caption continued to loop endlessly.

Watching the Detectives

Early evening the same day

Detective Chief Inspector Eric Deakins leaned back in his chair balanced precariously on its hind legs, his feet resting on a drawer pulled out from the desk. For a stout man in his mid-fifties, with the bleak prospect of retirement beginning to bite at his heels, it was probably a foolhardy trick to attempt.

He idly turned a clear polythene evidence bag in his hands as he stared out of his office window to the darkening horizons of the September evening.

***

He'd arrived at the scene of the crime a few hours earlier.

It had taken some time to get into the town, even with the siren wailing and flashing blue lights magnetically fixed to the roof of his un-marked car. He'd attempted to negotiate his way around a long queue of stationary traffic. Eventually, he gave up, unable to get even close to the bank. Instead, he parked up and walked the last hundred and fifty yards down the High Street. Something he resented having to do.

As he walked he could see fleeting glimpses of the cause of the problem through the exhaust fume choked gaps between the backed-up vehicles. A couple of yellow POLICE LINE DO NOT CROSS tapes had been stretched right across the road. Nothing could pass.

Not the fittest of men, his breath coming in short gasps as he walked, he could make out the familiar logo of The United Regional Bank on the small illuminated sign sticking out like a flag above the main bank signage. A handful of inquisitive onlookers and local media had gathered beneath it.

Corralling the immediate area were a couple of police cruisers, an incident van, and an ambulance, all with their lights flashing blue and red like a Turkish disco.

He made his noisy arrival at the yellow police perimeter tape, puffing and wheezing like the last man struggling past the finish line of the London marathon. By then, someone with a little more sense had at last taken control and reduced the crime scene tape to just half the width of the road. With the help of a local traffic officer and a contraflow system, the traffic was beginning to move again.

He ducked under the flimsy barrier, chest heaving, red–faced and sweaty. His mood, to say the least, was dark as he approached the nearest constable.

'I'm sorry sir, police line. No-one can cross it. You'll have to move back behind the tape,' he pompously announced.

DCI Deakins, unable to speak, raised his arm a little higher and with another deep gasp, thrust his proffered warrant card further into the officer's face.

Uncrossing his eyes, the young officer refocused on Deakins.

'Woops, sorry sir, I'm not used to this routine. It's the first bank robbery we've had since I joined the force.'

And as Deakins walked away, his attention already moving to a more senior policeman nearby, the constable raised his voice over the noise of the traffic.

'Still, it's all very exciting isn't it? I've never had to get the barriers out before.'

The senior officer at the scene, Superintendent Honeywell, recognised him as he approached.

'So Deakins, one of the senior members of CID has finally graced us with their presence,' he said frostily.

'Yes sir,' Deakins gasped, 'Sorry I'm late. The traffic coming into town was jammed solid for some reason,' he added with what he hoped was the subtlest note of insubordinate sarcasm that can be safely directed at a superior officer.

'So, what have you got here?' he asked as he finally got his breathing back under control.

'Well, it's a bloody bank robbery in case you haven't heard.' More sarcasm.

'Yes, I had heard sir.'

'Your assistant, Detective Sergeant Yates, managed to get here earlier, apparently without any trouble,' Honeywell said pointedly. 'She can take you through what we have so far,' his hand indicated the general direction of the bank.

'She's in there doing her job taking witness statements, I imagine,' he added impatiently as he walked off towards the gathered media, hoping an appearance on a news channel might be in the offing.

Inside the bank, tearful staff and a couple of customers sat together in a small group to the side of the room, most of them clutching cups of tea or sipping from bottled water. Finger print dusting and crime scene photography was already under way.

Deakins wandered in and glanced around the room for a first view of the scene.

'DS Yates around?' he said to a PC standing near the entrance.

The constable pointed over to an oak veneered door towards the rear of the room.

'She's in the manager's office with one of the members of staff, sir.'

Deakins nodded a thank you and walked over to the office. He tapped on the door, pushed it open a little and leaned in.

Detective Sergeant Debbie Yates was seated at the manager's desk. An obviously distressed bank manager sat opposite with a cup of tea rattling nervously in the saucer she was holding. The detective looked up at the interruption.

'You got a moment, Yates?' Deakins said from the door with a look that indicated he wanted a private conversation.

'Oh, yes, of course sir.' Pushing her chair back, she stood up.

'Mrs Bingham, would you mind waiting outside for a moment?'

Mrs Bingham, grateful for the interruption, put the cup and saucer down on her desk and left the room. Deakins closed the door and walked over to his young assistant. Yates was relieved to see him.

'Glad you finally made it sir, what took you so long?'

Deakins quickly explained the cause of the delay. The young detective agreed with a sigh.

'Yeah, it's the over enthusiastic new ones. They get common sense trained out of them.'

He quickly moved on to the robbery, asking what action she'd taken so far.

'Robinson and I have been taking down witness statements while they are still fresh in their heads. I hope that's OK with you, sir. I thought that would be the best thing to do until you got here.'

'Yeah, yeah. That's great, thanks. How far have you got?'

Debbie leafed through her notebook.

'The female clerk, ah, just a tick,' she flicked a couple of pages over. 'Yeah, here it is. Gulab Patel. She's the one at the till who had to hand over the cash. And Joan Bingham, the manager who I was just interviewing. According to her, she was in her office with the second man. He had arranged a meeting under the false pretence of raising a business loan. He made serious threatening noises if she didn't do as he asked'

'So she was a kind of hostage? Sounds a bit complicated. An inside job?' pondered Deakins.

'Don't think so.'

'Guns?' Deakins ventured.

'The witnesses said not. By the way, the get-away car is still parked outside.'

Deakins was surprised.

'I thought they escaped in a lorry?' He thought for a moment then decided. 'Show me the car. You can give me the SP on the way.'

Outside, ignoring the noisy chaos in the street, Deakins and Yates approached the 2005, metallic green Volvo.

'So where's the truck driver now?'

'He's inside the bank with the others, but I don't think he has much more to add to what we already know. He's getting a bit pissed off from waiting around. That and he wants to sort out his lorry.'

'Ah yes, the lorry. Any news on that?' Deakins asked as he started walking slowly around the car, peering through the windows.

'No, we're still looking. But we don't think it's too far because it had a bit of an argument with a bridge a few miles away,' she nodded down the High Street indicating the direction of the chase. 'The tipper bit at the back got torn off.'

Eric blinked and looked back at Debbie.

'You're kidding?'

Trying not to laugh, Debbie explained what happened to PC Evans.

'What, completely engulfed? Was he hurt?'

'No, he's fine. Suffering from shock, though. Took a while to free him. Car's a wreck as you can imagine.'

Deakins turned back to the Volvo, trying to stifle a laugh as he imagined the scene. He leaned through the open window of the driver's door taking care not to touch anything. He noticed the finger print dust on the wheel.

'No prints here I suppose?' he asked with little expectation.

'Clean for the most part sir, like everything else so far. It's most likely stolen, so what prints we did find are probably from the owner. As soon as we find out who he is we'll get a set of prints for comparison.'

As Deakins looked around the seat and the footwell, something caught his attention. '*A smoker?*' he wondered to himself.

He leaned back out and squatted down beside the door. Noticing just the slightest hint of grey dust on the road, '*Is that ash?*'

He went down on his knees and lowered his head for a look under the car but his over-indulged stomach prevented him from getting low enough for a clear view. Reluctantly, and with some effort, he laid himself out flat on the ground. He struggled to reach inside his jacket pocket from this position, but eventually extracted some tweezers and a clear polythene evidence bag.

Perhaps it was the wind or the draft from a passing bus that moved it, but there under the car was a single cigarette butt. Stretching his arm out to reach it, he carefully picked up the stub with the tweezers and placed it inside the evidence bag.

Groaning with the effort, he stood back up and, breathing heavily, turned to Debbie triumphantly waving the evidence bag like a winning lottery ticket.

'Well, you never know,' he said hopefully.

'Hmm, DNA perhaps?' DS Yates wondered.

'Could be. Could just be,' her boss replied over his shoulder as he started walking back to the bank.

***

DCI Deakins hefted his legs off of the drawer and tilted forward on his chair, placing all six legs safely on the ground. He turned impatiently, throwing the evidence bag on to the desk. There where now two of them. One held the cigarette end from under the car and another more recent one containing a cigarette butt discovered in the truck.

'Yates!' he shouted.

He heard the wheels of an old office chair squeal on the other side of the flimsy wall. A moment later, the door burst open with DS Yates clinging to the door handle.

'Boss?'

'Any news from forensics? They've been processing samples from the two cigarette butts for bloody hours. I thought these new DNA machines were supposed to be as fast as a whip. What about a database match?'

'Sorry, I've been typing out the witness statements. I'll give 'em another call.'

A couple of moments later, DS Yates tapped quickly on the door, pushed it ajar and thrust her head through the gap.

Deakins looked up hopefully.

'They're fairly confident the samples from both cigarettes contain DNA from the same person, but they haven't found a match in the DNA database so far. They said it's still early days yet.'

Her boss paused for a long moment before replying.

'Same DNA, so the same person smoked them. But whose? Have you got a DNA sample from the truck driver?' then adding as an afterthought. 'Does he even smoke?'

Yates quickly got the point. She wouldn't have been working on Deakins' team if she wasn't smart.

'I'll get on it now.'

The door slammed shut but Deakins had another thought, quickly got up and headed out through the door into the larger office beyond, bathed in the pallid florescent glow of energy saving lighting.

He wandered over to what his team called the Wailing Wall – a large white evidence board upon which would be pinned, taped and written the beginnings of any info and clues that might be relevant to the case.

It was looking pretty threadbare at the moment, but to be fair, the case had only just got up and running that afternoon. The fact that forensics had been able to deliver anything at all in such a short space of time was pretty miraculous. He'd just have to be patient.

What they had been able to stick up on the board in pretty short order were the three artist impression mug shots, which were based on a quick review of the bank's security tapes and the memories of the witnesses.

The male counter clerk had remembered hearing the robber shout out 'Alpha' to the one in the office just before they left, so Deakins had taken a leap of imagination and called the other one Beta. He didn't think they'd have taken the Greek alphabet further than that. There is no 'C' and the next Greek letter would have been Gamma. *'Na, not likely.'*

So, on the board above the 'Manager's Office' mug shot he had written 'Alpha'. Could he be the leader? So he added that bit of conjecture. And above the 'Clerk' bad guy sketch he had written 'Beta'. The drawing of the driver was much vaguer. A round bearded face wearing dark glasses, based on the memory of the only person who had had any kind of close visual contact, the traffic warden, and that was through the highly reflective glass of the windscreen.

So, some early wins. But it did feel as though they'd already plucked the easy to reach, low hanging fruit.

DS Yates strolled over to her boss at the Wailing Wall.

'I've finished the witness statements sir.'

'Good girl, that was quick.'

'Well, there wasn't a lot there really. The manager thought 'Alpha' was putting on a bit of a voice but she did remember seeing part of a rose tattoo showing on his right wrist.'

'Look,' Deakins said, 'Take any references like that, distinguishing features etc. and get them added to the mug shots.' Then, as an afterthought,

'I suppose we can assume they are wearing disguises, they made no attempt to hide their faces.'

'Most likely sir,' agreed Yates.

'Get new sketches done showing what they might look like clean shaven, shorter hair, no glasses,' Deakins said. 'Keep both sets on the board for the time being.'

'I'll get on to that,' Debbie said with what she hoped wasn't a too subtle glance at her watch as she turned to walk away. Deakins caught the theatrical message and glanced up at the office clock. 8.20 pm.

'Look, it's getting late Debbie,' raising his voice as Yates walked away. 'Sort it out tomorrow morning. Go home, for heaven's sake.'

He winced as he saw Superintendent Honeywell walking towards him across the office. He acknowledged him with a nod and turned back to the Wailing Wall.

'Not much added since I last looked Deakins,' Honeywell said as he joined him. 'Bit thin isn't it?'

'Early days, Superintendent. We'll catch them,' Deakins promised, hoping that would be the end of it, but also aware that Superintendent Honeywell never made an unnecessary journey down to the troops.

'I've got to give a press conference with the Chief tomorrow morning at 10 am.'

Here it comes, Eric thought to himself.

'He'll expect to be able to tell them something. I'm relying on you to come up with some crowd pleasing news.'

'I'll see what we can do.' Deakins said to the evidence board.

'Nine a.m. at the latest. My office.' Conversation terminated.

DCI Deakins turned and watched Honeywell wind his way through the untidy, desk strewn space of the CID office and then took his own shorter route back to his sanctuary at the far side of the room.

He dropped his arse down and re-balanced himself on the hind legs of his chair, planted his feet slowly, one at a time onto the desk drawer, heaved a

40

deep despondent breath of stale office air and stared out of the window into the dark night beyond.

'Bollocks!'

Won't Get Fooled Again

Three years ago

After leaving the army a Captain with military honours and a set of skills very useful in the mountains of Afghanistan but with no apparent advantage back in the civilised world, James Stack had an urgent need to make some quick money. Jim's next career specialisation and the cause of his ejection from the City and the comfortable civilian life he'd returned to, was precious metals.

Always a chancer, he saw an opportunity within the business of precious metals trading to make some very serious, but highly questionable money. His co-conspirator was V.P. Trade and Financial Integrity at Metro Metal Futures, Victor Avery, whom, he discovered, had high overheads and low morals. The scheme was simple enough, but would have been doomed were it not for Victor taking advantage of his highly respected position and unquestioned authority within the company to provide cast-iron cover for Jim as the scam progressed over the many months.

It relied on small incremental variations in spot prices per fine ounce during the course of what the industry calls the two Good Business Days that are allowed for delivery. That, and the fluctuation of currencies that it was either bought for, or rendered into.

The essential final step was the service provided by an anonymous third party fixer who operated deep within the shadows of The City. This individual's particular expertise was the almost miraculous ability to filter the value exchange with such a level of transparency, everything that came out the other end looked as clean as new sheets. To Victor Avery and James Stack, he was known only as Blackstone – a handle of sublime precision, borrowed from the nineteenth century magician and illusionist, Harry Blackstone.

Over the weeks and months, seemingly insignificant variants became very nice profits that both Jim and Victor were to share when the time was right. As it turned out, Victor had other plans which didn't include a share for Jim.

Victor had set up a shared account in Luxembourg, access to which required both parties to input their individual codes at the same time. Foolishly, Jim had agreed to an arrangement whereby a senior official at the small, private bank in Luxembourg held copies of both pass-codes, securely, on their behalf. Victor had persuaded Jim that this was a sensible precaution if one or the other became incapacitated for some reason. The surviving partner takes all. On the face of it a not unreasonable safeguard. They both carried the same risk. All fine and dandy. Except, he had unknowingly given his code, not to a bank official, but to Victor Avery.

In a further, devious act of self-preservation, the scheming Victor Avery had secretly put in place sufficient cover and distance to protect himself from the scam should it be discovered. His confidence was such that on the morning he heard a whisper the fraud was about to be uncovered, he just jumped right in and blew the whistle on what he told the authorities might be a 'problem on the floor'.

Jim had arrived at his desk in the thirty second floor offices of Metro Metal Futures for business as usual that morning. The buzz of energetic banter

43

carried across the floor between the young men and women, to each other in the room, and on phones to clients around the world. Each desk was piled with computer screens, three across and two high. Sets of numbers flashed red, yellow, and white in multiple columns down, while rows of figures marched like ticker tape across the screens, all offering different variants of the same seemingly chaotic data – an indecipherable puzzle of numbers and acronyms. For the uninitiated this could be mission control at Houston Space Centre for all they knew.

Yesterday had been an especially good day for Metro Metals Futures and their silent partners, the Scam Twins. The larger the deal, the more to be made on a most-for-you-but-a-little-for-us basis. Nothing too greedy. So, let's see what today brings.

Nothing good as it turned out.

With the Serious Fraud Office expected to turn up at any moment, Victor Avery asked Jim to come over to his office. A spacious room enjoying an enviable south west corner spot with views of south London in one direction and across Central to West London in the other.

When Jim entered the room, Victor was standing behind his imposing black glass and light oak desk, hands behind his back, staring out through the floor to ceiling plate glass windows at the awe-inspiring view of the Thames.

It was a view he never tired of. One of the world's great old rivers, with its endless sequence of bridges and ancient and modern architecture built on the shoulders of granite embankments that follow its serpentine course all the way back to the distant, haze filled horizon beyond.

Hearing Jim arrive he turned, walked over and looked him directly in the eyes.

'Take a seat,' he said grimly.

Jim did as he was asked. Something didn't feel right.

'We may have a problem, the SFO are on their way. It seems they know something about the little side business that's been taking place at Metro Metals.' He said this as though he had nothing to do with it.

If the wind was knocked out of Jim's sails by the news that the game was up, he was glad he was sitting down when Avery, pacing slowly back and forth across the office floor, gave him the next exciting piece of self-serving rationalisation.

'If we both go to prison we lose everything. They'll discover the pass-codes, and all our effort over the past two years will be for nothing. One of us has to protect the profits from our little enterprise and I'm obviously the best placed to do that. I'm afraid you're going to have to take the fall Jim. You can see the sense in what I'm saying can't you?'

Patronising and self-important, Victor Avery stopped pacing and sat on the edge of his desk. He watched the colour drain from James' face as he waited for a response.

Jim's mind was spinning as he came to terms with this ground-rocking shock wave.

'Come on Jim,' Avery urged. 'They're on their way. I believe they may actually be in the building now.' A skilled negotiator, he pushed harder.

'Roll with it Jim. I'll protect our investment and I promise your share will be safe and sound for when you...' He corrected what he was about to say. '...when you need it.'

Jim stood up. He wasn't giving up that easily.

'I'm not so sure Victor. Didn't you always say we were the two Musketeers? How can I trust you? I might feel safer if we were both in prison where I can keep an eye on you.'

Avery countered with a slow sad shake of his head.

'I'm afraid that's just not going to happen Jim,' he sneered. 'You don't think I haven't considered this outcome? I'm protected Jim. They won't be able to touch me.'

Then in a more conciliatory tone.

'Look Jim, trust me. It will be for the best. The money will be there when you get out. You can retire a very wealthy man. The alternative is to lose everything.'

His office phone bleeped. Avery grabbed it quickly to his ear.

'Yes?' He turned to look at Jim as he listened.

'Tell them to wait a moment.' Then to Jim as he replaced the phone. 'Too late. They're outside. You know what you have to do, don't you Jim?'

Jim collapsed back into his seat.

The next hour or so had a dream like quality to it as three officers from the SFO came into the office and confronted Jim with the evidence. There was nothing for it but to accept his fate. Avery had supplied all kinds of damning information: dates, amounts, enough detail for the SFO to unpick the fraud, but not implicate Avery. And most importantly, not reveal were the profit from the scam had gone.

Strangely, Victor Avery's name only came up as a stalwart defender of the trading regulators. A hero for god's sake. A complete whitewash!

It was conceivably true that if Jim told the fraud squad about Victor Avery's involvement, in all likelihood both parts of the pass-codes to the account would be discovered and all of the profits from the swindle lost. Or recovered depending on which side of the swindle you were on. And that was just too much effort and nerve shredding risk to throw away. He decided not to chance it.

Jim's defining character trait was a cool head. He took the fall reasoning that at least the full amount of profit from the fraud would remain intact in Luxembourg, and when he got out of prison he would claim his share as Victor Avery promised and perhaps a good chunk of Victor's share as well if he had anything to say about it. Well, he'd taken the fall hadn't he?

So, Jim kept Victor out of the investigation. Result? Victor Avery enjoying a stellar career ending up eventually in one of the most prestigious posts in the bullion world. Specifically, as head of security at the Bank of England. You couldn't make it up!

The irony that he had his own secret stash of money generated from the precious metals scam, secured in an account in Luxembourg and over which he now had full control, was probably lost on smug, self-regarding Victor Avery.

So, while all these glittering jewels were cast at Avery's feet, Jim took a career ending break in Parkhurst prison.

He was sentenced to four years but served two.

Jim endured every day with calm, Zen-like fortitude and patience. Reading in the daily newspapers about his ex-partner-in-crime's rise to prominence at the Bank of England only added steel to his resolve. He crafted his plans for revenge with an almost architectural eye for detail. All that was needed was a suitable opportunity.

Though Victor Avery had dealt cards to Jim from a treacherously rigged deck, Jim wasn't without his own Machiavellian nature. He had an ace up his sleeve.

***

On the day of his release from prison guess who wasn't there waiting at the gates, arms open wide and a big smile on his face to welcome James Stack back into the world? What a surprise!

Jim set about confronting Victor Avery. He did, after all, promise to keep Jim's stake safe. So to start with he would give him the benefit of the doubt and simply ask for his share. After all, they only had to input the two parts of the pass-code into the Luxembourg account. It was a long shot. Realistically, Jim had already mentally discounted a successful outcome to that scenario.

Turning Tables

There is a date circled in red in Victor Avery's calendar. For most of the time though it was cast to the back of his mind, as the day to day distractions of managing security at the Bank of England dominated his life.

You don't get such a prestigious job unless you have the right qualifications to degree level, Honours of course. Then a career path that demonstrates years of proven ability in the security industry at the highest level. Avery's discovery and timely tip off to the SFO of the 'problem on the floor' at Metro Metals Futures added yet another illustrious chapter to his glory bedecked CV.

Visits to other countries to share his knowledge of security management. Endless symposiums, back slapping industry awards, dinner engagements, visits from countless world banking professionals and, when he found time, the publication of yet another eagerly awaited volume on Ethics and the Security Industry. All this kept Victor Avery very busy indeed.

But every now and then, in a rare quiet moment, a tiny spider crawled across the back of his mind. He found the moment difficult to shrug off. He knew what it was of course. Nothing as prosaic as a guilty conscience, not for Victor Avery. No, this was simply an annoying detail that he might have to attend to in a rapidly approaching future date. The one circled in red.

It was on an ordinary unremarkable day that Victor Avery turned the page of his seven day desk diary to see what the new week had in store. And there it was. The only colour in a monochromatic two page spread. He was surprised how surprised he was.

***

It had taken Jim just a few days to feel completely adjusted to civilian life outside prison. He'd already been in touch with Charlie Dawson his ex-army buddy and former sergeant in his old command 'back in the day' as they say. Charlie, as easy going as ever and grateful for the company, was happy to help his former commanding officer. He gave Jim the use of the sofa for a few nights until he could find his own permanent living arrangements.

There may have been distance between them in rank, but Charlie's indefatigable optimism in some of the most dangerous situations in the bleak tribal regions of the Hindu Kush mountains bordering Afghanistan and Pakistan was hard to resist. In truth, even his constant comparisons to war movies in the middle of an unpromising counter-attack against seemingly overwhelming Taliban odds in Helmand Province, or during a bullet riddled siege around village ruins near their base, Camp Bastion, were a welcome distraction.

They remained in contact after Jim dropped his REFRAD (Release From Active Duty) resignation packet in the lap of his CO. He wanted out and no amount of counselling was going to change his mind. It took a bit more than the typical 6 months to process because Captain James Stack was an extremely experienced and valued officer. But in the end they had to let him go.

Charlie followed a little later and immediately looked Jim up. They had occasional drinks together in a local pub and Jim did what he could to help

Charlie find employment, but with cash running out, Jim needed to find employment as well. Even ex-army Captains need the occasional leg up and so, with the help of an old army friend already deeply entrenched and very influential within the banking business, he secured a job at Metro Metals Futures. A job that took care of just about all of his spare time.

In the end, Charlie found himself a job working as a glorified handyman on an oil rig off the coast of Scotland. It was during shore leave back in Aberdeen that he met the girl he would eventually divorce.

Three years later, who'd have guessed it? Here was his superior officer, Captain James Stack, just out of prison and sleeping on his couch.

***

It was the week after 'red circle' day that Avery got the call he hoped would never come.

The number wasn't difficult to find. Look it up. The Bank of England. They have a switchboard and everything. The trick is to get past it.

Anticipating the usual obstacles put in the path of any random person trying to reach someone who doesn't want to be reached, Jim did just a little research. The name of Avery's PA. This is always an important name to know. Treat her well and doors can be opened. Ears bent. Small favours done. Her name? Barbara Hamilton. Jim put that in his back pocket. It might come in useful later.

The next detail: who am I? He definitely couldn't use the name James Stack. So, who would Victor Avery take a call from? Pretending to be someone from within the industry is a fairly high risk strategy, after all, Avery knew everybody. Blow it, and Avery's radar will be on full alert. He's bound to be expecting Jim to make contact and Avery wants to avoid that at all costs.

Jim decided to go for the nuclear option. A name that would put the fear of God into Victor but who he would nonetheless take a call from.

Barbara Hamilton put the call through with the usual cool professionalism.

'David Grant from the Serious Fraud Office on the line,'

A pause, or was that hesitation? During which Avery was transported back to his office at Metro Metals over three years ago when David Grant and associates came marching in to begin their fraud investigation. At that moment, as they walked through his office door, he wasn't sure he was safe. But Jim Stack did take the fall and didn't implicate Avery. It was close. Too close. Victor Avery had been a very good boy since then.

'Put him through,' he said.

He heard a click and then the thin, ill-defined background noise of a room somewhere in London.

'Hello, David. It's been a while,' he said with slightly too much bravado. He calmed it down. 'What can I do for you?'

'You sounded a bit nervous there for a moment Victor.'

A long pause.

'James Stack. Why the subterfuge?'

Jim ignored the question.

'We have some business to complete, don't we Victor?'

'Business? I'm sorry, I'm not sure I understand. This is Victor Avery, Head of Security. Have you got the right department?'

Playing the blameless innocent. Typical.

'There's a Starbucks on King William Street. Be there in ten minutes. Don't think about refusing because, well, imagine what your PA Barbara would say once she hears all the dirt on you, Victor. Ten minutes.' Jim ended the call, leaving Avery holding the receiver to his ear connected to a dead line.

***

Jim was already sitting at a table, nursing a cappuccino in Starbucks when he made the call to Victor Avery. He'd deliberately chosen a table set in a recess towards the back. No point in drawing unnecessary attention to himself, or Avery, if he turned up.

Conveniently, at this time of the morning you can practically have your pick of the tables. The hiatus doesn't last long. Meetings over, they start to crowd in again. Presumably, for more networking over a 'Grande iced half-caf triple mocha latte macchiato,' chosen to impress all within earshot just how desperately cool they were, as they shout their absurd order to the Barista. '*Only in the City*' Jim thought.

For himself, he had ordered simple. A small cappuccino. '*One tall cappuccino coming up!*' Why do they screw around with the language?

As Jim took a sip, he looked up just as Victor Avery entered. He'd made good time. The Bank of England, also known fondly as the Old Lady of Threadneedle Street, is but a short walk from the coffee house in King William Street. But just making your way out of the fortress like building itself can take time. It covers a huge area of prime London real estate.

At last, here it was. Jim had waited a long time for this moment. He'd taken the fall and served two of the four years term he'd been given.

'Coffee?' Jim asked as Victor sat down. Avery just sat there, arms folded, looking directly at Jim. He didn't look happy.

'We have an arrangement Victor. An agreement.'

Jim leaned in across the table.

'We have a contract. A fifty-fifty share of profits.' He said in a low threatening voice. 'I served time to protect those profits. You know why I'm here. You know what I want. I need your pass-code. It's time to collect my share as agreed.'

Avery just sat there and gently shook his head. His mouth set in a sly smirk.

'I have no idea what you're talking about. You were convicted of serious fraud against clients of Metro Metals Futures. You went to prison for it and as far as I'm concerned our professional relationship ended back then.'

It was Jim's turn to shake his head. He moved in just a little closer.

'Listen Avery,' Jim's voice now a lethal whisper. 'You've got my share of a sizable chunk of money. Where is it? Still in Luxembourg? You'll be making a very big mistake if you underestimate me. So come on. The password. Now!' He almost spat the last word out in barely controlled anger.

Avery looked on imperiously, eyebrows arched as though accidently encountering some unpleasant beggar in the street. He unfolded his arms as he stood up, placed his hands on the table and leaned forward towards Jim.

'No James. There are no such profits as you say,' Avery sneered. 'There is nothing to connect me to you and your tawdry little scam. If there was I'm quite certain I'd have heard about it by now.' He hissed the words out, not wanting to be over-heard, his face screwed into a red grimace.

'It didn't come up during the investigation. There is no evidence against me. That's why you and you alone went to prison.'

Jim leaned back in his chair, folded his arms and stared up at Avery for a moment.

'You'd better take care of yourself Victor,' he said with a grin. 'That blood pressure will kill you if you're not careful and I need you alive to get my money.'

Avery took a breath to calm himself. He glanced at his watch.

'You've had all the time I'm going to give you Stack.'

Then, with a sneer, as he turned to go,

'It's over. Don't contact me again.'

Dismissing Jim, he started to leave. He'd only taken a few steps when he heard Jim call out.

'Avery!'

He kept walking until he heard the four words that changed everything.

'I have a recording.'

That stopped him. He froze between the tables for a moment but didn't turn.

'I'll be in touch,' Jim said. And in a final dig, 'Have a nice day.'

Avery started his journey again, winding his way through the handful of arriving customers. Through the door and a right turn out into the sunlit street. A final glimpse and he was gone.

He didn't look happy.

Thick as Thieves

How to Rob the Bank of England

November

A few weeks passed, during which they undertook another bank robbery, barely making a getaway or a profit. The only change in their modus operandi was to use false beards and moustaches instead of growing them over a couple of weeks or so. It dawned on them that there was a danger that as their beards grew, they would start to look like the artists impressions put out by the police after the first robbery. Which meant the closer they got to the day of a heist, the more they would look like the perpetrators!

The police were sniffing around but they didn't seem to have any real leads, none they were prepared to tell the press about anyway. Out of the three of them, Charlie and Toni were getting the most rattled. It was getting seriously risky, particularly as they had to assume the banking industry was probably taking preventative measures in order to stop people like Jim, Charlie, and Toni, just walking in off the streets and helping themselves.

It couldn't last much longer. Pack it in or prison. It was bound to end one way or the other.

The gang were at a disillusioned low when Hollywood and Zero got a call from Jim telling them to come over for an urgent meeting.

Despite travelling from different parts of London, Zero and Hollywood arrived in the street outside Jim's address at pretty much the same time. Charlie pressed the button on the apartment building's intercom system. They stood there, furtively glancing up and down the street, shuffling feet and hands stuffed into pockets, against the November chill while they waited for Jim to operate the electronic door switch. Both Charlie and Toni were apprehensive about this unexpected call.

A click, and then Jim's voice.

'Yeah?'

'It's us.'

'Come up.'

A buzz as the electronic latch released the door. Charlie pushed the door open and they walk the two flights up to Jim's apartment.

'What do you reckon this is all about Hollywood?' Zero asked.

'Don't ask me. Jim's been a bit quiet these last few days. Maybe he's calling it a day. Maybe it's nothing.'

They were about to be surprised.

The door to Jim's flat was slightly ajar. Charlie pushed it open and they stepped through.

A small, dark hallway took them past a kitchen on the left, not much larger than a telephone kiosk. Dishes from Jim's lunch still waiting to be washed – the aroma of cooking still present in the air. Toni sniffed approvingly. Garlic? Definitely. Herbs too. Probably marjoram and oregano. Some kind of pasta dish he reckoned. It smelt delicious, reminding him of his mother's Italian cooking.

Along with his other skills, Jim fancied himself as something of a cook. He knew how to take care of himself on the street, in the bedroom, and in the kitchen.

The combined bathroom and WC faced the kitchen. A few short steps further down on the right was the door to the apartment's only other room. Jim's bedroom.

Rent in this increasingly desirable corner of London was getting expensive which made affordable living space harder to find. Nonetheless, the end of the short hallway opened out into a bright, reasonably sized and eclectically decorated living room. Good, comfortable furnishings in their day, now a little on the tired and shabby side.

Not that he didn't have taste. No, James Stack had bags of that. It was more to do with the result of Jim's initial shortage of ready cash after he was released from prison almost three months ago. But more recently the reluctance to waltz into Harrods with a Tesco bag full of stolen money to pay for any tasteful, if expensive suite of furniture and coordinated designer bauble that happened to catch his eye. An observant salesperson might find that very slightly suspicious.

Large Georgian windows looked out across the road to the upper floors of buildings that were built both before and after the war. The random placing of the post war architecture conveying a telling story of where the German bombs fell.

They found Jim relaxing casually on a sofa near a window, a bright pool of early Winter afternoon sunlight reflected off a nearby office tower picking him out like a yellow gelled spotlight. He was on the phone, but he looked up and waved for them to take a seat.

The two made themselves comfortable on the other couch.

'Charlie. Why don't you make some coffee or something? I won't be a mo,' Jim said, his hand covering the phone.

It was a bit more than a 'mo' later that Charlie and Toni found themselves together on the couch. Coffee made, drunk, and empty cups sitting on the coffee table in front of them, as neglected as they were. Zero looking absently at Jim, Hollywood staring randomly around the room, fingers drumming on the arm of the sofa.

Jim finally concluded his call as the sun, dropping lower in the sky, disappeared behind a building. He apologised for keeping them waiting and, after some friendly small talk, hit Charlie with the last thing he expected Jim to ask him.

'Hollywood, run that Goldfinger plot past me one more time.'

Stunned by Jim's sudden interest in a story that he had dismissed as pointless the last time Charlie brought it up, he wondered whether the stress of the two bank robberies had finally driven him over the edge.

He gave Jim a sideways, *'are you winding me up?'* look through one half-closed eye and turned to Toni to check he wasn't in on the joke. If anything, as far as Charlie could judge, Toni seemed just as surprised.

So, Hollywood explained the plot of Goldfinger one more time – albeit in his own random, arse-about-face, kind of way.

When Hollywood eventually dragged his endlessly embellished summary over the finishing line, Jim put his hands behind his head, closed his eyes and leaned back into the sofa thoughtfully. His usual habit of grinding his jaws when he was thinking was accompanied by the slight turning of his head back and forth, as though he was placing, swapping, removing, and reordering things on a large board

59

visible only to him. It was clear he was coming to an important decision.

Silence descended in the room. Only the muted noise from the city outside intruded.

The weak Winter sun finally made another appearance through a gap in the City skyline, casting warm, straw coloured rectangles over the apartment furnishings. Reflections from shiny surfaces throwing smaller, random shapes of dappled light into the darker recesses of the room.

Charlie turned to look at Toni and gave him a *'what's this all about?'* shrug. Toni returned the gesture.

They didn't have to wait long. Jim opened his eyes and unclasped his hands from behind his head. He leaned forward towards the other two. Their modest bank robbing enterprise was about to be given a very large shot of steroids.

'OK. We're going to rob the Bank of England,' he said in a calm, matter-of-fact voice.

Toni and Charlie reacted to this extraordinary proclamation by sitting bolt upright with their heads raised up like a couple of alarmed meerkats.

'And here's how we're going to do it,' Jim continued. 'We turn the Goldfinger plot upside down. Stand the whole thing on its head.'

With their mouths gaping open, Jim had Charlie and Toni's astonished attention.

'I've been kicking this 'Goldfinger Plot' around and it seems to me that it does have some merit, if you look at it from the other end of the telescope.'

The two listening gang members reacted with predictable, and not unreasonable disbelief. Words like: 'Impossible.' 'Can't be done.' 'What, like dig a tunnel?' 'Go in guns blazing?' 'Are you crazy?' And in a particularly defensive tone from Hollywood,

'Hey, Jimbo, it's just a movie, not a training video,' spilled out in Jim's direction.

'I hear you guys, but please bear with me for a moment,' Jim pleaded.

'I think there's a way to rob the Bank of England but you don't do it by going in through the front door, or digging a tunnel, in fact we're not going anywhere near it. We're going to wait for the gold to come to us!'

They didn't interrupt, so Jim continued.

'The bank's vaults are pretty much impregnable, I think we can take that as a given, right? Bank of England security is confident all bases are covered – or so they believe.'

'But, if you can convince them an apocalyptic event is about to happen they are probably going to do whatever it takes to defend themselves against it.'

'Sorry...a poly what?' Hollywood said.

'Something bad,' Zero explained.

Jim ignored the interruption.

'Did you know that the Bank of England holds gold not just for the UK economy but for many other countries as well? As you can imagine, there's plenty of it. Many thousands of tons of foreign gold stacked on pallets. In fact, there's actually more gold in the Bank of England than Fort Knox. Enough neatly stacked bars of gold to bury a very dangerous needle in a haystack.'

More stunned looks from Charlie and Toni. Toni went to say something but Jim held up his hand to stop him.

'So, how do you get the gold out of the Bank of England?' Jim asked rhetorically. 'Well, it's the foreign gold that's the Bank's Achilles heel.'

'That phone call earlier was from a friend of mine from the Aldermaston Atomic Weapons

Establishment. He's a very clever chap. It turns out you don't need a large atomic device like they had in Goldfinger if all you want to do is contaminate the gold with radiation.'

'This is all sounding a bit wild Jim. It's way out of our depth,' Toni said.

'Let me finish guys,' Jim urged. 'You only need a few gold bars that have been hollowed out to make enough space for a small explosive device and quantities of some extremely radioactive substance. This substance will be blown into the air by the explosive charge and carried by the vaults air circulation system to settle on most of the other gold throughout the bank, irradiating it and rendering it untouchable for…well, quite a long time.'

'But hang on, that's exactly the Goldfinger plot isn't it,' Charlie countered. 'You said something about looking down the wrong end of a telescope. Doing it differently?'

'Exactly! Because we're not going to do it!'

'Wait a minute. We are going to do it? We're not going to do it? Which is it?' Zero asked.

'Pay attention and I'll tell you.'

'The bank receives large quantities of gold from many different countries and it's constantly moved about within the bank as the owners of the gold buy and sell, depending on the needs of their economies. Bank security will be led to believe that one of these countries, name currently unknown, has become the victim of a criminal gang. The Bank of England is the first target in a plan to undermine the world gold bullion market by contaminating major gold holdings thereby rendering them untradeable,' Jim explained.

'They plan to achieve this by placing radioactive material and an explosive propellant and timer into several hollowed out gold bars. Bank of England security will be led to believe that this toxic shipment is already stored somewhere within the Bank of England's vaults, and has been in place for a time span of more than a year. The gang has deliberately made the time scale vague to allow as much internal shuffling of the gold as possible. The result? Growing uncertainty as to which shipment or country might be involved and where any individual bars of that gold consignment might now be.'

'Time is not on the Bank of England's side because security will suspect the perpetrators have no reason to delay once they have revealed their audacious plan. Therefore, a contaminating explosion could occur at any time. They may only have hours!'

'They'll never be able to find this needle in a haystack within the time they believe they have left. Only one thing is certain though and it's the only bright spot. The British gold will not be the source of the problem. So what will their instincts tell them? Save the British gold. And how would they do that...?'

'Take the British gold out of the vault,' Hollywood and Zero chorused.

'Bingo! They know that the problem lies within the foreign gold so they'll leave the foreign gold where it is and take the uncontaminated British gold out. It's a lot of gold and they'll need to move it somewhere safe. And that, well, it's our golden opportunity, to borrow an extremely relevant phrase. Anyway, the gold would be out of the bank and vulnerable.'

'It's bloody brilliant! For the first time I can't think of a movie like it,' Charlie said.

'Yes, clever. But how much gold are we talking about here? And where would they take it? What kind of transport would they use? The security. How are we...I mean...?' Toni said shaking his head and holding his hands out in supplication towards Jim.

'Zero, I'm working on that,' Jim said patiently.

'Wait a minute,' Charlie said in a triumphant tone, 'I think I've spotted a wrinkle.'

'What have I missed?' Jim asked, resignation in his voice, expecting the usual, unhelpful 'Hollywoodism.'

'Why would these foreign gangsters bother to tell the Bank anything about what they're up to?'

'Hey that's a good point,' Toni joined in. 'Why don't they just keep quiet and let the bomb thing go off?'

'That's right,' Charlie butted in excitedly. 'It's not in their interest to let the Bank know. The whole point of the plan is to make sure the thing goes bang.'

Jim gave Charlie and Toni a nod of respect.

'Well done. You've both been paying attention, I'm impressed.'

'So, how would the Bank know if the gang don't tell 'em?' Hollywood pressed.

'And why would they tell them, Jim?' Zero added.

Pausing for a moment, Jim responded thoughtfully.

'It's a fair point. What our hypothetical gang wants is to increase the value of its own gold. It's purely a financial gain thing isn't it?'

Searching hesitantly for the solution, he started to draw the threads of the answer out of thin air.

'Well, if they're only in it for financial gain, they have no interest in getting people hurt,' he extemporised, gaining confidence as his idea coalesced.

'That's it! The reason they tell them, is to give the Bank a chance to clear people away from the imminent explosions and radio-active contamination. This isn't some psychopathic, cat loving, Bond villain character, out for total world domination. This is just greed, pure and simple.'

'Yeah, that makes sense,' Charlie said.

'It's all a bit humanitarian, but I'll buy it,' Toni agreed.

'Well, let's hope the Bank of England does,' Jim added.

'So, when do we do it?' Charlie asked.

'Now that is a very good question,' Jim said. 'Not soon, that's for sure. There's too much to sort out. But be sure of this, guys, once we pick a date it's going to happen very quickly. Over a very short period of time.'

An inspired Hollywood throws in a cinema classic.

'To screw-up the words of Rob Scheider in Jaws, We're going to need a bigger gang.'

'Yeah, we'll need an extra pair of hands or two,' agreed Zero. 'Got anyone in mind Jim?'

'Give me a break guys,' Jim countered irritably. 'Look, I didn't say it was going to be easy. To pull this off we're going to need some extra hands as you say, but we also need some very well placed help and I do have one very particular person in mind. But this guy is going to need a little persuading.'

Telephone Man

Retrieving the smart phone

For all of his scheming, Victor Avery's arrogant self-confidence didn't allow for the possibility that anyone else could be as crafty as him.

How could he know that during the progress of the Metro Metals scam, Jim had recorded many of their chats on a smart phone hidden in his pocket?

Circumspect as they were, these potentially incriminating conversations carried enough damning detail to form the basis of an insurance scheme. To protect him from what? The unexpected spanner in the works for one. What did he know about Blackstone? That strange, mercurial figure on the edges of the scam. And that private bank in Luxembourg, the custodians of the account containing the spoils. Might they need a timely prodding when their conscience starts to prick? They are, after all, unwitting partners in the scheme. Maybe. But right at the top of a short list of reasons, was slippery Victor Avery.

There might come a time when Jim will need insurance against that most primeval of human motives: Greed – with a sub-clause covering self-interest and its yellow streaked sibling – self-preservation.

The only problem was that Jim didn't hide the smartphone he'd used to make the recordings in his own desk for fear it might be discovered. So he'd surreptitiously stashed it away in a folder filed at the back of a nearby colleague's desk drawer.

You can call James Stack a cynic if you like, but his confidence in the security of his chosen hiding place was founded on the not unreasonable belief that nobody bothers to read Health and Safety documents. The folder was innocently labelled 'Fire Drill.'

He needed that file now. Did his colleague still work at Metro Metal Futures?

They say revenge is a dish best served cold and Jim was a very patient man.

Now that he was committed to the Bank of England scheme, he needed the help of a well-placed insider, such as Victor Avery, and a means to persuade this key member of the Bank of England management that refusal was not an option – which meant he needed the smart phone.

So how was he going to do that small thing?

**

It all nearly went completely pear shaped the first time he tried to gain access to the offices of Metro Metals Futures in One Canada Square, commonly known as Canary Wharf. He just tried to brazen it out and walk straight in amongst a crowd of others. He should have known. Security helped him back on to the street. Well, you don't get far without a kosher security tag but he was surprised just how far he had managed to get. It was *so* close.

He had taken the subway to Canary Wharf. The train stopped at the station in the normal way but unusually, though not exclusively for the London Underground network, there is a glass wall at the platforms edge. Automatic doors arranged along its length match the positions of the train doors when it came to a halt. Both sets of doors open together to provide access to and from the train. A not unreasonable precaution in an effort to keep the dangers of the electrified rails and the high speed arrival of the train itself away from the curiously suicidal.

He arrived at the surface and main lobby of One Canada Square by way of a magnificent, cathedral like escalator hall. Not difficult. However, getting access to the upper office floors is a tougher trick, because security is usually as water tight as a fish's arse.

His main gambit was to use his old Metro Metals security card. He swiped it across one of the terminals and, as expected, it denied access. Well, it was three years out of date, after all.

His journey was deliberately timed to join the happy throng of workers arriving by the thousands in the morning rush hour. There were always one or two whose card occasionally didn't work for some reason or other. Perhaps it was system overload, who knows?

The overworked security guards habitually just came over and, after a cursory inspection, allowed them through.

That's what happened this time. A quick flash of the Metro Metals card, his finger covering the date, and he was through. Not bad!

He walked over to the lifts. It was a tall building, but even at nearly eight hundred feet high it was a mere foothill by comparison to other majestic edifices soaring skywards at heights beyond two thousand feet in other parts of the world. Thirty two lifts serve the building. Jim took one to the thirty second floor where Metro Metals Futures had their offices.

The lift stopped and he stepped out into a lobby area. A bunch of other passengers pushed past him heading towards the doors of other businesses on that floor. Across the lobby another lift arrived, the doors opened and out-flowed more office workers. He joined several walking towards the double glass doors of Metro Metal's reception. He thought he recognised one of them, but didn't get anything back that suggested a light had gone on.

He didn't need his card this time. He simply walked through with the others. Not bad at all!

And here he was, at the very edge of the trading floor. He could see his old desk a few rows down and to the left of that, just by the window, the desk where he'd secreted the smart phone. Nobody there at the moment. My god he was so close, might he actually do it?

Nobody was paying attention to him. They were all busy chatting to each other, wandering around randomly from desk to desk with cups of coffee or staring at the flashing numbers on computer screens, just as they had always done.

He'd only taken a couple of steps towards the unmanned desk when he heard a voice behind him.

'Excuse me sir. Can I help you?'

'*Shit!*' He stopped, managed to arrange the equivalent of a friendly smile on an innocent face and turned.

'Sorry?' He said.

'And you are...?' The voice of authority from a security uniform. 'Can I see your security pass please, sir?'

There was nothing else he could do so he showed his old Metro Metals employees card. He tried to slip his finger over it to hide the date, but the security guard simply took the card from him.

After the briefest of inspections, the guard looked back up at Jim.

'Hmm, this card is very out of date sir.' And then, 'You're not entitled to be on this floor. Would you come with me please?'

Jim followed the guard back through to the reception area. The guard held the door open. Jim took a quick look back before walking through and in that brief moment saw a slim, attractive woman with short blond hair return to her desk with a cup of coffee in her hand. It was the desk by the window. The one with the Fire Drill folder containing the smart phone.

He tried for another quick glance before the door closed. What could he see? What could he remember? Smart, petite. Dark trouser suit. Some kind of scarf, blue or blue green? White blouse. Dark shoes. Heels? Thousands of women dress like that in the City, but he was sure he would remember her face. She was beautiful.

In the reception area, the guard called for assistance from central security operations and then turned to Jim.

'What is your name sir? And what are you doing here?'

There was nothing for it, Jim would have to bluff his way out.

'I'm James Stack. I used to work here, but I've been away for some time. I just wanted to see if any of my old colleagues still worked here. You know, give me a first chance for any jobs that may be going.'

The guard wasn't convinced.

'Well, they've got a Human Resources department for that sort of thing sir. That would have been the correct way to go about looking for a job wouldn't it?'

A second security guard arrived from Central Casting. A man whose personality permanently typecast him for the roll of petty official.

'What have we got here then?' he said.

'Well, I don't think it's anything to worry about,' the first guard surmised, taking a more forgiving approach.

'A former employee. Just escort him out of the building,' adding, 'I've got his old security pass. I think that's the end of it.'

'I see,' the other guard said with a nasal sneer. He turned to inspect Jim.

'So, sneaking around were you?' He looked Jim up and down, then turned back to the other guard.

'OK, leave it to me.'

'Come on you. Out!' he said, putting a hand on Jim's arm.

'No touching if you don't mind,' Jim said politely at first. The guard ignored him, tightened his grip and tugged.

Jim stood his ground and leaned into the guards face.

'Take your hand off. I'm coming,' his voice carried the authority of an officer used to unquestioned command in the battlefield – the bully deflated like leaky balloon.

Grateful to be out on the street, Jim did a quick debrief. What had he achieved? Well, not exactly nothing.

***

It had been a stupid plan, not even a plan really, but his old 'Keep It Simple' army training hadn't worked this time. He needed a bit of luck as well.

He needed a more subtle approach.

Unsurprisingly, after all this time, Jim's old colleague who worked at the desk by the window had moved on. But occupying it now, though seen only in the briefest of glimpses, was a very attractive young woman. If he was able get to know her, perhaps she could return the smart phone to him. This task had both risk and pleasure attached to it. Still, a man's got to do, as they say.

Her name, it turned out, was Summer.

Hello, I Love You, Won't You Tell Me Your Name?

Retrieving the smart phone: 2nd Attempt

Jim lurked down in the great escalator hall below One Canada Square. He found a corner to the side that gave him a good view of the escalators themselves. To anyone watching, he was simply passing the time reading a newspaper while waiting for a friend.

He had no idea if she was a user of the tube network, but you've got to start somewhere.

After this morning's near miss at Metro Metals he had decided to return to his flat and pass the day working on the next bank robbery. Simple considerations, like which bank and where? These were what he concentrated on for now. All very small fry compared to the big-time behemoth of a con that was brooding menacingly from some not so far off future date.

Such was the enormity of the Bank of England job, it needed plenty of capital to have any chance of a successful outcome: planning, money, third party resources – and luck.

He phoned Charlie and Toni and told them to expect a meeting later in the week. They rotated the venues in turn, so it was going to be at Toni's place in Clerkenwell. For security reasons he insisted they communicate by mobile phone only. No emails, no texts, no trail. Probably time for a change of phone numbers as well.

The planning was a distraction. A means to pass the time until the evening. He made little real progress because he couldn't get the task of recovering the phone, and her, out of his mind.

So, will she use the underground? If so, what time does she quit work? Some of these bright young things work till stupid o'clock. But then of course, they earn the money.

Another question. Will he recognise her after such a fleeting view? The City is full of attractive women wearing short blonde hair and dark trouser suits. Oh yes, and heels. But still, he thought he'd be able to pick her out.

He started his watch at five pm. It wasn't long before the hall and escalators were seething with the tired and homebound. The only thing preventing it from parodying a scene from Charlie Chaplin's 'Modern Times' was the very real sense of prosperity. Jim smiled at the thought, 'Christ! Hollywood would be proud of me.'

'Wait a minute! Is that her?' Jim tried to get a better view. She was just about to step off the escalator. The tide of commuters engulfed her as she strode into their wake. She was a little smaller than most but he could just make out the blonde hair.

He pushed his way into the crowd, forcing a path as near to her as he could get. The wave of people fanned out onto the platform just as a train arrived. She had peeled off to the left and was still some way ahead as the doors opened.

Nothing. Just the backs of people fighting to squeeze on board. The doors closed and the train started to move. The section of carriage she had entered was going to pass him so he stood and waited – boxed in by the press of humanity trying to refill an already crowded platform area.

Through the windows he could see the crush of people, arms raised to the hand rails. Tightly packed though they were, each inhabited a tiny island of private, impenetrable space, beyond which no-one else existed.

A warm draft of air blew along the platform as the train started picking up speed, the pitch of its whining motors climbing higher. The carriage – her carriage – took its turn to pass and there she was, with her back to the window, arm raised as she clung to the hand rail. If only she would turn her head. Then, just at the point the carriage was passing closest to him, he got a full profile and then a three quarter angle as she turned her shoulders. Fleeting though the view was it was enough for Jim to be certain. It wasn't her. Very nice though, whoever she was.

Fighting the flow of travellers, it took Jim a while to return to his position in the escalator hall.

For the rest of his watch he had one other heart stopping close call and plenty of other similar looking pretty girls that kept him entertained.

As the crowds started to thin out he took the risk of leaving to get a cup of coffee to go. He returned to his position with it, sipping occasionally. The hall became eerily quiet except for the quiet hum of escalator machinery and the mournful sound of an arriving train echoing through the tunnel. Apart from the odd late worker and a few couples passing through, the place felt almost abandoned. He gave it until nine o'clock.

He'd try again tomorrow morning.

***

An early start. Six thirty. He took the same position, but came equipped with coffee and bagel.

Same as last night. Except, of course, the tide of humanity was heading in the opposite direction.

He gave up at nine thirty. No point in waiting any longer, after all, she was in the office during his failed attempt yesterday morning at eight forty-five.

He took the tube to Bank and walked from there back to his flat near Liverpool Street Station.

Bank station is pretty much opposite the Bank of England which gave Jim a moment of thoughtful reflection about the larger game plan as he walked past its vast bulk.

***

London Underground is not the only way to commute to offices in Canary Wharf. You could take a bus. Not likely, he thought. Taxi? Could be. That could make it a little trickier.

More likely though was London's novel elevated rapid transit system known as the Docklands Light Railway.

The following morning, he took the Jubilee Line back to the tube station at Canary Wharf and then walked up to the DLR station that rose above the street.

It was another early start with no way of knowing from which direction she might come. The platform formed a central island with trains arriving from both directions on either side. He should get a good view from here he hoped.

Armed once again with coffee and bagel he started his vigil.

A couple of early close calls lowered his mood to pessimistic. It just didn't look good. This was turning out to be a hopeless plan.

Then, just as his mood couldn't get worse, two trains arrived at the same time. Twice as many commuters getting off. A chaotic rush towards and past him. He tried to hold his coffee away to avoid it being knocked, but one commuter brushed so close his arm was pushed back sharply against him, spilling his coffee down his coat.

The woman turned to apologise...and there she was! Just as he remembered her.

'I'm so sorry,' she said absently before turning to walk on. A soft American accent. He didn't expect that for some reason.

Jim stood there frozen in mouth-gaping surprise for a micro-moment, before snapping awake and rushing to catch up with her. She was already making her way down the stairs and out of sight as he squeezed a passage through the packed flow of commuters, all heading in the same direction.

When he caught up with her what was he going to say? He hadn't given this critical bit of the plan a moment's thought.

Well, he'd better think of something now, he was almost alongside her.

'That wasn't much of an apology?' '*Oh God,*' Jim squirmed. '*What a prat.*'

Still walking briskly she turned to him.

'Sorry? What?' her voice had an irritated ring to it.

Jim kept pace with her.

'The coffee. My coat's ruined.'

Her stride didn't slow, but she glanced down at Jim's coat.

'It doesn't look too bad to me, but look, if you want me to pay to get it cleaned.' She was all business, but started to reach into her purse.

Jim had to admit there wasn't much coffee left in the cup when it spilt. But that wasn't the point. He had to keep this conversation going.

'How about just replacing the coffee? There's a place near here.' *'Christ! That sounded so lame.'* 'There's a better place. I'm on my way there now.'

'Sounds good to me.'

He followed her to one of the smarter cafés. An Italian Deli on Reuters Plaza overlooking the water. It took a couple of minutes, but it was on the way to the office block where Metro Metals was located.

He had a chance to get a better look at her as they walked. A little shorter than him, so maybe five foot eight in heels. The blond hair hanging in a cute bob had the hint of some brunette streaks. Hard to see her face properly as she was just half a step ahead of him.

Under the short winter coat, she was wearing the same tailored trouser suit as before, or so he thought. The scarf was different, claret with some sort of modern yellow pattern, fine wool and quite long. The outfit looked expensive, but what did he know?

With such a difference in her choice of clothes, he was surprised he recognised her at all. That is until they entered the noisy deli and he got a good look at her face reflected in the long mirror behind the counter. No question it was her. She was unforgettably lovely.

As they stood in the queue, she turned to him.

'Well? What do you want?' she asked in a diffident tone that perfectly conveyed her disdain for a man who would oblige her to buy a replacement coffee under such circumstances.

Jim almost forgot why he was there for a moment and just managed to stop himself saying, '*My smart phone.*'

'Ah, a cappuccino thanks.'

The queue moved at the usual glacial pace, but while they waited Jim tried some small talk.

'You work around here then?' he ventured, immediately regretting the blindingly obvious. Noting the '*are you serious?*' look on her face, he tried a quick recovery.

'Of course you do.' he said, laughing.

'Yes, I work in the clouds up in One Canada Square.' She said in a softer voice.

Jim thought, '*The clouds, that's just where you'd expect to find an angel. Glad I didn't say that out loud!*'

'I used to work up there for my sins. What a rat race,' he said instead.

'Oh? Who did you work for?'

'I was in precious metal trading.'

She turned her head to him with renewed interest.

'That's the game I'm in at the moment. Ever heard of Metro Metals Futures? It's not the biggest player.'

Jim played it cool. He had to choose his moment. This was not it.

'Yeah, I've heard of it.'

Further talk was interrupted by the server who simply turned from the last customer to her, and without a word or a smile, asked what she wanted with a much practiced raise of her eyebrows and a slight upward nod of her head. She may even have been chewing gum. Sullen would describe her temperament, though the server would probably object to that and claim she was just overworked.

'Angel' placed the order. Turns out she was a simple soul. Black coffee to go.

They moved down the counter past the barista working the La Spaziale, and on to the crowded delivery area.

'So you're an American,' Jim said in attempt at casual conversation while they waited.

'Actually, I'm Canadian,' she said with the resigned tone of someone who has to correct that assumption many times a day.

'Look, I'm really sorry, I've got a tin ear for accents.'

'Don't worry, I'm used to it,' She actually smiled as she said it.

'One Cappuccino and a black coffee to go!'

They both reached for their drinks and took them over to the condiments island for sugar, wooden stirrers, and flavour shakers.

'Angel' turned to say goodbye to Jim but he caught her just before the words came out.

'Look, have you got a moment. Let's take our drinks over there,' pointing to a couple of tall chairs by the window that had just become vacant.

She hesitated.

'Please. Just a couple of minutes.'

She looked at her watch and shrugged.

'Why not?'

Jim was already moving towards the chairs, eager to claim them before someone else grabbed the coveted window location. His arms open in a silent gesture for her to take a seat.

'Angel' joined him and as she sat down, Jim introduced himself.

'Hi, I'm James Stack. Please call me Jim,' he said as he offered his hand.

'James,' she considered the name as though it was an intellectual conundrum and then took his hand.

'I'm Summer,' she left it there.

'Now that is a beautiful name. It suits you.'

'Thanks,' she said, stirring a full sachet of sugar into her coffee.

'Look, I'm sorry about your coat. I'm very accident prone. Just clumsy I guess.' She took a sip of coffee.

'Hard to imagine. You move like a ballet dancer.'

Summer didn't respond. She just stared out of the window clasping the warm cup in her hands.

Jim tried a brighter note in the hope of moving the conversation towards the hidden point of the meeting.

'So, you work at Metro Metals? Been there long?'

'A few months.'

Then she asked the million dollar question.

'What about you? What business are you in?'

Jim took a deep breath.

'What if I told you I used to work at Metro Metals Futures?'

She examined Jim's face.

'Now that would be a coincidence.' she said with just a hint of suspicion. And then, after a sip of coffee, she sat upright and gave Jim a reproachful look,

'Is it a coincidence?'

Jim turned to look out of the window. He needed a moment to consider how he was going to couch his reply.

Summer now fully engaged, pressed him again.

'Mr. Stack, is this meeting a coincidence?'

The sudden formality worried him. He decided to try the truth and see how that worked. Well, it's better than just making stuff up as he went along. It could get him into deeper trouble.

He turned and looked straight into her beautiful face.

'I used to work at Metro Metals. That was quite a while ago. I won't explain why I left.'

She was still listening so he pressed on.

'Suffice it to say I left in a hurry and wasn't able to take all of my possessions with me.'

Her look turned frosty – still beautiful, but frosty.

'What has any of this to do with me?' She started to get out of her chair to leave.

'Please bear with me Summer. Let me explain,' he implored.

She stood there, ready to leave in a hurry, but curiosity held her attention for a moment.

'I left behind a smart phone. It holds some very important personal information. The problem is I didn't leave it in my desk. I didn't want it to be found so I placed it in another desk. One nearby,' he stopped to let that sink in for a moment.

'My desk,' she said emphatically. She was smart.

'You put it in my desk. But why on Earth do you think it will still be there. And by the way, how the hell did you know I worked at that desk?'

Jim explained with what he hoped was disarming honesty.

'Yesterday morning I tried to retrieve it. I still had my old Metro Metals pass. I got as far as the trading floor, believe it or not. I was just a few yards away from the desk. Your desk. That's when I was stopped. As I was being invited to leave, I saw you returning to it.'

Summer stood there for a moment, just looking at Jim. She joined the dots.

'And you want me to find this smart phone and give it back to you?' Summer stood there slowly shaking her head as she worked through what she had just heard.

'And you just waited on the platform in the hope of seeing me.' It wasn't a question, just a statement of fact.

'Well, it was a bit more than that, but essentially that's about it,' Jim replied, adding. 'And a bit of luck. You bumping into me. I really wasn't sure I'd remember what you looked like.'

'I'm not sure I'm flattered by that,' she said in a lighter tone.

Amid the noise of the cafe there was silence between them for a moment as they looked at each other. Jim wondering what happens next.

She broke the silence.

'So, how long has the phone been in my desk?'

'Quite a long time.'

Summer considered this for a moment.

'I don't understand. Why do you think it's still there? I'm using the desk and I haven't seen anything like that in the drawers.'

'Have you noticed any folders in the larger bottom drawer?'

'Yes, documents I've placed there. There's nothing there, just the usual Health and Safety stuff.'

Jim urged her on.

'Have you checked inside the Health and Safety folders? There's one called Fire Drill.'

'No-one looks at Health and Safety notices.' She closed her eyes and slowly nodded her head and gave a small laugh as it dawned on her. She looked at him with renewed respect.

'Very clever. It might still be there.'

'So, will you get it for me?' Jim asked in his most persuasive voice. His face a picture of imploring supplication that would've embarrassed a Labrador puppy.

'Is this illegal? I won't do anything illegal.'

'It's just personal, Summer. Absolutely nothing illegal I guarantee it,' Jim pleaded hopefully.

Summer stood there for a moment, chewing it over.

'OK. Meet me here tomorrow same time. Coffees are on you.'

She took her coffee cup, turned, and left.

Jim watched her as she disappeared into the busy pedestrian area outside and beyond the view of the window.

He let out a quiet breathy whistle.

'Well that went better than it had a right to,' he thought to himself.

Police and Thieves

December

Two bank robberies and almost nothing to show for it. The Wailing Wall has a few more mug shots to decorate it. These were accompanied by captions, headings, brief summaries, and some red connecting lines that go from the witness and CCTV generated mug shots, to their related best guess mug shots an artist had worked up. Guesses based on how the villains may actually look without disguises. The main difference from a few weeks ago was that the board now bore the names of two bank robberies. It was an unhappy mess.

Perched on Detective Sergeant Yates' desk, DCI Deakins went over everything for the umpteenth time. Debbie Yates, leaning back in her chair, counted the leads on her fingers as though a new lead would magically appear.

She waved her forefinger.

'We have what we think is a good resemblance of the perpetrators.'

'Yes, but nobody recognises them, so they can't be accurate,' Deakins countered.

Yates added her middle finger.

'We know their modus operandi.'

'But what does that give us? They use the bank's customer relationships against them. The disguises have changed so there's no way to anticipate who's a villain, until it's too late.'

'Well, there's the DNA evidence,' Debbie said as she held up a third finger.

'It's brought us nothing,' Deakins said in total frustration. 'There's just no clear match in the

85

database. You'd think that three guys who've embarked on a crime spree would have a bit of form!'

DC Robinson wandered over with a piece of paper. 'Boss, here's a curious one for you.'

'I can't deal with that now John, leave it in my office.'

Robinson walked away leaving Yates and Deakins no further forward. Nothing magical happened. The case remained as it was – moribund.

An hour passed during which Eric Deakins popped out to purchase a few groceries from the local Tesco Express.

When he returned to his office, he threw the bag on the floor, pulled open the middle drawer of his desk, took out his lunch box and placed it on the desk. It was as he peeled off the Tupperware lid that his eye caught the title of the document Robinson had left for him. It was partially covered by the polythene container.

He pushed the box to one side and picked up the note. As he read, its meaning dawned on him. He got up, leaned through the open door and called Robinson over.

'When did this come in?'

'Well, I was out when it landed on my desk boss, so it must have come in before nine this morning.' Robinson said as he crossed room.

'Christ! This might be what we've been waiting for Yates.'

'What's that sir?' Yates said coming over to join Robinson.

'A breakthrough!'

***

It took two attempts to reach CID in south London. The first took him to a message service for a Croydon massage parlour. Yates got him the correct number and he finally got through to DI Russell.

'This is DCI Deakins, Helmsford Constabulary. I've got a DNA match report here from you guys. What can you tell me about it?'

'Hang on a minute. I'll put you through to DI Jennings. I think it's his case.'

Click...pause. The briefest hint of something from Vivaldi's Four Seasons, then...*click*.

'Yes? DI Jennings?'

'This is DCI Deakins at Helmsford Constabulary. I've got a DNA match report from you,' he repeated. 'What can you tell me about it?'

'Hi. Yes, I thought this might interest you. We had a break-in at a pub a few days ago. From what we can see from the crappy CCTV pictures it was a couple of teenagers. Not professionals, anyway.'

Deakins heart sank, but he listened anyway.

'They broke in, damaged the till, which was empty, of course. But they managed to nick a few bottles of spirits.'

Deakins interrupted.

'Look, I can't see what this has to do with me...?'

'Stay with me a moment. One of them cut themselves on the glass as they broke in – or out. Anyway, we ran it through DNA a few days ago and it came back with a partial match for something you've been trying to match on the database.'

Deakins thought for a moment.

'How partial was this match?'

'Familial. Pretty strong connection.'

Familial, as the word implied, meant there was a strong family connection to the DNA sample from the cigarette butt.

Deakins sat up and leaned into the desk, fully tuned in.

'You got a name?'

'No we haven't, he hasn't got a record. At least not one that includes a DNA profile.'

Deakins sank back into his chair.

'But we're pretty sure we'll catch this kid. When we do, I'll get straight back to you.'

'Thanks for your help anyway. Really appreciated.'

'By the way,' DI Jennings asked. 'How is that bank robbery investigation going?'

'Don't ask.'

Double Agent

January

Jim went through the list of hoops the con had to jump through in order to have a hope of succeeding. They went under the general heading of: *How do you convince the Bank of England that...*

1: There is a conspiracy in progress right now within the vaults of the bank – a plot with the deadly purpose of contaminating much of the gold bullion stored there with radio-active material?

2: Once you've achieved that small thing, how do you put the suggestion in their collective mind that it would be impossible to check every single individual bar of gold within a narrow time frame?

3: Make them believe that amongst all four thousand five hundred tonnes of bullion, they can be certain that only the British inventory does not contain any of the tampered gold bars.

4: Persuade them that the best plan would be to get the 'clean' British gold out of the bank and to a place of safety – away from the threat of imminent contamination.

And 5: They've only got twenty-four hours!

Jim knew of one person who might be able to help.

Time to reacquaint Victor Avery, Head of Security at the Bank of England with his past.

***

Deep within the walled fortress of the Bank of England a telephone rang. It was answered with the curt pomposity of a person supremely confident in their place at the top of the food chain.

'Yes?'

'David Grant of the SFO for you Victor.' Barbara couldn't be sure, but was that a 'gulp' she heard at the other end of the line just before she pressed the button to transfer the call?

'Hello Victor. Listen to this...'

***

Jim couldn't get the same table at Starbucks in King William Street. The café was busier than last time for some reason. Still, he made himself comfortable and reasonably unobtrusive at a table half hidden under the stairway.

His call to Avery had cheered him up, especially when he played him just a snippet of one of the recordings.

He sat, stirred some sugar into his coffee and waited for Avery to arrive.

***

Summer had turned up the next morning as promised with the smart phone. She had made a good point about its value, as the battery was of course as flat as a pancake.

As pleased as Jim was about finally getting hold of the phone, he was infinitely happier to see Summer. He wondered if he could push his luck a bit further.

They chatted and drank their coffee. Jim wasn't keen on a full kiss and tell revelation at this point. The kiss definitely, the rest could come later. It turned out that she might be up for a 'later' in the form of a see-how-it-goes, date. A lunch, somewhere nearby, later in the week.

He actually had a spring in his step when he left. It felt good.

***

Ten minutes he'd given Avery, as before, so he settled down with his coffee and waited.

He unrolled his newspaper and glanced at the front page. Usual nightmare about terrorist plots. Threat Level up-graded to 'Oh shit!' Everyone told not to be alarmed. He turned the page.

Looks like the politicians are deep into election mode. It's January and elections are next May. Christ! Four more months of it.

***

A little heads up on Politics in the UK.

There are a number of political flavours to choose from but in truth there are only two main contenders. 'This Lot' and 'The Other Lot'.

'This Lot' are any party that's in power at the moment and 'The Other Lot' condemn them obsessively – blowing raspberries from the wings.

Someone from another planet would compare their policies and not find much difference between them. They both claim to want to protect the National Health Service, want to provide welfare to help when it's needed, good schools, and a decent living wage for all. The difference between them is in the manner in which these worthy ambitions are paid for.

One 'Lot' prefers to tax and, if high taxes don't bring in the bacon – borrow. The other 'Lot' believes it should be provided strictly through taxation and by the way, keep those taxes as low as possible so that John and Jane taxpayer have money left to spend as they choose. Borrow, only as a last resort.

Both parties claim to appeal to the centre ground.

Somehow it all evens itself out and they both get a go at governing the good people of this green and pleasant land.

'The Other Lot' had been in power for a goodly long time and completely emptied the treasury to meet the promises they had made at each General Election. Indeed, so voracious was their appetite for spending that to pay the cost of their promises they sold almost fifty percent of the UK gold stored in the vaults of the Bank of England, amounting to some 350 tonnes. When that wasn't enough, they borrowed like the Greeks.

Then came the worst banking crisis in recent history of the world and the borrowing got ratcheted up to eye watering levels. To use the terrorist threat level as a comparison, we were at 'Oh shit!'

'This Lot' had been in power for four years or so and in an attempt to reduce the level of debt they introduced the unpopular concept of austerity. Some pundits predict the good people of Great Britain have had just about enough of belt tightening.

So, in all likelihood, at the next Election the political roundabout would turn once again.

***

Absorbed in his newspaper he didn't notice at first as someone shuffled into the bench seat on the other side of the table.

Jim looked up. Victor Avery was sitting back in the seat with his arms folded, his scowling face half hidden in the darkness of the recess under the stairs.

'Ah, Victor. It's been a while. Would you like a coffee?' Jim said folding away the paper.

Avery shook his head slowly and leaned forward.

'What is this all about Stack?' Avery was coming on all hard man.

'If this is an attempt at blackmail I can tell you now, to avoid wasting any more time, I'm untouchable.' It was an impressive attempt at a whispered threat.

Jim leaned in to Avery.

'You did hear your voice in the recording I played to you, didn't you Victor?'

'Who's to say it was my voice? Could have been anybody.'

'Would you like to hear more? I've got hours of it.'

'I doubt it.' Calling what he hoped was Jim's bluff.

Jim had been able to find a charger for the phone and though he'd given it a full charge, he couldn't be sure how long the old battery would hold out.

He brought the smart phone out of his pocket and held it in his hand on the table. A couple of touches and swipes and he was into the folder with the recordings. They weren't labelled as such but did have dates automatically attributed to each separate file.

He spoke as he browsed to one good example,

'You must be able to remember our little chats Victor? Think back. Any particular detail of our scam you'd rather not hear?'

Avery tried to appear unimpressed. He leaned back, arms folded again with a slight sneer on his face, challenging James.

Jim found the date he was looking for and plugged headphones into the socket. He pressed play and fast forwarded to a particular section. Stopping, he wound back a bit, listened, and put it on pause.

He handed the headphones to Avery.

Avery took them suspiciously, staring into Jim's eyes, expecting...no, hoping for a trick. This better not be for real. He held one of the phones to his ear, cupping the other ear – his eyes fixed on Jim.

Jim tapped the screen to play the recording.

It was as though Avery had teleported back to his old office at Metro Metals Futures. He recognised the background sound instantly. The familiar buzz of the trading floor beyond his door.

His voice sounded distant, as though he was over at his desk. From what he was saying he was reviewing something on his laptop screen. His voice got clearer as he got up and walked over to where the mobile phone recorder, and presumably Jim were on the couch.

His and Jim's voices were as clear as a bell, there was absolutely no misunderstanding the nature of the conversation.

It even included ounces traded, profits made for MMF, and money that Victor Avery and James Stack would receive once their skimmed share had passed through Blackstone. For Christ's sake, they even talked about the Luxembourg account. It was incontestable evidence of his involvement in a major fraud.

Jim watched Avery grow pale as he listened.

Eventually, Avery slowly removed the earphone, his chin dropped to his chest for a moment.

'There's quite a bit more of this stuff. I didn't realise quite how much I'd recorded,' Jim said almost cheerfully.

Cornered, Avery submitted to the inevitable.

'OK Stack. You'll get your money.'

He may be a hard man to impress under normal circumstances, but Victor Avery's earlier stone faced rejection of Jim following his release from jail had now magically transformed into one of uncharacteristic malleability.

Copies? Of course. Safe and secure. Envelopes held in the protective care of lawyers, to be opened in the event of something happening to Jim.

'My share? We're beyond that Victor. I'll tell you what I want.'

So, Jim set about drawing a very precise picture of what he wanted Avery to do. He told him about the Goldfinger plan and what Victor's part in it would be.

Pale faced and submissive, Victor Avery was eventually persuaded that the worries of certain job loss, permanent exclusion from the industry, a lengthy jail term, reputation ruined and a lifetime of poverty, could be avoided – there was a happier alternative. He would benefit from significant remuneration in cash and without a blemish on his character, simply for providing the very tiniest morsel of help to Jim's enterprise.

A bell had rung, a light gone on, and the tumblers of a lock had fallen into place. With his keen sense of self-preservation linked to the prospect of a substantial payment, he needed no further persuasion – Victor Avery was open for business.

As Jim brought the conversation to an end, he added a final thought.

'I'll need to keep in touch with you Victor. I can't keep using the name David Grant from the SFO, your PA, Barbara, will get suspicious.'

'Don't call the switchboard. Here's my mobile number.' He took out a pen and wrote the number down on a paper napkin.

'If I'm not alone I won't be able to talk to you. You'd better call in the evening.'

He pushed the napkin over to Jim.

Avery looked drained.

'Are we done here, Stack?'

'For the time being. I'll be in touch.'

This time it was Jim's turn to get up and walk away, leaving Victor Avery sitting in the shadows, looking the very essence of an extremely worried man.

The most essential element of the plan was in place.

Owner of a Lonely Heart

Later in the week

She had agreed to lunch, somewhere busy. Nothing too intimate. After all, what did she know about James, apart from the superficially obvious fact that he was good looking? Charming too, she was prepared to admit. Let's face it, after deliberately setting out to find her, he'd then talked her into getting his phone and she went right along with it – that was a whole lot of charm right there.

After meeting him the following morning and agreeing to a quick lunch, she'd spent the next couple of days admonishing herself for being such a mug.

Even so, she was intrigued by this enigmatic man, James Stack. Perhaps even attracted.

***

Jim waited by the phone booth outside Jamie's Italian at Churchill Place on the East side of Canary Wharf. He checked his watch again. One forty-five. She could take her lunches pretty much as she wanted, within reason, so a late lunch was agreed. At least most of the crush would start to ease around that time.

He jammed his hands deep into his coat pockets, hunched his shoulders and turned the lapels of his coat up against the winter chill – his breath turned to misty ghosts as it left his mouth. He took another look at his watch. Then, from behind, as someone touch his shoulder, he heard the sound of a warm Canadian voice.

'Hi.'

He turned and there she was.

'Sorry I'm late.' She smiled as she said it.

'That's OK, Come on, let's get inside.'

They didn't have long to wait for a table. They had to raise their voices above the noise of other diners but with luck it would start to thin out soon. Jim hoped so, because he didn't think shouting at Summer for an hour or so was going help him set a romantic mood. And that, Jim realized, was exactly what he wanted to do.

Jim ordered the Burger. Summer settled on a Crispy Soft Shell Crab dish, supposedly one of Jamie's specials.

Two glasses of white house wine arrived and they talked, and the time passed.

Jim discovered that Summer was only doing temporary agency work, which she didn't expect to last much longer at Metro Metals.

She revealed that she had been married. An English guy. The idiot had had an affair. She found out. A friend, for heaven's sake.

All in all she was pretty bored with her life at the moment.

Then, of course, she wanted to know something about him. Tricky.

He began by talking about his career in the army.

'I made Captain and was involved in Special Forces in Afghanistan. It was a mixture of periods of utter boredom spiced up with some pretty insane stuff.'

'Wow! That sounds really intense.'

'Sounds exciting, I suppose, but I needed to move on. I came back to England and moved to London. Got a job as a precious metals trader at Metro Metals.'

'You said you left Metro in a hurry. At least I think that's what you said. I'm curious. What kind of a hurry?' There was a playful tone in her voice.

'Well,' Jim paused for a moment. It was then he noticed that much of the background noise in the restaurant had finally died down as people left to return to their offices. He became thoughtful, his eyes fixed on his half empty glass of wine on the table, his fingers slowly rotating the stem.

'I don't want to say something that....' He tried again. 'You may not want a second date once I've told you.'

'Who said this was a first date?'

'Fair point. Look, no matter how I dress it up, it's not pretty, so here goes.'

Jim gave her the full version including the two years in prison. He left it there. The things that came next in the career of James Stack were not the kind of cards he wanted to lay on the table. Not right now. Later – maybe.

'So there it is.' He looked up. 'You did ask.'

She was leaning forward with her elbows on the table, her hands clasped in front of her mouth, one finger gently brushing her lips.

'Well, that's some story,' she said eventually. 'James Stack you are not a boring man.' She actually seemed impressed.

'What about the phone? Why did you really want that?'

'I had an accomplice who escaped justice and kept my share of the profits. I recorded some of our conversations. I needed some leverage.'

'So, what happens next?'

'Well I hope you'll let me take you to dinner.'

'No, I mean have you used your leverage yet?'

'So, no dinner?'

'Maybe,' she teased. 'I want to know what happened next. Or what will happen next.'

'It's already happened. He didn't seem very happy, but I think I can safely say that he's decided to be helpful.'

Summer nodded thoughtfully.

'Good. I'm glad. It seems to me that you certainly deserve it after what you went through.'

Jim relaxed.

'I'm glad you see it that way. I must admit I'm a bit surprised, though.'

'Don't judge me, James. We've only just met.'

Encouraged, Jim tried again.

'So, does that mean dinner?'

'Yes, I think so,' she said softly.

'Saturday?'

'OK.'

Summer insisted they split the bill. Jim helped her with her coat and then walked with her back towards her office, high in the upper levels of One Canada Square, the majestic edifice that soared up before them. It towered above the newer skyscrapers, reaching into the cloudless powder-blue sky, all sparkling glass and gleaming stainless steel in the chilly mid-winter sunlight.

Before they parted she gave him her mobile number.

Jim watched as she walked away and then headed for the tube station with the single blissful thought, *'She calls me James, not Jim.'*

Taking Care of Business

Early February

'So guys, on the sorted side we have the outline of a plan,' Jim said. 'Well, to be fair, we have a bit more than that. We have an outrageous but potentially executable plan, subject to some loose ends,' he added with more than a little sangfroid.

***

They had gathered in Toni Zeterio's semi-detached house buried in the back streets of Clerkenwell in the borough of Islington, London. A patch that still holds a large community of Italian Brits whose descendants originally migrated to the area way back in the mid eighteen-hundreds.

To call the house Zero's was pushing the truth because it was in fact owned by his Italian mother, Floriana, who still lived there. She moved there after leaving her husband Lionel in Luton, deciding to remain in England and live amongst fellow Italians in London, rather than return to Naples.

The house was partly paid for out of the divorce settlement and by Lionel's monthly child care contributions until Anthony was eighteen. Floriana, now sixty two, was still trying to keep up with the remaining mortgage repayments through waitressing jobs provided by friendly owners of local Italian restaurants. The house, though, was now worth considerably more than she paid for it. A classic example of asset rich and cash poor.

So Anthony lived with his mother in their three bed, one bathroom semi, among a community of mainly Italian macho friends, all of whom had cool Italian names. His mother had a cool Italian maiden name but she was stuck with her ex-husbands surname, Pendergrass. She couldn't be bothered to go through all the bureaucratic crap to get it changed. Anyway, to an Italian, Pendergrass is exotic!

Anthony had no such reticence. As soon as he was eighteen he changed his name by deed-poll to Toni Zeterio. His mother, who didn't re-marry, was quietly pleased.

Later, he fled the nest and spent a number of years with his relatives in Naples. It was here that his interest in crime was nurtured. Toni took a tentative place among the foot soldiers of a local gang run by an uncle.

He wasn't expected to take part in any of the serious stuff, just keep a look out and run errands.

One such errand required a visit to his extended family in New York. A period that equipped him with all kinds of nefarious skills.

He stayed long enough to fall in love with a beautiful distant cousin. Though she played him along in what he now realised were deliberately clandestine trysts, his love for her was hopelessly unrequited. The final nail in the coffin being the moment she married her long term fiancé. He really should have seen it coming.

For a twenty five year old it was a bit late in the day for doe eyed puppy love. He sank into a fug of morbid self-pity which left him so out of salts that he lost all enthusiasm for the drugs and protection racket business.

At the urging of senior members of his New York 'family', he returned to Naples. There he could lick his wounds, safely nestled in the loving bosom of the gangster family he had come to know so well.

He had more girlfriends but nothing came close to his one true love in New York. Eventually, he returned to London, ostensibly to get a job and go straight. More to please his mother since he was living with her again.

Like all Italian mothers it delighted her greatly to have her son back home where he belonged – living with her. She pampered and fussed over him, reminding him time and again that no woman would treat him as well as his mother does. Given his experience in New York, Toni conceded that it might just be true.

And so, for the last few years, Toni had settled back into a comfortable and undemanding life at home with his mother. He was thoroughly bored.

Then he bumped into Charlie who introduced him to James Stack.

***

'Look Jim, it all seems very clever and all that, but don't you think it's a bit top heavy?' Zero asked. 'You know, the whole thing depending on one man who you've blackmailed into doing it. How dependable is he?'

'That's right. He's what, Head of Security at the Bank of England?' Charlie probed. 'He's bound to have friends in high places he can call upon to look you up and scare you off.'

'I can assure you,' Jim said. 'The last thing this man wants is friends in high places getting involved. I've got him on a very tight leash. He will do what I want him to do.'

'Jeez, Jim, what on earth do you have on him? Cosy family snaps with boy scouts?' Toni asked.

'Don't worry about that sort of detail. His balls are mine for the moment.'

'What I'm trying to say,' Toni pressed Jim. 'I don't see how this bloke can simply say, "Oh dear, I've just received a letter out of the blue from some gangsters who have put explosive gold and radiation into our vaults". Won't they want to know how he got the letter or whatever? There has to be a trail or something.'

'That's right,' Hollywood joined in. 'He's going to need some kind of evidence. How does he know what he knows? Who told him?'

'Come on guys, one thing at a time. Listen, this is the way I think it should go down.'

Jim set out the next steps in his plan.

'The Bank must be completely convinced.'

The others nod in agreement.

'The onus is on Avery to do the convincing,' Jim continued. 'And I can assure you that he can be very convincing. But he doesn't work on his own. He runs the security department and relies on his staff to keep him abreast of things.'

Jim got up and walked over to the window, staring out into the rain washed street, red tail lights from passing traffic reduced to a stream of distorted lens flares through the rain streaked window pane.

He continued absently to himself. Wanting to hear the plan out loud for the first time – to hear how it sounded – to see if it made any sense.

'The job of the Bank of England depository is to hold gold safely until it's called for by its owners. They don't just turn up at the door and say "I've got 10 tonnes of gold in the back of my van, do you mind sticking it in your vault for a while?" Nothing arrives that they don't expect. There are no surprises.'

He turned round to look at the other two.

Charlie spotted a possible weakness in the plan.

'I can see how the bit where they are persuaded to move the gold out of the Bank just might work, but then what? Has anyone thought about that small detail? You know, the bit where we have to take the gold out of their hands, or trucks, or whatever?'

Toni is shocked by the sudden appearance of the blindingly obvious.

'You're right, I was so focused on Jim's crazy plan I just hadn't thought about what happens next.'

'Yeah, getting the gold out of the Bank is starting to look like the easy part,' Hollywood replied glumly.

'Unless of course, Jim plans to get Hollywood in as one of their drivers. He has had some experience driving a truck recently,' Zero added with undisguised mirth.

'Give it a rest,' Hollywood countered – bored with the constant references.

And then he looked directly at Jim.

'Is that the plan? Me, one of the drivers?'

'Well, I suppose that could be a solution couldn't it?' Jim said. Then more seriously, 'We have to consider far more than that. If we manage to relieve them of the gold, where do we take it and how do we turn it into cash? We have to find solutions to all of these problems, guys.'

Jim looked over at Zero.

'Why don't you get in touch with your old friends in Italy and America, Toni? You may have some useful family resources, if you know what I mean. See if they'd want to get involved, capiche?'

Zero grabbed this suggestion with both hands. This was his opportunity to ingratiate his way back into the mainstream of the family business, so he was very enthusiastic.

'Count on me Jim. I know just the people we need for this kind of thing.'

That was probably stretching the truth, but he'd make some calls and see how far it took him.

Jim started to wind things up.

'Charlie, check out some of your contacts who know something about warehousing. Nothing too big or far away. Discrete, easy to get to, but hard to locate.'

Then in a deadly serious tone to both of them.

'Listen you two, don't give anything away. Nobody needs to know any of the finer details. Just tell them we have a way to get the gold out, but say nothing about how we plan to do it, that's ours to know and nobody else's, at least for the time being.'

He paused to look each man in the eye.

'This is all fact finding. Yes?'

Toni and Charlie nod agreement.

'Yeah, I can do that, No worries mate,' Charlie added. 'Never let you down before have I, sir?' The last word a reminder that he was Jim's old, reliable, army buddy.

'Jim, are we really going to do this?' he added nervously. 'I mean, this is scary stuff, you know, robbing the Bank of England. It's big league, hard core, villainy. Serious prison sentences. You know, I'm just saying...'

Jim was already making his way out of the room when he turned to Hollywood.

'Stay cool Charlie. You wanted just one final big score. We all did.'

A thoughtful moment passed between them. The only sound was the noise of the traffic in the wet street outside tuning up for the slow Pavane of the evening rush hour. Jim took a breath and said breezily,

'Look, we still have one more bank job to do. I'll get back to you on that, so both of you be available to meet at my place next week.'

Charlie followed Jim out of the room into the hallway. Jim opened the front door and stepped out into the rain flecked night. Just before he closed the door behind him, he turned to Charlie.

'Have faith, Charlie. Have I ever let you down?' He winked, turned, and was gone.

Charlie went back into the living room. He tried to sound cheerful.

'How about a brew then, Zero?'

'Yeah. Good idea, Hollywood my friend.'

Toni, still buzzing with the unexpected opportunity to show off his criminal connections to these small-time amateurs, slipped out to the kitchen were his mother spent most of her time. The sound of cups and saucers rattling on the kitchen counter and a kettle being filled from the cold tap filtered through to the living room. Definitely his mother making the tea. Toni would have used mugs.

Alone for a moment, Charlie had a chance to think about Jim's last words. He was used to Jim's mercurial style, but he felt he wasn't being given the whole story. He couldn't put his finger on it, but he was sure Jim knew more than he was telling.

Then, as he pulled himself abruptly into the present, a chill frosted his spine. The thought of one more bank job gave him the shivers.

'Third time unlucky,' he thought to himself.

With a Little Help from My Friends

Early February

'Why are we having this conversation, Toni?' Franco Borriello asked in his impatient, New York Italian manner. 'You've told me nothing. I'm a busy man. I'm here for one day and I've given you this time as a favour to your uncle.'

Franco was a short, thick set man in his sixties. His hair – what was left of it, had been dyed black and brushed passed his ears into a DA at the back, just touching the collar of his beige, double breasted cashmere coat. Annoyance caused his eyes to bulge out of his doughy face. Or it could be a thyroid problem. Either way, he had the demeanour of a New York mafia patriarch, used to unquestioned, fawning obedience.

He popped the Paracetamol he'd been holding into his mouth and took a swig of water from the glass tumbler. He swallowed, screwing his eyes against the pain drilling into his forehead. Jet lag. *'Why does it only happen when I fly to Europe?'* he thought. Lifting his glasses and rubbing his eyes with his thumb and forefinger, he took a moment to calm himself.

'Now, tell me Toni, what is it you want from me?'

They were seated in the lobby of a smart hotel south of Piccadilly in Central London. Franco Borriello had caught the late night flight to London for a meeting with business associates at The Montgomery Hotel in Covent Garden. The plan was for a quick turnaround back to New York on the redeye tomorrow morning. He was annoyed they had no suite for him at the Montgomery and he had to put up with the inconvenience of this dump, five star though it may be.

Over the years, the business in New York had morphed from pure criminal activity to pure criminal activity disguised as innocent banking and finance.

Jim, aware of Toni's apprenticeship in Naples and New York, had asked him to get in touch with his relatives to see what they could bring to the party. He knew this was a dangerous step. These syndicates had access to people with a vast range of 'talent'. Skills that enabled them to operate in a broad sphere of criminal activities.

These ranged from; the subtle, hard to trace, and highly profitable 'internet credit card scam': the ever popular drugs and money-laundering game: onwards through main stream brute-force 'criminality' – there's a whole list of interesting choices under that heading – and downwards to 'contract wet-work'. And of course, banking and finance. This last subdivision providing a valuable interface between the legitimate and criminal world. It was a very dirty business.

Toni had tried to be circumspect about the Bank of England project, hoping he could raise Franco's interest without giving too much away. But Franco was having none of it.

'I'm sitting here because you want my help,' he said. 'Don't tease me like I'm some kind'a virgin schoolgirl, Toni. Have some respect.'

So, leaning in to Franco, to be sure he couldn't be overheard in the lobby, Toni gave Franco the name of the target and a brief outline of their plan.

Franco listened in silent, open mouthed astonishment.

'This is a joke, isn't it Toni?' easy to anger and now with his head feeling like it was clamped in a vice, Franco raged.

'You've taken my valuable time to talk about some stupid schoolboy prank? Even a child knows this is the one bank that can't be busted into.' Realizing he could be overheard he lowered his voice.

'I'm outta here, Toni, and I think you should go get your head examined and stop wasting my time.'

'But Mr. Borriello, we're not going to break into it, you don't under...' Toni pleaded.

'Forget it!' Franco put a hand up to stop him. Then he heaved himself slowly out of the deep leather chair and stood there looking down at Toni.

'Are you married yet Toni?'

'Married? No, Mr. Borriello I...'

'Find yourself a girl. Get married and have some kids.'

He picked up his briefcase, turned, and walked out into the street, the model of a conventional business man going to another tedious meeting. Except that as he approached the door, a stockily built man materialised out of the shadows and joined him. Franco Borriello never travelled alone.

Toni sat there for a moment going over what had just happened, or more accurately, hadn't happened.

The Third Bank Job: The Recce

Same day

Getting around the southern half of England north of London is easy if you're heading north or south, but it's like threading wool through a tapestry trying to get across country from east to west. No single thread will get you from A to B.

Jim took a large scale map with him on the recce of his chosen target. There were two to check out. One was the primary. It was this location that he needed to ensure had the correct layout demanded by their bank robbing template. Well, it had worked the last two times. If it ain't broke, as they say.

This town was extremely close to the A1 – a key artery, down which flows much of the vehicular life blood of the British economy.

He parked up near the target bank, a traditional institution with a proud heritage going back 150 years or so. It had recently been swallowed by a thrusting operation called Citizens Personal Banking Trust. This tiny outpost however, had not yet benefited from the shiny, open plan face lift that had turned so many other branches into soulless, high street clones.

This was good!

He ambled up to the nearest counter, proffered a £20 note and asked for change for the parking metre. Then he ambled out.

Back in his car, Jim unbuttoned his coat and removed the GoPro video camera from the Velcro strap around his chest.

Because his GoPro had no means to view what had been recorded, he'd installed a GoPro app on his smart phone that synced to the camera using GoPro's in-built Wi-Fi. He used it now to find the recording he'd just made.

The high definition video footage showed an extremely wide view of the bank interior seen through an enlarged button hole in his coat. The picture – clear as a bell – confirmed what Jim had seen in his brief visit. A street door into a small lobby where a cash machine was installed. An internal door gives access to the main banking area with the familiar arrangement of cash counters down the left hand side. Two glass cubicles were set off to the right. Presumably these were for interviews and obviously a relatively recent addition in an attempt to give the timeworn interior a modern gloss.

The old, solid wood panelled door on the back wall was what interested Jim. It had a sign halfway down that bore the legend 'Manager'. Jim thought to himself, '*God bless these old relics of the past. How they did love their privacy.*' There were no windows. So the bank got a big fat 'tick'.

Next on the list. The getaway.

Jim took his portable satnav from its mounting on the windscreen and switched it on. It took 30 seconds or so for it to see a couple of satellites. He'd printed out three different scale street maps of the area. One showing a wide view of the whole town and associated routes through and around it. Another was a larger scale view of the centre of the town showing every road that led off of the high street. The third was a very large scale map with the bank set off to the right hand side and the A1 highway slicing through top to bottom on the left. A distance of little more than 200 yards or so apart.

He fixed the GoPro back onto his chest harness, set it to record and buttoned his coat.

Once out of the car and with the sat-nav in his hand, he followed the back streets in the direction of the A1 using the sat-nav to confirm his position. The street that got him closest to the A1 ended with a pedestrian tunnel which passed through the grass covered embankment supporting the highway just a little over 15 feet above.

It was a quiet residential area. A side road running parallel to the A1 was lined with old terraced houses that faced the embankment to the left and right of him. He wondered who would want to live next to a main highway with all that traffic noise 24 hours a day.

This town, like many of a similar size that have a motorway near them, didn't have direct access within the town. You had to drive out of town to get on to it.

Jim looked around to see if anyone was nearby or watching from windows. No people. No traffic. Just what you'd expect in a sleepy back street. Confident he was not being observed, he started climbing up the embankment, not quite vertical, but it certainly felt like it by the time he got to the top. He reached a stubby barrier separating the highway from the fifteen foot drop. It was all that prevented him from getting onto the A1 itself.

He climbed over and there he was, standing on the rubbish strewn verge of the noisy, multi-lane, thoroughfare. This made him very visible to all the passing traffic which could at any moment include a traffic cop.

He quickly made a note of the sat-nav coordinates. Then he took out his stop watch, set it to zero, punched the button and began to retrace his route back to the high street at a good fast walk. He must remember to add a few seconds to allow for the quick slide down the embankment. A journey that smeared a green patch along the seat of his pants after losing his footing on the damp grass

Back in the car, with the route fresh in his mind, he took the map with the largest scale and inked a yellow highlight along the streets to the A1 under-pass, making notes at various points including the height and angle of the embankment itself and the precise satellite navigation coordinates. He then noted the time on the stop watch, added 30 seconds for the climb up and wrote that down as well.

He unbuttoned his coat, detached the GoPro from its harness and turned it off.

The escape route got a big fat 'Check'

This part of the plan was good to go.

The secondary target was some way away from the primary and it took time to get there because there was no local on-ramp to the motorway. But the journey back was considerably quicker, and this was the route he timed.

The principal planning for bank robbery number three was now in place.

With a Little Help from My Friends

Reprise

Early the following morning

The LED street lamps and enormous flashing animated advertising displays of Piccadilly Circus provided a permanent Las Vegas-like brilliance that pushed back the dark of the early February morning. Large flakes of cold, wet snow fell heavily out of the black sky to melt on the damp pavement. The place was deserted apart from a lone street sweeper that motored across the empty plaza before disappearing up Regent Street. Added to that depressing scene was the tricky task Toni Zeterio faced in a few moments.

Yesterday had been a disaster. He'd set out to gain the help of Franco Borriello, the head of one of New York's leading crime syndicate families. Toni knew him a little from his time working for the 'business' some years ago. His uncle in Naples had arranged the re-introduction as a favour. And as a favour to his uncle, Franco had agreed to meet Toni when he was next in London.

As far as Franco was concerned, the meeting took place, time was wasted, tempers were lost – mainly Franco's – and duty fulfilled.

If he had heard of the expression he might have added – 'End of!'

Franco had an early flight back to New York from London Heathrow. The red eye. The thought of it irritated him more than a little.

He was already awake and washing down another couple of Paracetamols from the packet on the bedside table when the phone rang with the hotel's early morning, personal wake-up call.

Toni had taken the tube to Piccadilly – a lonely ride at that time of the morning. From there he made his way on foot the short distance to the hotel.

He rounded a corner and saw the warm tungsten glow of the hotel foyer flooding out into the cold street, illuminating a taxi parked outside. By the cloud of exhaust rising slowly into the freezing air, the taxi's motor was running.

As Toni approached, the concierge stepped down the three short carpeted stairs towards the taxi and opened the door. Moments later Borriello's henchman walked out and stood in the street next to him, his short black coat hanging open over a frame as solid as a vault door, weapon easy to reach. He waited with his back to Toni. Franco followed shortly after and boarded the cab. The side of beef turned and climbed in. They were travelling light, briefcases only.

Walking quickly to catch up, Toni stepped around the concierge and leaned into the open door of the taxi. Borriello's security guy went into full alert, gave him a threatening look and put a thick forearm across the frame of the open door, barring Toni from getting any further. His other hand moved towards the inside of his coat.

Franco looked seriously shocked. In another scenario, on another day, this could have been an assassination attempt.

Shock quickly changed to surprise and relief as Franco recognised Toni. The side of beef was still in shield mode.

'Toni!' Franco said. 'What are you doing here? Don't you know I'm on my way to the airport? I don't have time for this.'

'Please, Mr. Borriello, let me...'

'Enough! We said all that had to be said yesterday. It's over.'

'Look, there's much more to it. I know it may sound crazy, but please give me one more chance to show you how it can work.'

'Close the door Toni, I'm going to the airport. Driver. Let's go.'

'Well I can't mate, until you close the bloody door can I?'

'Toni. Close the door,' Franco shouted.

The driver revved the taxi motor and started to inch slowly away.

Toni put one foot inside the door and hopped on the other to keep up.

'Look mate are you getting in or what?' The driver shouted.

Toni didn't need another invitation. He gave a big shove and pushed his way through beefy guy, tripping over his legs and landing on the floor at Borriello's feet. The henchman made a move to grab him and haul him out. But Franco relented.

'OK, OK. You're coming to the airport with us. Are you satisfied?'

Beefy guy slammed the door shut and the taxi picked up speed.

'Listen Toni. This better be good. You've got thirty minutes. Now sit down for Pete's sake, you're crowding me.'

Toni picked himself up, lowered the rear facing, flip-down jump seat on Franco's side and sat down. Franco grimaced from a sudden throb of pain as his headache reached five on the Richter scale. He popped a Paracetamol in his mouth and removed his glasses to give his eyes another squeeze.

He put his glasses back on, leaned back in his seat and closed his eyes in an attempt to relax. He took a long, deep breath – almost a sigh, before speaking.

'OK, Toni. What is it you haven't told me yet about this great plan?' He said, resigning himself to the inevitable.

'Thank you, Mr. Borriello. I'm sorry about interrupting you like this but you won't regret it.'

'Yeah, yeah. I already do. Now get on with it.'

And so Toni told him – everything.

Can't Get Enough

The following Weekend

The first thing Jim did when he arrived back from his recce was to call Summer. She'd been on his mind from the day he first had coffee with her at the café on Canary Wharf three weeks ago.

Lunch at Jamie's had led to dinner the following Saturday in the West End. That happy evening, in what Summer insisted should be a neutral location, somewhere they both had to travel to, moved the relationship further along.

Summer had just arrived home from work and was closing the door to her apartment in Greenwich when her mobile rang. She saw that it was Jim and answered it quickly, holding the phone between her head and shoulder while struggling to free herself of her winter coat.

'James, hi. I've just got in.'

She fussed around her modern, open plan flat, switching on lights and unpacking a bag of groceries in the kitchen as she spoke.

'How's your day been?' she said as she adjusted the thermostat to put some warmth into the cold apartment.

'Busy,' Jim said. 'Been out and about visiting places. You know. Boring stuff really.'

They chatted for a bit. Small talk. And then Jim asked.

'So, how about the weekend?'

'What about the weekend?' She teased back at him.

'Well, it's a collection of days, most people like to think starts on Friday night and goes on through

119

Saturday and Sunday. It's a kind of work free zone,' Jim teased back.

'Yeah, I've heard of it,' she said, throwing herself onto the couch, kicking her shoes off and turning to lay full length with her feet up on the cushions.

'So what about it?'

'Well, dinner tomorrow night for a start. We could go out, or I could cook something at my place?'

'You mean man food?' she joked back.

'Hey, I'm not such a bad cook. I might surprise you.'

'James, you're just one surprise after another.'

She still wasn't ready to commit. Not yet.

'Look, I'd love to have dinner with you on Friday. Err, oh that is tomorrow isn't it? OK, dinner tomorrow night would be nice.'

'My place?' Jim asked hopefully.

She paused for a moment.

'Do you know Greenwich?'

'Not very well.'

'There's a place opposite Greenwich Market that's pretty good. Great fish if you like sea food.'

'I like it already. Fish on Friday. Very traditional.'

'Not as traditional as you think. It's Turkish!'

They spent the next ten minutes or so chatting idly before finally agreeing to meet in the restaurant at eight the following night.

The restaurant wasn't difficult to find. It was just as Summer had described, exactly opposite Greenwich Market. He made sure he was there a little early. This was one date he didn't want to arrive fashionably late for.

He was delighted when Summer arrived bang on time. A good sign. She spotted him from the door and made her way over to the corner table he'd reserved.

He'd specifically asked for somewhere discrete and intimate. As it turned out, by the time he got there the restaurant was already buzzing. This was obviously one of Greenwich's most popular Friday night eating destinations.

He watched Summer as she walked across the restaurant and around the other tables towards him. Other guys were watching her too, trying to disguise their quick, covert glances from their own female companions. And no wonder. She looked fabulous.

Gone was the tailored city business suit she had worn on the last two occasions. This was different. Relaxed, on her home turf, she was dressed for comfort: a pink tailored blazer over a simple white t-shirt, tucked into tight fitting blue jeans. Her winter coat carried casually over her arm.

He stood up as she arrived, took her coat and placed it over a chair and leaned in to kiss her cheek. She responded in an easy, familiar way.

Seated at the table, the noise of the restaurant blurred into an easy to ignore buzz in the background.

As far as they were concerned, they were the only people in this room.

The evening passed with great food, delicious wine, and easy conversation. By the time they had drunk the last sip of wine and moved on to the subject of coffee, they were literally, the only people in the room.

It was Summer who suggested coffee at her place instead. Her apartment, after all, was only a short walk away. It seemed so natural.

So that's what they did.

**

They spent the whole weekend in Greenwich, never moving far from Summer's apartment. Breakfast? Very late. Lunch and dinner were casual affairs of pub food, Bistros and Italian.

Jim shopped for a few items of clothing and a toothbrush. He hadn't assumed anything would develop between them, though he had fervently hoped it would. Jim wondered what Summer would have said if he had turned up at the restaurant on Friday night with an overnight bag – what would any girl have said!

Typically, like any city dweller in any city the world over, Jim had promised himself he'd eventually get around to seeing all the stuff tourists come to London to see.

Greenwich had a lot to offer. The Cutty Sark was an impressive living museum down on the Thames water front. The National Maritime Museum and the Millennium Dome each deserve some of your time. If they don't do it for you, the Fan Museum might float your boat, as they say.

On Sunday, after lunch, they enjoyed the long walk up Crooms Hill to visit the Greenwich Observatory where Greenwich Mean Time is measured. But just as importantly, it's the place where you can stand on the precise point on the globe that represents zero degrees Longitude.

Summer had her arm through Jim's, chatting easily together as they strolled up the hill.

'Well, I'm going to be out of work soon,' Summer said.

'Oh? Why is that?'

'I was only working at Metro Metals temporarily, as you know. My contract got rolled on a couple of times, but from the end of the month I'm back struggling along with the rest of the huddled masses looking for work.'

'How do you feel about that?' Jim asked.

'What do you mean, James? No income. It's a bit scary. I've got bills to pay.'

'What I meant is, do you have ambitions to do something completely different? Or are you content to stay doing nine to five for ever?'

'Something different would make a change. Something a little more adventurous.'

'Adventurous?' Jim said. 'How do you mean?'

'I'm not sure. Something surprising. Perhaps something that arrives out of the blue.'

Jim pushed a bit more.

'Adventure tends to carry some risks.'

'There are all kinds of risks James. Handing your money over to an investor carries risks. Crossing the road carries risks,' she said. 'The thing you did at Metro Metals carried a big risk. It was a hell of a gamble. How did you feel when you were in the middle of it?'

'That's a good question.' Jim turned the thought over in his mind for a while before giving Summer his answer.

'I'd been in the thick of it with Special Forces in Afghanistan. There were quiet times but even then you couldn't be sure someone hadn't infiltrated the camp with an IED.'

'IED?'

'Improvised explosive device. You had to keep your eye out for them, the bastards hid them all over the place out in the country. It was the sorties into the hills and mountains to winkle out Taliban or Al-Qaida rebels that could be seriously dangerous though,' Jim said. 'I suppose coming back to a safe life in the UK, free of that kind of tension, felt dull by comparison. The Metro Metals scam gave me a good shot of the adrenalin I'd been missing.'

They neared the top of the hill and approached the observatory.

'I could definitely use a good shot of adrenalin,' Summer said with a laugh. 'But I'm not sure I'm ready for the risks. Perhaps I'm destined for a conventional, quiet life.'

They walked onto the cobbled courtyard of the observatory. A brass strip had been permanently fixed along the ground to represent the Prime Meridian longitudinal line that slices the Earth from North Pole to South Pole, dividing the world into eastern and western hemispheres.

Jim stopped and turned to stand directly in front of Summer. Taking hold of her hands, he looked into her blue eyes, smiled, and then asked her to look down. She saw that her feet were straddling the brass strip. One foot in the eastern hemisphere, the other in the west.

'If you had the chance to change the direction of your life, which way would you turn Summer?' Jim asked.

'Certainty or adventure? More of the same, or a little more spice?'

Summer stared at her feet for a moment and then slowly tilted her head back up to look Jim directly in the eyes. Nodding her head thoughtfully, she gave Jim the most enigmatic of smiles. A mischievous look that Jim struggled to decode.

The Third Bank Job: The Set Up

The following week

The intercom buzzed.

'Yeah?'

'It's Toni.'

'Come on up.'

He pressed the button to open the street door downstairs, left his apartment door ajar, and returned to his newspaper on the sofa.

A few moments later Toni breezed in and dumped himself down into the sofa opposite.

'So how did it go with that girl then?' he said cheerfully.

'Summer? Really good Toni. Really good,' Jim said over the top of his newspaper.

'You seeing her again?'

'Oh, yeah.' Jim said with a smile.

'Has she got a sister?'

'No, I don't think so. Anyway, it's about time you found yourself a girl Zero, you can't go on living with your mother.'

Toni was struck by the comment.

'You're the second person to say that to me recently, Jim. Saying it is easy. Finding a girl, now that's not so easy, especially at my age,' Toni said mournfully.

'What are you Toni, 36?'

'38.'

'Still time, my friend. She's out there somewhere, but you've got to put some effort into it. Use some of that Italian charm.'

Jim put his newspaper to one side.

'Talking of Italians, how did you get on with your relatives? Did you manage to make any useful contacts?'

Toni lit up.

'Like I told you before, Jim, my contacts are as solid as they come. I had a big meeting with the boss from New York,' Toni boasted.

Jim was impressed.

'New York.'

'That's right. Franco Borriello,' Toni bragged. He paused to let that sink in. 'He was here in London for a meeting and he gave me some of his very valuable time before he flew back to the States. He doesn't do that for just anybody, Jim. We're, you know, family. Blood.'

Jim gave a cautious welcome to the news.

'That sounds impressive. So, what will he bring to our party?'

'Anything we want Jim.' Toni said smugly

'Anything!' Jim said. 'That could be a lot of help. I presume this would all be locally sourced. We don't want a bunch of New York heavies getting involved.'

'They've got all the people with all the skills we're gonna need right here in London. We just got to tell them what we want and when.'

Jim thought about that for a moment.

'And what do they want for all this generosity?'

'Well, they don't want wages, they want a share of the takings of course.'

'Why are they so eager to provide all this on those terms, Toni? What did you tell them?' Jim asked suspiciously. 'You didn't tell them the whole plan did you?'

'No, no,' Toni replied in a panic. 'It's all good. I only told them the bare essentials. You know, just the headlines like you said.'

'And that was enough for them?'

'Yeah, they could see we had a good plan. I just told my friend Franco to trust me and that was good enough for him.'

Jim left it there.

'That's brilliant Toni, I think we've made a great start. With your contacts, pretty much everything is in place.'

'But what shall I tell them we need, Jim? Those Bank of England security trucks might be armed when they move the gold. It could be bloody dangerous.'

They were interrupted by the door buzzer. Jim indicated for Toni to answer it.

'That'll be Charlie.'

Toni pressed the buzzer and cracked the apartment door open. He went back to the sofa. Jim had followed Toni as far as the kitchen to refill the coffee percolator.

Charlie barged through the door, slammed it shut and went straight through to the living room, a little breathless from running up the stairs.

'Hey Toni, where's Jim?'

'I'm in the kitchen. What do you want – tea or coffee?' Jim shouted.

'Toni wants his usual coffee and you know me. A brew up as always.'

Five minutes passed. Jim returned gripping three hot mugs which he put down awkwardly on the coffee table, trying not to spill them.

'Hey Charlie, any news on warehouses?'

'I'm still working on it Jim. It's a little trickier than I thought. There's one idea that might fly, but it'll need more work.'

'What's that then?' Jim encouraged him.

'Containers.'

'Containers. That sounds interesting. What did you have in mind?'

'Well, several containers, but only one to hold the gold. We use a temporary warehouse location which I have yet to source, by the way, and load everything into one of the containers. Then we move all of the containers around and park them in places like lorry parks, transport cafes. We could even fake up some road works and leave one there. You know, keep 'em separate. Never keeping them in one place for long. But leaving them in plain sight. Like a shell game.'

'I like it Charlie, for you that's almost subtle.' Jim said. 'Keep working on it and see if you can find that warehouse.'

'Will do, Jim.'

'But why keep the gold in one container only? Why not split the gold across all of the containers? That way we reduce our losses if they did find one,' Jim said.

They nodded in agreement.

Jim picked up his coffee, took a sip then added another thought.

'You know, we're talking about tonnes and tonnes of gold here. We can afford to lose quite a bit. In fact I don't think we should even try to take it all, just a sizable chunk. We don't have to be greedy.'

Charlie and Toni agreed up to a point.

'We have to consider our new partners Jim, they'll want to be in on the planning,' Toni said.

'Partners!' Jim responded.

'What partners are these, Jim?' Charlie asked.

'Toni has made contact with his friends and family in the States. Seems like they want to come on board.'

'Toni, we need the help of professionals but I hadn't thought of them as partners, more like shareholders.'

'We can't do this alone, Jim. These guys will expect to be in right at the beginning. They've got the experience and the expertise.'

'Yeah, I know that Toni. But I'm running this operation, you'd better make sure they know, OK?'

'Yeah, that's all cool Jim. They understand,' Toni said. 'They have a guy here in London who wants to meet you. What shall I do? It's your call Jim.'

Jim gave it some thought while he drank his coffee.

'OK, we'll talk about that later. But right now I want to talk about the next bank robbery, which by the way, is on for next week.'

Charlie sat bolt upright.

'Jeez, that's soon Jim. You must have been busy.' He sounded alarmed.

'Relax Charlie, I've got it all set up but we're going to do it a little differently from the last two times.'

Toni chipped in.

'How different are we talking Jim?'

'The same technique as before within the bank, Toni, so make sure you've got your disguise ready. Perhaps some changes to it would be a good idea. Keep 'em guessing,' Jim said. 'But Charlie, you're going to have a bigger role.'

'Me? What kind of bigger role?' He sounded worried.

'We're going to try a distraction ploy. You know, smoke and mirrors, to make the getaway cleaner.'

'I'm all for an easier escape, the last two were hairy to say the least.'

'I knew I could rely on you Charlie,' Jim said, bringing a large envelope out from under the newspaper on the coffee table. 'Have a look at these maps of the town, guys. The larger one shows the general area. Notice the bank circled in yellow highlighter. Now, see over to the left, the A1 motorway is not far from the high street.'

'That's the getaway route, yeah?' Charlie asked.

'That's right Charlie, you don't park outside the bank this time. We'll meet you on the A1, right above where the pedestrian underpass is.'

'Wait a minute Jim, that's a hell of a risk isn't it? The timing's got to be right on the money. I can't hang around on the shoulder of the A1. Some traffic cop might stop by and ask questions.'

'Yeah, I've considered that. That's why there's a second part to the plan, and that's where you come in, Charlie.'

'I can't wait to hear this, Jim. I was only mildly terrified before.'

'Nothing you can't handle, Charlie. Just imagine you're about to take on the Taliban in the Hindu Kush mountains. Is anything scarier than that?'

'I was *trained* to take on the Taliban, Jim.'

'Well the people we're facing this time won't have guns, so it's not life or death is it? Get a grip.'

'Yeah, I hear you Jim. So what is it you want me to do?'

Jim took out the large scale map with all his notations on it from the recce.

'First, I want you both to take a close look at the route from the bank and pay attention to my notes.' When you've done that I've got some video for you both to watch.'

'And me?' Charlie asked.

'Hang on Charlie, I'll get to your part in a minute. You're gonna love it.'

'Now I really am worried.'

The Third Bank Job

Second week in March: Morning

The high street wasn't busy. The busy days tended to be the regular market days on Tuesday and Saturdays. That was when hordes of out-of-towners swelled the shopping population of Belford.

Today wasn't a market day so the shops and businesses were left to struggle with the meagre footfall offered by the handful of locals. The ones left behind once the battalions of commuters had left for London.

And it's why James Stack chose that day for the robbery.

Jim had made the appointment with the manager on the premise that he represented a consortium that was planning to build a supermarket on local farm land soon to be made available. They wanted the opinion of the towns' most influential business people to get a measure of the viability of their business plan. You can always rely on vanity to open doors.

He arrived alone at the appointed time and waited in the main bank area for the manager to come out and greet him. He looked around and noticed one teller at the counter. Another clerk was busy taking care of business with a customer in one of the glass interview cubicles. Only a couple of customers would be in line ahead of Toni if he arrived now.

The manager came out only a couple of minutes behind schedule. He shook Jim's hand enthusiastically in a double handed grip while apologising for the delay.

'Mr. Samuels, so good to meet you. I'm Brian Coal. Do come through, won't you?'

He took Jim through to his office. As he entered, Jim turned and caught a glimpse of Toni arriving just as the manager closed the door.

'*Good man,*' Jim thought. '*I hope his disguise stands close scrutiny.*'

Toni had gone for an auburn coloured wig, side burns and pencil thin moustache. He'd also given his teeth some serious dental decay and tobacco staining on his fingers. Reflective coated lenses set in dark chunky frames removed the need for coloured contact lenses. He still fattened his face with cotton balls as before. A check jacket, beige slacks, cloth cap and tan leather brogues completed his disguise.

With his tonsorial adornments, he looked like a picture from a 1950's mail order catalogue. All that was missing was an elegant briar pipe in his hand and a jaunty pose. He reckoned people would be so busy looking at his disgusting teeth they wouldn't remember his face. Just one person stood ahead of him in line.

In the office, Jim sat on the threadbare cloth cushion of an upright wooden chair facing a large, time worn, mahogany desk. The youthful manager was seated in his comfortably padded red leather chair behind it.

'This will all be going soon,' he said to Jim, sweeping his hand around the office in a gesture of apology for the aging furnishings. In his hand he held the business card Jim had passed to him as he sat down.

'Really? That's a shame. I do like tradition, don't you?' Jim said. Adopting a plummy voice – the very essence of aristocratic breeding – a perfect match for his immaculately tailored, deep blue, Saville Row, chalk stripe, English wool suit and pink silk tie. He had dyed his hair blond and fixed a matching moustache in place.

'Well, it's all about efficiency isn't it? That and the new corporate look they're rolling out to all the old branches of Citizens Personal Banking Trust,' he said. 'We've got to move with the times, Mr. Samuels. Move with the times as they say.' He gave a flourish of his hand as though sweeping everything away.

'I imagine that's the way of the world Brian, whether we like it or not.'

'Now, to business,' the manager said. 'A new supermarket is it? That'll put some life into this town, Mr. Samuels. No doubt about it. How can I be of assistance?'

The truth is, supermarkets tended to suck the life *out* of a town, but business was business as far as Brian Coal was concerned.

Jim glanced at his watch, then bent down, picked up his briefcase and put it on his lap. He popped the latches and opened the lid so that the contents were hidden from the manager. A good thing because it contained just three things. None of them related to the business of supermarkets: Jim's leather gloves, a lightweight fabric hoodie and a ratchet wrench.

'Well Brian, I'll tell you how you can help me,' Jim said as he put the leather gloves on. 'I have a very urgent need for money.'

'Money?' Brian said with surprise. 'I thought you had a consortium of investors for that sort of thing?'

'A consortium of sorts, Brian.'

Jim put his hand into the open briefcase and took hold of the ratchet wrench, keeping it hidden within the case.

'Now I want you to pay very close attention Brian. I am holding a gun here.'

The manager sat bolt upright not sure how to respond.

'Mr. Samuels, is this a joke? I'm not sure I appreciate it if it is,' he said with a nervous laugh.

'Oh, I'm sure you're aware of the previous bank robberies. The last manger was shot. But of course you'll know that, won't you?'

The look of alarm showed he had the manager's full attention.

'I know he injured his arm but I didn't know he was shot.'

I can assure you he was, because I shot him,' Jim said calmly.

In fact, after the last robbery, the manager had fallen over a chair in his haste to leave his office. He'd dislocated his shoulder on the table just after Jim and Toni had exited the bank. It was serious enough that he was taken to hospital.

Still holding the wrench in his right hand, Jim put his other hand into the case and turned the ratchet a couple of times. It gave a very loud double-click. An effect that anyone who'd ever seen an action movie might assume was a gun being cocked.

The manager sat back in his chair, his hands half raised in the air as though in surrender.

'You must know the routine, Brian,' Jim said confidently. 'The phone will ring any second now. It will be one of your counter clerks who is being told to read a note placed before her. The note has a set of very precise instructions, one of which is to call you in your office and confirm you are being held at gun point. She will expect you to confirm this. You will then tell your clerk to do whatever the man says.'

Seconds after he finished explaining the rules, the phone rang.

'Pick it up,' Jim commanded gruffly.

The manager leaned over and picked the handset up, hands shaking.

Jim gave him a threatening look and nodded to the phone.

'Hello?' Brian managed feebly, staring back at Jim.

A moment of silence passed as he listened to the voice at the other end, his head swivelled towards Jim. Terrified eyes flicking between Jim's face and the briefcase.

'Y-Yes,' he stuttered. 'Do as the man says. Don't take any risks. Just do it.' Hands shaking, he replaced the phone. It took a couple of attempts to get the handset to sit back in place properly.

'Now what?' he said, his voice breaking into falsetto.

'We wait...quietly and calmly.'

***

The clerk had read the hand written note held to the hardened glass screen. It was very clear in its demands. The man pushed a folded cloth sack through the gap at the bottom of the screen.

There were other customers being served at the other teller's position. The clerk looked over to see if they'd noticed what was going on. Well, she knew what this was. She'd read about it in the newspapers, and of course they'd talked about it in the bank. 'The Hostage Heist' they'd called it. Two bank robberies using the same method. Two robbers, one who took the manager hostage in his office and the clerk at the cash till hands the money over to his accomplice.

The accomplice was standing in front of her right now holding the message to the window. Which meant the manager had been taken hostage and she had to do as instructed.

He glared at her through his thin rimmed glasses. His eyes were blue. She'd remember that when the police asked for a description. He hadn't actually spoken yet, but she'd be listening keenly. She reckoned she was pretty good with accents. Let's see now, he's what about five foot eight? Greying hair, must be in his fifties.

'Don't just stand there, get on with it,' Charlie Dawson growled in his best Sheffield accent. Not a bad Joe Cocker if he was up for a Joe Cocker sound-alike competition.

She opened the drawer and took out all the notes, stuffing as much as she could into the large bag. It bulged so much it was difficult to push through the gap between the glass screen and the well in the counter. It was a tight fit and for a moment she didn't think it would go through. But he grabbed his side and between them, pushing and shoving, it burst out the other side tearing the bag in half. Twenty and fifty pound notes fluttering to the ground. He bent down and scooped them up with one hand, while he held the other torn half of the bag in the other. When he stood up, the clerk was still standing there wide eyed and open mouthed. Now though, there was another woman standing next to her.

'What's going on here?' the other woman demanded.

The clerk turned at the sound of her voice.

'But you're supposed to be...?' The clerk's words petered out.

'Come on, quickly. Push the rest of the cash through.' Charlie demanded.

'Leave it!' The woman ordered.

No point in getting into an argument. Charlie moved closer to the microphone to the left of the screen.

'Don't move. Don't call the police,' he whispered menacingly, giving both women an intimidating look in turn. 'Your manager...,' he made a slicing motion across his throat with his thumb. 'Understand?'

The clerk gave a quick nod in the direction of the woman standing next to her.

'This is the manager.'

By now the other clerk had stopped serving his customer and both turned to watch the scene.

Charlie was quick to recover.

'Well, have a nice day,' he said with a laugh as he turned to leave.

He exited the bank smartly, bumping into two new customers on his way out. He walked down the high street a little, before slipping between two parked cars and crossing over to a side road. He took a quick look back up the high street before turning off. No one seemed to be pursuing him.

A little way down the street on the right, a dirt access road took him to a row of small, rundown garages. He had the key to number six. He walked down the row counting off as he went. He got to number six and put the small key into the lock in middle of the handle. It wouldn't turn. He tried again. Both ways this time. Nothing. Shit!

Did he count correctly? He stepped back and nodded off each garage door until he got to number six. The one he was standing in front of.

There was another row of garages behind him. Did he count the wrong row? He counted off six doors on the other side, walked over and tried the key. Nothing. Shit! Panic! He could hear the whine of police sirens in the distance.

He thought about it for a second. Jim's directions were very clear, as always. He even had a photo. He reached into his jacket pocket and pulled it out. Yes definitely these garages. He turned the picture over. Written carefully on the back were instructions. Odd numbers on the left, even on the right. Christ! He'd forgotten.

He went back to the row opposite and counted two, four, six. Three doors in. He tried the key. Yes!

He quickly pulled the cantilevered door up and there was the car, a blue Ford Sierra, ten years old and as common as muck. He stepped into the cramped space between the car and the garage wall. Pulled the keys out of his pocket, opened the door as far as it would go and squeezed in.

He wasn't alone. Next to him in the passenger seat was what looked like a petite older woman wearing a dark blue Niqab covering her head and shoulders down to her waist. A small space allowed her face to be visible, but only just. She was already strapped in.

'Hello darling, cold night?' Charlie said to the shop dummy.

On her lap was a black Burka decorated in small sequins. He pulled it over his head and down, covering him to his waist. It would go all the way to his feet if he stood up, but there was no point. He glanced in the mirror. His face was barely visible through the letter box opening.

'Hmm, an improvement.'

He got the motor started and drove slowly out of the garage, stopping once he'd cleared the door. He got out, closed the garage door, locking it before returning to the car.

This was it. Fingers crossed he should be parked on the A1 in about half an hour. Jim had reckoned the likelihood of two Asian women driving an old Ford Sierra being stopped was remote. But as he drove slowly down the high street, back past the bank, he felt distinctly vulnerable. His heart was pounding and he was beginning to sweat. That was probably because the car's heater was jammed on high. He had to crack a window to stop the windscreen steaming up.

From behind he could hear the sound of police sirens heading to the town centre. One, obviously a local crew, passed him noisily with lights flashing.

Nobody looked. He was invisible.

It took ten minutes to get to the main on ramp for the A1. Once on the south bound carriageway he saw a steady stream of police cars flying past on the other carriageway heading north. Lights flashing sirens blaring. Heading back the way he'd come.

The plan was that after fifteen minutes on the motorway Charlie would call Jim.

Taking his mobile from his trouser pocket turned out to be tricky. What with the seat belt strapped across his chest and all the folds of the Burka getting in the way.

'Christ, how do these women get on with this gear?' he wondered.

After a few seconds of frustrating rummaging, while at the same time trying not to wander into vehicles passing him in the outer lane, he managed to find his pocket and fish out his phone. Using one hand, he speed dialled Jim. Just one ring. That's all Jim said he wanted.

**

All was calm in the manager's office. Brian Coal, stressed and jumpy, was behaving himself. His eyes never leaving Jim.

Jim on the other hand attempted a relaxed pose with his legs crossed, his hand on the 'gun' hidden behind the lid of the briefcase. In fact, he was probably as stressed as the manager, he just hoped it didn't show.

Time does strange things when danger threatens. Stress causes your body clock to race ahead and what seems to be an interminable passage of time may only be seconds.

'Why hasn't Charlie called?' He wondered. *'What's gone wrong?'*

His heart started to beat harder and faster. He started to consider a plan B if Charlie didn't make it to the A1 rendezvous.

A bright ring from his mobile snapped him alert. He waited. Just the one ring. It was Charlie.

They had ten minutes to get to the rendezvous point.

Ninety seconds later he heard a shout from Toni from within the bank.

'Alpha!'

That's all he needed. He stood up and leaned over the desk to the manager.

'OK Brian, we're leaving,' Jim said still maintaining the posh accent.

'Listen very carefully. We're taking the clerk with us. Nothing will happen to her if you stay put in your chair. Don't call the police and DON'T leave the office. Understand?'

'Yes...I understand.'

'What do you understand Brian?'

'I've got to stay here in the office and don't call the police.'

'Good man Brian.'

Jim started to leave, but as an afterthought, he took the ratchet wrench from the briefcase and laid it on the desk in front of the manager.

'Brian? Take this and get your nuts tightened.'

He snapped the case shut and left.

Toni was already at the street door by the time Jim caught up with him. The clerk was still standing where he'd left her, behind the glass screen at the counter. The other customer and clerk turned to stare at them as they left. They were probably wondering why anyone would shout 'Alpha' at the top of their voice for no apparent reason. Must be one of those medical conditions you hear about.

Now, as they walked quickly away from the bank, it was just a question of following the route to the A1 pedestrian underpass. They had five minutes to get there.

Toni had three large fat bags stuffed with cash. A good haul. He gave one for Jim to carry as they speed walked. No running. Nothing to attract attention. Jim hid the bulging cloth bag under his jacket as best he could.

Once they'd safely turned the first corner, Toni removed his jacket and threw it into a garden. He was wearing a grey jumper underneath. Jim did the same with his dark suit jacket and tie. He took the lightweight fabric hoodie from the case, put it on, and hid the bag of money underneath it. He wiped the case clean and stuffed it between a short brick wall and hedge that marked the boundary of the shabby Victorian houses they were passing.

All this was done in seconds as they kept up the fast walk to the underpass.

In the old Ford Sierra the two Asian ladies were still motoring steadily southward down the A1. Charlie could see the pedestrian overpass just ahead. He put on the emergency blinkers and pulled over. This was the bit that bothered him. The rules are, you're not supposed to park on the hard shoulder except in an emergency. Traffic cops tend to stop and ask questions if you're just sitting there. There's no way Charlie would pass that test. If the police stopped it was game over.

The Sierra came to a standstill right over the underpass and Charlie pulled the hand brake on. With both indicators going, most motorists would recognise this as an emergency.

He kept the engine turning over and waited.

'Bollocks!'

Charlie looked in the rear view mirror and saw the flashing lights of a police car speeding down the outside lane towards him. All the cars in front either slowing down to the speed limit or pulling over to let it pass.

'Here it comes. This could be it,' he said to the manikin next to him.

But the car just sped past. The officer in the passenger seat giving the old Ford Sierra and its occupants a bored glance as it went by.

'Probably gonna turn round at a junction and head back up to join the other cops in Stebbingbrook. They all want a part of the action,' Charlie thought.

After it had passed, two heads popped up furtively behind the barrier. Took a quick look to make sure it was clear and stepped over. They went for the rear passenger doors. The doors wouldn't open.

'Come on Charlie, the doors are locked for Christ sake!' Jim shouted.

No central locking. Charlie cursed as he undid his seat belt. He reached over to pull the lock buttons up. Jim's side behind him was hard to reach and he only just managed it. The other door was impossible. Jim got in and opened it for Toni.

'Charlie, come on, let's go,' Jim shouted as Charlie wasted time re-attaching his seatbelt.

Once the old Sierra had re-joined the traffic the three bank robbers started to relax.

'So, how did it go?' Charlie asked.

'Better than expected. We were almost like real professionals,' Toni replied with a laugh. 'How about you Charlie? If that is you under there.'

'Yeah, good. There's been nothing but cop cars rushing up the A1. They can only be going to my little robbery. There can't be any police left south of the county.'

They drove on in silence for a while as they headed towards London. All three of them watching the last fifteen minutes of their lives in their heads, like the replay of a scene in a Catch-Up TV download.

Charlie broke the silence. The one man robbery and subsequent get-away had taken its toll on him.

'Listen guys, I gotta tell you, I'm still buzzing from the adrenalin rush. Look at my hands,' he took one hand from the steering wheel. It was visibly shaking. He gave a nervous laugh.

'I'd still rather be up to my neck in bad guys back at Helmand.'

'You did great, Charlie,' Jim said. 'I knew you would.'

'You were right, Jim. Once I put the message up on the window, our reputation took over. The clerk had obviously heard what had happened before. She followed through just as you predicted she would. She never questioned if we had the bank manger hostage or not, she just assumed we did.'

'Good man,' Jim said. 'Distraction. That's the name of the game. Send everybody up to the north of the county.'

As he drove, Charlie reached down into the passenger foot-well. He brought up the ripped bag and waved it for Jim and Toni to see – notes falling out onto the shop dummy's lap.

'Little bonus for us.'

Jim and Toni looked at each other and laughed.

'Way to go, Charlie,' Jim said.

The mood lightened.

'Can you see anything through that get up?' Toni asked.

'Enough, but its bloody warm inside here. I can't get the heater turned down either.'

'Well if you and your girlfriend can get us back home without banging into anything, we'd be grateful.'

A quick laugh, followed by a period of silence. Toni noticed that Jim seemed to have dozed off. How was he able to do that after the stress of the last hour or so? Then a thought occurred to him.

'Hollywood. No movies?'

'Funny that, Zero. I can't think of anything that's like what we've just done.'

"Yeah, well now we're moving into the seriously big-time thanks to you. What do you think about that?'

Charlie gave that some thought. When he did speak, Toni detect a slight trace of unease.

'Do you know what, Zero? I wish I'd kept my bloody mouth shut.'

Doubleback

Same day

'When did this happen?' an exasperated DCI Eric Deakins shouted down the phone. He turned to get Detective Sergeant Debbie Yates attention across the room but she was already staring at him, alarmed by the tone of his voice.

His hand covered the mobile as he spoke to her.

'They've just hit another bank. Get your things, we're off to...,' then to the phone. 'Where did you say it happened?'

A pause. Then to Yates.

'Stebbingbrook,' he said. 'We'll need all the toys, Yates – prints, pictures. See if you can get one of those portable DNA profiling things over there as well.'

Debbie indicated she was on to it. Eric Deakins tapped his mobile off and put it in his pocket as he headed for the door to catch up with Yates. He stopped and looked around the CID office.

'Anyone seen DC Robinson?' He shouted across to the two remaining officers in the room.

'He's following up on that break-in at the Audi dealership sir.'

'Call him, will you? I need him over in Stebbingbrook ASAP. Let him know it's another bank robbery. You can pick up on the Audi case for the time being.'

'Yes sir!' a delighted younger officer was grateful for the opportunity to get his teeth into a real case at last.

Deakins didn't wait for the junior detective's reply.

Blue light flashing and siren wailing, Eric Deakins and Debbie Yates wove their way across the north of the county, through congested country roads and eventually, the freedom of the A1 motorway.

On the way, Deakins got another call.

'What?... At the same time?...' He looked at Yates as he spoke. 'So, where did this one happen?... Belford! But that's twenty miles back the other way.'

'You're not going to believe this.'

'Another bank robbery, boss?'

'Yeah, and we're heading away from it at eighty miles an hour.'

'What do you want to do, go back?'

'No, I'll tell you what we'll do,' Deakins said. 'We'll go to the first one, we're nearer it anyway. Have a quick look, then I'll jump in the car and go to the second one.'

'Coincidence do you think, sir?'

'Coincidence?' Deakins pondered. 'I don't think so. Seeing the distance between them it could be a distraction robbery. You know, get everyone up to the north of the county while the real robbers get away.'

'Very clever if you can pull it off.'

'They may well have done just that.'

He clicked the police radio to send.

'Control. This is DCI Deakins.'

Static, then a thin metallic response.

'Control.'

'What have you sent over to the second bank robbery at Belford? Have you got anything left?'

'We're on to that now sir. One car is there already.'

'Well done. I'll be heading there myself after dropping Detective Sergeant Yates off at the bank in Stebbingbrook. Let them know, will you?'

147

'Will do.'

'Oh, one more thing. Contact DC Robertson. Tell him to go straight to Belford.'

They arrived at the scene of the bank robbery in Stebbingbrook only twenty minutes after the phone call and twenty-five minutes after the robbery. On the way, two or three police cruisers passed them on the south bound carriageway, heading down to the scene at Belford.

Nevertheless, there were still so many police cars parked in the road outside the bank, it looked like an annual national law enforcement convention. DCI Deakins reckoned every patrol car in the two counties constabulary area must be there.

'Those cheeky, clever sods! They'll be miles away by now,' Deakins said.

They parked as close as they could get, which was not close. Eric Deakins could see that it was starting to thin out though. Someone had decided enough was enough and was starting to get the cars back on duty. A couple moved off with greater speed – lights and sirens clearing the road ahead. Probably heading down to Belford.

Yates got out and headed for the bank. Deakins got out and walked around the car to get in the driver's side. He'd decided against going into the bank himself. Better, he thought, to go straight back down to Belford crime scene and start his investigation. He'd wait to hear the report from Sergeant Yates when she turned up later at Belford.

The robbery at Belford, he reckoned, was the main event, if his theory about the robbery at Stebbingbrook being a distraction was correct.

On the drive down he thought it through. If this was, as he suspected, the third of the so-called Hostage Heists, then only three people were involved. If that was still the case, how did they spread the work between them to do two banks at the same time, or did they in fact have some additional help?

The whole bloody thing had got as confusing as hell. He'd got Superintendent Honeywell on his case because of lack of progress. And now the press would be all over it again like a rash.

Well, at least there was a good chance that at last they'd made a mistake and left some clues. Over confidence might have set in. Arrogance even. With any luck, it would be third time unlucky.

***

DC Robertson had been taking statements from the clerk and was about to move on to the manager when DCI Deakins walked in gasping. He leaned heavily on the frame of the door before going over and collapsing on a chair by one of the glass interview rooms: hands on his knees, head up in the air like a goldfish breaking the surface in a fishbowl – heaving for air.

By the time he'd got to the bank, the area was surrounded by police cars and media wagons. Sky News had even managed to get a crew over, up-linked and live. A reporter was doing a stand up to camera outside the bank.

'*What the hell could they possibly know already?*' He wondered. As he walked past he heard the woman reporter saying something about '...will this be another unsolved case for the Helmsford police?' '*Great!*'

No sign of Honeywell yet. It wouldn't be long though, what with all the journalists and cameras jamming the pavement. He was such a media tart.

With all the cars parked outside he couldn't get close to the bank, *again*, and had to park way down the road. A walk of any length didn't do it for DCI Deakins.

'You OK sir?' Robertson asked.

'Me? Oh yeah...*gasp*...I'm good. Give me a...*heave*...Give me a minute. What have you...*gasp*...got for me?'

DC Robinson gave Eric a concerned look before running through his report.

'Well, it's definitely the same bunch sir. You know, same modus operandi and all.'

He paused to see if his boss wanted to say anything. Apparently not.

'I've already taken a statement from,' he glanced at his note book. 'Mrs Susan Everett. Ah, she's the bank teller.'

Nothing. Just a nod and a flick of a hand indicating for him to continue.

'She remembers a man who had an appointment with the manager – a Mr. Brian Coal. He's over there,' pointing to a man sitting at a table with another staff member. 'Shortly after he went into the manager's office, another man arrived and queued at her counter position. She's given a fairly detailed description of the man, specifically remembers his bad teeth.'

He went on to tell DCI Deakins what happened and, as he had already suggested, it did indeed appear to be the same routine.

'He shouted out 'Alpha' when he had the money and then ran to the door. That was when the other man came out of Mr. Coal's office.'

'Anything else?' Eric said, his breathing almost back under control.

'No, that's pretty much all from her for the moment sir. Oh, apart from one thing.'

'Oh? What's that?'

'The manager didn't come out of the office for quite a while for some reason. The clerk, Mrs Everett, went in to see if he was alright. He seemed extremely relieved to see her.'

'Right, I think it's time to chat with the manager, Mr...?'

'Coal, sir.'

'Oh, can you organise some coffee for me Robinson? I'll be in the manager's office.'

He walked over to the manager, introduced himself and followed him in to his office.

Seated in the chair only recently vacated by James Stack, he pulled out his notebook and a pen from his jacket inside pocket. Brian Coal had seated himself nervously in his leather chair behind his desk: back straight, forearms on the table, head down and eyes on the ratchet wrench. He looked uncomfortable.

When Deakins spoke to begin the interview, the manager's head snapped up like a spring, his mind returning to the present.

Brian Coal told it pretty much as it was, carefully avoiding anything that might cast him in a less than heroic light.

'I'm curious, Mr. Coal, why did you wait so long in your office after...,' he looked at his notes. 'Mr. Samuels left?'

There was an embarrassed silence for a moment.

'He told me to wait here and not move and not call the police.'

'Once he was out of the bank, surely you would have been safe to do just that. Weren't you worried about your other staff?'

'Oh, yes, I forgot to mention. He said they were leaving with Mrs Everett, ah, the clerk? You know, taking her hostage.'

'So you believed they had taken the clerk with them?'

'That's right. How could I know any different?' he said, pulling himself together and assuming more authority. 'He was very threatening. He had a gun and...' He froze.

'A gun?'

'It was hidden behind the lid of his briefcase,' he replied weakly.

'So you didn't actually see it?'

'No, but he told me he'd shot the manager during the last robbery.'

'He told you that did he?' Deakins said. 'The manager wasn't shot during the last robbery. In fact, no guns were used.'

The manager just sat there forlornly staring back down at the ratchet wrench on the desk in front of him. Oh, how he wished he'd had the foresight to remove it.'

'What is that?' Deakins asked.

The manager went to pick it up to hand to the detective.

'Don't touch it! Leave it where it is please.'

The manager's hand shot back.

'I think it's a tool of some kind,' he said meekly.

'A wrench,' said Deakins as he stood up and leaned over the desk for a closer look. 'Is it yours?'

'No, Mr. Samuels left it there.'

'Why would he do that? What happened?'

'He had that in his briefcase. He was clicking it. I suppose he was trying to make it sound like a gun. When he got up to leave, he came over and put it down on the desk in front of me.'

'I'll bet you were relieved it wasn't a real gun? What did he say?'

'What do you mean?'

'When he put the wrench down in front of you, he was making a point. It would have been safer for him to take it with him. Did he say anything?'

'Let me think, maybe.'

'Maybe? I'd have thought pretty much everything the man said would be fairly memorable.' Deakins said with his pen ready, hovering above his notebook.

'Look, he may have said something about tightening some nuts.'

'Can you give me the precise words please, Mr. Coal? Every detail is important.'

Brian Coal couldn't avoid it any longer.

'He said I should use it to get my nuts tightened.' He turned away and looked at the wall in an attempt to recover some dignity.

DCI Deakins tried to smother a snigger as he wrote it down. He had to admit, he did have some admiration for this villain, whoever he was. At least he had a sense of humour.

Street Fighting Man

Later that day

The three of them were sitting in Jim's living room chatting and laughing. The cash lay in piles on the coffee table. Lots of it. This job had been the best of the three. Jim had fixed drinks. A beer for Charlie, red wine for Toni, and a double whiskey for himself. After what happened on the way back, he needed it.

***

They had driven up to the top floor of a multi-storey car park in north London, changed their clothes, and removed their disguises. They stuffed the shop dummy in the boot and walked over to the exit stairs. A second car they'd parked earlier the same day waited for them in the shadows of one of the darker corners on the level below.

They climbed in and stayed until it got dark, which was around six p.m. at that time of year. They'd left a couple of canvas shoulder bags and a nylon kit bag in the car to carry the cash. One each. Toni got out with his shoulder bag and made his way back to Jim's alone. Charlie then drove out of the car park and dropped Jim with his kit bag near a London Overground station a few miles away. He then drove over to the West End of London, found a quiet side road and parked in whatever space was available.

Like much of London, pretty much all of the parking bays were for local residents only, so his car would probably piss someone off. Well, it was going to get discovered at some point. As long as they didn't connect it to him.

Even though they had all kept their gloves on, he gave the interior a quick wipe with a paper cloth, screwed it up and put it in his pocket. A quick look around to see if anyone was paying any attention. Not a soul. Well, no one nearby anyway.

He got out with his shoulder bag and made his way to the nearest bus stop. The closest was on Brompton Road opposite Harrods. He wanted a bus that would get him back over to east central. That should give him just a short walk to Jim's place off Brick Lane. It turned out he needed two connections to get close.

***

Charlie had dropped Jim near Gospel Oak to catch an Overground connection to Shoreditch High Street. From there it was a fifteen minute walk to his apartment near Brick Lane. A walk he'd done many times.

There was no direct route. It was one dog leg after another. Sometimes along a brightly lit and busy main road, then a cut through quiet residential back streets before a stretch of high street again. It was during the deserted back road journey that things started to go wrong.

He'd passed a pub where early evening drinkers were standing outside smoking and chatting. A few people, mostly young men, were heading into or away from the pub. He took a turn to the left along a street lined with three storey Victorian and Edwardian houses – all awaiting their turn to be gentrified. Only two street lights were working near the junctions at either end and another blinked intermittently a third of the way in. Some warm tungsten light spilled from a couple of ground floor windows, but mostly the street was dark between the pools of pale street light that book-ended the road.

He heard the soft footsteps coming up at a fast walk behind him. He'd been aware of the two guys since passing the pub. Tall black and skinny, short white: late teens, early twenties at the most. He increased his pace, but they kept up, a measured distance behind. He knew this street a little. *'What were they waiting for?'* Jim wondered. He got an immediate answer.

One guy, the tall black one, suddenly ran past Jim and disappeared off to the left. The street may have been dark in places but way back at the junction, a car took a right hand turn and its headlights, though far away, threw the briefest of light down the street, casting a long faint shadow of the youth behind him. He was much closer. It was about now that Jim wished he'd kept the wrench.

He could see it now, a dark space between a couple of houses. Time to cross the road. No way he wanted to get into a fight – not with all the cash in his kit bag. This would be a serious pay day for a couple of opportunist muggers. That was just not going to happen, Jim decided. He'd had some tough training, courtesy of Special Forces, but he wasn't invincible. Sure, he could take these guys on but he might not walk away from it.

As he moved over to the edge of the pavement, the tall black guy stepped out and blocked him. Short white came up behind and took hold of one of the fabric handles on the end of the kit bag.

So, no choice. It was going to be a street brawl, like it or not. He jumped up and gave tall black guy a

156

good hard kick in the chest. Short white had a good grip on the handle, but so did Jim. He threw the bag up and round in a big wide circle over his head causing short white to spin round and jerk his arm up behind his back. Jim pushed his arm up further, but short white still had a hold. It must have been painful. Jim gave him a hard shove head first onto the bonnet of a parked Range Rover and the grip relaxed. The head butt to pressed steel was hard enough to kick off the alarm. Good. Noise and flashing amber light. That should get some attention.

Tall black guy was back on him now with a powerful punch to the side of his head from behind. Enough to disorient him for a moment. Somehow he managed to remain standing. The guy was going for a kick, but he could see it coming during one of the brief flashes of the Range Rover hazard lights.

He stepped to one side and caught the leg as it came through, raising it as high as he could. With tall black guy behind him hopping on one foot, Jim turned back with a sweeping kick of his own, catching tall black guy hard between the legs. He was rewarded with very satisfying cry of pain.

Lights started to turn on in nearby houses, a couple of front doors opened. One man stood staring out into the dark street. All he could see in the darkness was fleeting frozen images of three guys fighting in the intermittent amber light of the Range Rover's alarm. It looked like the flickering motion of a silent movie.

Tall black guy was bent over, staring at the pavement and cupping his injury with both hands. Jim thought it only polite to say goodnight with a hard kick up into his face. He turned and saw that short white was trying to get back up so he gave him a good night kiss as well.

A few of the good people of the neighbourhood had already started to walk cautiously towards him, calling out to see if he was alright. Jim told them he was fine. As they approached, tall black guy and short white picked themselves up and fled off down the street.

One of the locals, obviously the owner of the Range Rover, came over and clicked the alarm off. He was moaning about possible damage to his car and was beginning to suggest Jim might know something about that. A few more people sauntered over, emboldened by the ones already there. Someone mentioned they'd already called the police and that was when Jim thanked them and took off in a hurry.

He was home in another five minutes to the distant sound of a police siren echoing mournfully amongst the city buildings. Toni was already there, waiting in the street. Charlie arrived twenty minutes later.

***

It wasn't a bad haul judging by the amount of cash on the large coffee table in Jims apartment, what with the unexpected extra loot from Charlie's diversion robbery. That one was only supposed to look like a copycat job to get the police over to the other side of the county. The ploy had worked so successfully that they'd got away completely clean. As far as they knew, anyway.

Jim refilled his tumbler from the bottle of whiskey standing amongst the cash on the table, and raised it to the other two.

'Here's to you two. Well done guys.'

They each raised their glasses and took a swig. Toni reached over for the red wine, refilled his glass and returned the compliment.

'Well done back at you, James Stack. That was quite a plan. I never doubted it for a moment.'

'Me neither,' Charlie said. 'But I swear the stress is screwing with me love life, Jim.'

'What love life is that, Hollywood, the expensive kind?' Jim joked. 'Anyway, we should have enough cash to keep our heads down until the Bank of England caper.' Jim gestured to the cash. 'Look, we all need a bit of petty cash now to pay our own personal bills and some spending money. I think we can afford a grand each.'

Charlie had already downed two beers. He got up from the couch and headed for the bathroom.

'I need a piss suddenly.'

'Do me a favour Hollywood.'

'What's that?'

'Don't pee on the carpet OK? Oh, and help yourself to another beer from the fridge on your way back.'

'No worries, Jim. Copy that – no peeing on the carpet,' Charlie laughed as he said it.

While Charlie was away for a few moments Jim turned to Toni.

'OK, Toni. Goldfinger is a go. Can you make contact with whoever it is want's to meet me? The sooner the better.'

'I'll sort it out tomorrow, Jim.' Toni said as he downed the last drop of red wine from his glass.

It was as simple as that. The Bank of England job was on.

Under Pressure

The following day

The recent Hostage Heist bank robberies had forced the content on the Wailing Wall to spread across to a second board. They now had the names of a third and fourth bank in heavy marker pen along the top of the second board. Below that were new artist impressions of the three perpetrators, based on the memory of the new witnesses. These were set alongside typically unhelpful frame grabs from the CCTV cameras of both banks.

It appeared that the men at the cash counters of both banks had decided cloth caps were this year's 'must have' item for the fashion conscious bank robber. Which was something of a nuisance because CCTV cameras tend to be mounted high on walls and from that angle the peak of a cloth cap hides much of the face.

DS Yates walked over to stand next to a forlorn DCI Deakins.

'How did it go sir?'

'Brutal. I've got till the end of the week to come up with something or Honeywell will give the case to someone else.'

'So I can take it he wasn't happy then?'

Eric Deakins gave a short laugh.

'It's politics, Debbie. He knows we can only work with the information we've got, but he has to show the commissioner that he's on top of it.'

'Well I don't want to make your day any bleaker, but while you were with Honeywell, forensics came back with nothing on the torn half of the cloth sack just bits of prints and fragments of DNA. They're checking to see if any part matches the DNA from the cigarette butts.'

DCI Deakins thought for a while.

'Any news on how the Stebbingbrook robber got away?'

'He was seen walking away from the bank down the high street. Town Council CCTV shows him turning off into a side street. We're searching that road, knocking on doors seeing if anyone saw anything based of the description we have of him. There is one interesting place. A row of old garages. He could have had a car parked there.'

'Do you know who owns these garages?'

'We're checking on that now.'

Eric stepped back from the boards and thought for another moment.

'Do you think the Stebbingbrook robber picked the others up?' he said. 'What is the time line for both robberies? Could he have got down to Belford in time?'

DS Yates went back to her desk and put an Excel document up on her PC. She tapped in the heading, Stebbingbrook, and then a row of times taken from her note book.

'What have you got in the way of timings sir?'

Deakins went to his office to get his notebook and came over to Yates's desk. He flicked through to the relevant pages. He gave Yates the times and she typed a second heading, Belford, and a second row of figures. When she'd finished she sat back and turned to her boss.

'Well, there's about half an hour between them. Stebbingbrook then Belford in that order.'

'It's tight, but do-able, if nothing goes wrong.'

'And in the half hour down to Belford he would have seen all our cars heading past him going the other way,' Deakins said.

'That was both skilful planning and some very good luck,' Deakins added with grudging respect.

'So, if he dashed down the A1 to Belford, were did he pick the other two up?' Yates asked.

'Just what I was thinking,' Deakins said. 'No one saw them get in a car, as far as we know, and a high street CCTV camera was helpfully pointing in the other direction. It would have taken him too much time to drive into the town centre, so I think they would have had to go to him.'

'Let's have a look at a Google map of Belford,' she was doing it as she said it.

A few keystrokes and they were hovering over the town centre. The A1 cut through to the left.

'Go in a bit and see what kind of journey it would be to get to the A1 from the bank,' Deakins said with growing enthusiasm.

She zoomed in a bit until it was clear that using only a few streets they could get to within touching distance of the A1. A brisk, but easy walk.

'Let me put street view up,' Yates said.

She dragged the little orange man icon over the junction were the side street met the A1 and there it was.

'It's an underpass and an embankment up to the A1. Easy to climb.' Deakins said enthusiastically.

'You think he parked above the underpass sir?'

'It's the only way it would work,' Deakins said. 'Put a call out and see if any officers can remember seeing anything when they drove past.'

'Good idea sir, you never know,' Yates said. 'I'll get on to it now.' She was doing it as she said it.

'Oh, and get some officers to search those streets to see if they dumped anything along the way: clothing, disguises, the briefcase?'

Deakins heard the phone ring in his office. He was in a better mood as he walked over. He wasn't sure how much further forward knowing they had parked on the A1 at Belford would push the investigation, but it was something. Progress.

He grabbed the phone and fell back into his chair. 'Hello, DCI Eric Deakins.'

He pushed his chair back on its hind legs and lazily propped his feet on the drawer. He listened for a moment then abruptly took his feet off the drawer and put the chair back on its four legs. He had the phone to his ear, upright and as alert as a meerkat.

'So you've got a name? I'm on my way.'

***

Deakins and Yates arrived at Croydon CID a couple of hours after the call from DI Jennings. The traffic was as bad as ever crossing London. Christ he was glad he didn't work here. Sure, the crimes were more plentiful, that was true, but you just waste your time sitting in your car. Even with the blues and twos annoying the neighbourhood, there was just nowhere for the traffic to get out of the way to.

'You're a bit late sir, but never mind, let's get over there,' DI Jennings said. 'I'll fill you in on the way over.'

Deakins apologised on behalf of himself and Yates, blamed the traffic, and climbed into the detective's car.

'We've got a woman police officer keeping the mother company till we get there,' Jennings said.

'So, what happened?' Yates asked.

'Well, as expected, the kid eventually got caught trying to rob a shop. There were two of them.'

'How did you know which one was the one we're interested in?' Yates asked.

'That's was easy. He still had a plaster on from where he cut himself the last time.'

Deakins laughed at that.

'Jesus, I wish all detective work was that easy.'

'We arrested and charged both boys. I say boys but one was nineteen and the other one was just sixteen – the one you're interested in that is. The mother came down to pick him up and the kid was released in his mother's charge. The case comes up in a couple of weeks.'

'So, what is the mother's name?' Eric Deakins asked.

'She's married to a local businessman called Shalit. Respectable family. Typical kid gone off the rails situation.'

'Why does that happen?' Yates mused. 'When you've got everything going for you?'

The point was agreed by everyone in silence until they arrived at Mrs Shalit's house. A large, modern, detached property in a well-to-do belt of countryside south of Croydon. They pulled up behind a police car already parked on the expensively paved driveway.

Mrs Shalit welcomed them in frostily. This was obviously something she wanted nothing to do with.

Too bad.

She took them into a large, bright kitchen. Natural light flooded the room through a row of glazed, bi-fold doors that led out to the garden. Mrs Shalit invited them to take a seat in the tall chairs that surrounded the breakfast bar, but they declined the offer. Deakins noticed the police woman standing nearby as they came in, a cup of tea already finished on the counter. She'd obviously been relaxing in one of the chairs before they came in. No offer of tea or coffee for the newcomers though, which Deakins could have definitely used right then.

Jennings introduced Deakins, and Deakins introduced Yates, then they got down to business.

'Mrs. Shalit, thank you for allowing my colleagues from Helmsford Constabulary to talk to you. I'm sure they won't be long. They have a completely different case they're working on and believe you might be able to help.'

'I honestly don't see how I can be of help if it's not to do with my son,' she said.

'Well, indirectly it is to do with your son, but nothing that he has done wrong, so don't worry, Mrs. Shalit,' Deakins said.

Mrs Shalit didn't respond.

'How long have you been married to Mr. Shalit?'

'About six years.'

'Apart from your son do you have any other children of your son's age?'

'No, we have a daughter. She's four and a half. Why? Where is this leading?' she asked suspiciously.

'So obviously, your son has a different father,' Yates said.

There was a pause before she responded.

'When I was seventeen. It's really none of your business. My husband adopted him after we got married. He's been very good with him. If you knew my boy you'd know this business is just not like him. It's these other idiots he started hanging around with.'

'Mrs. Shalit, I understand. Please let me finish,' Deakins said. 'Your son's father, are you still in contact with him? Can you give me his name?'

'Is this about Charlie?' She asked.

'Charlie who?' Yates asked.

'Charlie Dawson. He is Peter's father.'

Yates jotted that down.

'Do you know where he lives now, Mrs. Shalit?'

'Good grief Inspector, that was years ago. He did send some money from Scotland when he worked there for a while. And then the money stopped.'

'Is he Scottish?'

'No, he's very English, from around London when I knew him.'

'Do you have a picture of him, Mrs. Shalit?'

'No, sorry. What has he done? Why are you looking for him?'

'Sorry, we can't reveal that at the moment,' Yates said. 'Do you mind having a look at these pictures and see if you could pick him out for us?'

Yates placed the portfolio of drawings and CCTV stills on the counter. Three slightly different sets of drawings and three sets of grainy stills showing ill-defined faces from strange angles.

'Well, it was a long time ago, and Charlie was a lot younger, but I suppose if I had to choose, perhaps this one is the closest to what he might look like now.' She said pointing to the drawing of the round faced, bearded and sunglass wearing sketch.

'He was a skinny boy back then, but he might have put on some weight.'

'Age?' Yates asked. 'You know, when you knew him?'

'Older than me, I think he was nineteen.' Mrs. Shalit reminisced. 'I remember that he was a gentle boy, but he did have a restless spirit. He wanted to see the world. I suppose everyone's a bit like that at that age.'

DCI Deakins nodded his understanding.

'If you can think of any other information please do get in touch, Mrs. Shalit,' Deakins said as he handed her a card.

They thanked her and left.

Running With the Devil

A couple of days later

The food was good. Well, as he was paying so it bloody well should be. The last band was a second on the bill jazz quartet. He was surprised how much he enjoyed them.

He'd never been to Ronnie Scott's before. The venue was discretely lit. Tiered galleries snuggling under a low ceiling. Each table dressed with individual table lamps. He could see why it was a popular place. Lots of couples and a few tables with parties of six or seven. There were some regulars who knew the place well. Not full, but busy enough for a mid-week. The main event was due on in about twenty minutes. Quite a big band by the way the stage crew were setting up mics and music stands.

Cool jazz was playing quietly in the background as the low murmur of conversation buzzed around the room.

They were sitting in a booth to the right of the stage but a little further back. Him and Gerry Conners, the guy who ran the London end of Franco Borriello's business.

'So, you like jazz?' Conners asked.

'Well, I liked that.'

'The Stan Raydon Quartet. I always try to see them when they're in the UK,' Conners said. 'The next set is a much bigger sound, lots of brass, full on, big band jazz arrangements.'

Jim could hear a hint of Irish in Conners' voice.

'How long have you known Franco Borriello?' Jim asked, wanting to move the conversation on.

'I worked for him in New York for a while some time ago,' Conners said. 'I even met Toni Zeterio then but he wasn't what you'd call an executive, if you know what I mean. He was just a gofer.'

Jim wasn't surprised by that news. He always thought Zero was flexible with the truth. He lived with his mother, for heaven's sake.

A waiter walked past their table, so Jim grabbed her attention and started to order another round. Conners stopped him.

'No, let me Jim, what are you having? Another whisky?'

'Better not, just a small beer.'

Gerry Conners was medium height, dark hair turning silver. Or maybe it was highlighted, hard to tell in this light. His square face had a permanent day's growth of beard, popular back in the nineties. He guessed he was about forty-five. There was an easy charm about him, but Jim thought it disguised a steel-hard ruthlessness.

He decided it was time to get down to business.

'Gerry, what do you know about our project?'

'Your project,' he mused. 'That's an interesting way to put it. I know what I've been told by Franco after his conversation with Toni in London. Franco is not easily impressed, Jim, but this scheme... shall we say it caught his imagination.'

'I'm glad he was impressed,' Jim said. 'But how much did Toni tell Franco?'

'Well James, he obviously told him enough. He called it the Goldfinger plot,' Conners leaned in towards Jim. 'He wouldn't have flown me over to New York for a meeting if he didn't think it was worth it. He said he wanted part of the action, Jim, and that's why we're talking now.'

'I'm glad he's taking it seriously,' there was a sarcastic note to Jim's reply.

'Seriously? The biggest privatisation of national assets since Attila the Hun put Italy on his shopping list?' Conners laughed as he said it. 'Who could resist it Jim?' And then in a deadly serious tone,

'Franco's relying on me to see that it gets done.'

Then Conners got really serious.

'Let me tell you who you're dealing with here, just so's we're clear,' Conners said, leaning in and putting his arm around the back of Jim's seat all close and intimidating. 'We are an international organisation that's extremely successful in any venture we get involved in. We have access to large resources and we bring these assets to bear to solve any problem that confronts us.'

Jim just sat there listening, determined not to be intimidated.

'Let me put it another way, Jim. At this time, because of the way we deploy our 'assets', we do not have any problems. If a problem pops up, we crush it back down. Your little project simply presents us with a challenge. A problem that will be solved through brutally effective deployment of our assets. My boss, Franco Borriello, does not like problems, they make him unhappy. Am I making myself clear, Jim?'

Jim was still thinking about how Conners had emphasised the word 'brutally'.

The waiter arrived and placed their fresh drinks on the table. Conners signed the bar bill, lifted his shot glass in a toast to Jim, and took a swig.

'Believe me James, Franco is not a man you want to make unhappy.'

'So, to partners,' Jim said as he raised his beer glass.

'Yeah, you could say that Jim, it's just a question of knowing who the junior partner is.' Conners winked at Jim as he said it.

That wasn't the way Jim saw it.

'You think we're the junior partner, is that it?'

Conners gave a sneering cough of a laugh.

'Be realistic, Jim. Your plan gets the 'product' out into the fresh air. It's clever, but all the risks lie in harvesting the 'product' and then getting it to a place of safety. I'll grant you the initial part is clever and unconventional, but we're going to be doing all the heavy lifting – supplying the brute force. You were looking for help and you've found it.' Conners got deadly serious again.

'We're coming on board, Jim. We're going to be supplying the expertise and taking a lion's share of the risks. That doesn't come cheap, if you know what I mean.'

'I'm not sure I do, Gerry. Perhaps you'd better spell it out for me?'

Conners didn't hesitate to get stuck in.

'Your little outfit James, it's a joke. You've done what, two or three small bank jobs? You're all just waiting to be picked up by the police.'

Conners was relishing this assassination of Jim's criminal career.

'Wake up, man. You're amateurs. This is way out of your league. Sure, your little scheme gets the initial set-up in place, but we take care of the rest of it. That sounds like a big investment that deserves a big reward to me.'

Jim could see where this was going.

'Put a number to it, Conners.'

Gerry Conners stood up with his glass in his hand and looked down at Jim.

'We'll give you twenty percent.'

An emphatic statement from someone who knew he had a winning hand. Conners downed the last drop from his glass and put it on the table. He leaned in to Jim.

'We know about Victor Avery, James.' With that bombshell the meeting was over. He didn't wait for a reply, he simply turned and walked off. Two large guys at a nearby table got up and followed him as he weaved his way through to the exit.

Jim watched them leave, then turned back to his drink. So, now he knew that Toni had spilled everything to Franco Borriello, including Jim's relationship with Victor Avery. This was a set-back. But Toni doesn't know about the recordings on the phone surely? That stuff was Jim's exclusive leverage over Avery and the only way Jim could make the Goldfinger plot work. That was a wrinkle right there. Jim knew that anyone who had access to that leverage had the keys to the plan.

If the London mob had a way into Avery then they didn't need Jim and twenty percent would look generous. On the other hand, Jim reasoned, the London mob was not a charitable organisation. They wouldn't give anything away unless they had to. Therefore, because they didn't have the leverage, they still need James Stack and his boys.

His thoughts were interrupted by the sound of a loud, crackling brass section playing short stabbing blasts to a seriously fast, syncopated arrangement for drums, double bass, guitar, and piano that tore through Cole Porters 'Just One of Those Things'.

'Very appropriate' Jim thought as he leaned back in his chair to listen. He was here now, tickets bought and paid for. Might as well stick around to enjoy an evening of superb big band jazz.

Though, as good as the music was, he couldn't prevent his mind from wandering back to the Avery problem. There were lots of questions. Practical things to which only Victor Avery knew the answers.

As confident as Gerry Conners was about the abilities of his mob getting their part of the job done, their involvement was pointless if the bullion didn't come to the surface. Nothing could progress until he had more strategic information from Avery.

The Goldfinger scheme needed to move up another gear.

The Dinner Party

End of March

A dozen men and women sat around the dinner table, all dressed to impress – a small group of London's elite, some with their partners. Most were bankers. Where there are bankers, politicians are never far away. This one was with his partner, a German interior designer called Freddie.

As they always did for such occasions, Victor and his wife had brought in a private chef to create a sumptuous meal in their own large kitchen – a pretentiously over-equipped manifestation of Avery's ego.

Fine wines appropriate for each course were furnished from Victor's own cellar.

The result, as always, was a wonderful and highly productive evening in the rarefied company of the so called great and the good.

Victor sat back in his chair, cradling a fine Delamain twenty-five year old cognac in his cupped hand. He warmed the dark caramel liquid so that its exquisite flowery oak aroma drifted up for him to inhale. An utterly satisfying experience made even more gratifying when in the company of people who had the ability to further his career.

The politician alone, if the polls are to be believed, could be in a position soon to recommend some sort of gong. He'd settle for a CBE – Commander of the British Empire. He liked the sound of that. But he hoped for a Knighthood for services to banking. Perhaps he was being too presumptuous, but it was only a matter of time he thought. Looks like he'd backed the right horse – eventually. Victor's allegiance was a very flexibly commodity.

Everything was at it should be. It felt as though the gods were smiling on him – one of their favoured sons. Nothing could spoil his evening.

And then the phone rang.

His wife was just returning from her regular fussy inspections in the kitchen and was in the hall when it rang, so she answered it.

'Hello, Avery residence.'

'Can I speak to Mr. Avery please?'

'Well, I'm very sorry, Mr. Avery is not available. Perhaps you could call back tomorrow. Try his office then.'

'I'm sorry, this is urgent. I'm aware that Mr. Avery is home.'

Victor Avery had left the table heading to the cellar for another bottle of wine when he passed his wife in the hall.

'Who is it?' he asked with little interest, his hand already on the cellar door knob.

She put her hand over the mouth piece of the phone.

'I don't know. He says it's urgent.'

He walked back and took the phone.

'Look, who is this? I'm very busy at the moment,' he said irritably.

His wife watched as Avery's face went pale. He turned his back on her as he spoke. All the pleasantries of the evening evaporating.

'What do you want?' he said gradually composing himself. It had been a month since he'd seen James Stack. He'd put that unpleasant business to the furthest reaches of the back of his mind.

'We need to speak. I have some questions that need answering,' Jim said.

'Can't it wait until tomorrow for heaven's sake?'

'I'd rather speak now and your evening looks like it's coming to an end anyway.'

Avery pulled up at this.

'What do you mean? Where are you?'

'I'm outside standing by my car. Come out here or I'll knock on the door. That'll attract some attention amongst your dinner guests.'

As he said that, two expensively soused guests walked past laughing and talking with self-absorbed familiarity. They were heading towards the front door. One indicated with a cigarette packet that they were going outside for a smoke.

'I'm coming outside. Don't say anything until I'm there.' He slammed the phone down and followed the man and woman smokers to the door.

It was a chilly night and Jim pulled his coat tighter as he took a couple of gravel crunching steps towards the elegant oak panelled front door of Avery's grand Georgian mansion. He stopped, hidden in the darkness near the parked Maybach's and Bentley's, when the front door suddenly opened and a rectangle of bright light spilled out onto the driveway. Two people stepped through into the cavernous, white Doric columned portico. They stood there lighting cigarettes, laughing and chatting animatedly, unaware of the man standing further back in the shadows.

Behind them came Avery, making polite excuses as he squeezed passed and walked away from the house towards Jim.

Avery didn't look happy. Good.

'What do you want Stack? I said you could use my home number when you needed to contact me privately, not to invite yourself round.'

'Well, I'm here now. I've some questions about procedures at the Bank that you can answer for me, Avery.'

'What, now?' Avery said, exasperated. 'I'm in the middle of a dinner party for god's sake. Can't it wait?'

Jim reached into his inside coat pocket and pulled out a sheet of paper.

'Here's a list of things that only you know and now I want to know them as well.'

'Such as?'

'The most important one is this,' he said indicating the first heading on the sheet of paper.

'But as you can see, there are a few other critical things on the list.'

'My god, Stack! This could end my career if I tell you this kind of thing.'

'I thought we'd been through all of this, Avery. It's not just your career that's in the balance. It's your freedom. So listen, I need this information and I need it now.'

The two inebriated smokers on the porch, bored with their conversation and with cigarettes glowing between their fingers, wandered over to Avery and Jim. Eager for fresh news.

'So Victor, who have we got here?' The woman said looking Jim up and down appreciatively.

'Oh, it's no one Sarah, just someone I know. He's on his way now.'

'Oh no, that's not fair,' she said. 'It's a cold night. Bring him in. It's the least you can do.'

Then, turning to her companion.

'There's plenty of Victor's delicious wine left, it would be a shame to waste it, wouldn't it darling?'

'That's right Victor,' darling said. 'Invite him in. I'm sure the others would like to meet him.'

His female companion turned to Jim.

'I'm sorry, Victor's so rude. And you are?'

'James Stack,' he said offering his hand.

'Well hello to you James Stack,' Sarah purred.

She put her arm through Jim's and together with darling, walked him back in to the house, leaving Avery standing there in open mouthed astonishment. *'How is this possible? He came here to threaten me and now he's an effing dinner guest!'* he said to himself.

Seated at the table an hour later Jim was enjoying himself enormously to Avery's obvious discomfort and judging by the glass of cognac in his hand, at his great expense as well. They wanted to know who this new guest was. This mysterious friend of Victor Avery. How long had they known each other? They were even more fascinated by Jim's earlier career in the army. A captain no less, with stories of adventures in Afghanistan to enliven their own gilded but dull lives.

Eventually though, to Avery's relief, the guests started to leave. Chauffeurs arrived to take them back to their pieds-a-terre in London. Only one couple were staying overnight and they had retired to bed earlier. Avery's wife had thrown in the towel soon after Jim arrived.

Finally, Jim and Avery were on their own.

'OK, Stack, enough civility. Get out.'

'Don't worry Avery, I'm going,' Jim said as he got up from the table and started moving towards the door. 'But remember that list. I want answers. You're the man that makes those strategic security decisions. You know what's going to happen, so you have the advantage of forward planning.'

'It's not that easy, Stack.'

'Oh, I don't know Victor. Think about it. When the shit hits the fan you'll have a couple of hours at the most to deliver a workable solution. You'll look like a god when you come up with a practical plan seemingly off the top of your head.'

Never one to miss an opportunity, Avery couldn't help but chew on that intriguing prospect.

They were at the door now.

'I'll have something for you in a couple of days. Call me then.' He started to close the door but Jim pushed his hand against it.

'Two other things I need to know that aren't on that list.'

'Oh, what are they, Stack?' Avery said impatiently.

'I want those Luxembourg bank codes.'

'Look, it's not as simple as that Stack. It's not just me you're going to have to deal with.'

'That's a problem you'll have to solve.'

Eager to get rid of Jim, Avery pushed harder against the door.

'One more thing, Avery,' Jim said through the narrowing gap.

'And what's that?'

'Who is Blackstone?'

The door slammed shut leaving him standing there in the cold night air.

Jim returned to his car and switched on the engine. His breath a frosty mist as he waited for the engine to warm up. His attention was drawn to the rear view mirror as another car parked further back in the darkness switch its headlights on. Whoever it was, they must have been waiting for him to leave. One of the guests?

Jim waited and after a moment the other car pulled out and drove slowly past him. A chauffeur was driving but he could just make out the passenger in the back silhouetted against the curtained light from the great house beyond.

He gave it a couple of minutes – after the red tail lights had completely disappeared and only the orange glow from the distant motorway remained – before he pulled out and began his journey home.

Jim wondered what that was all about. Unexplained events made him nervous. Was he being watched he wondered? And if so, who by?

Tell Me Sweet Little Lies

Mid-April

The Belford bank robbery had been knocked off of the front pages of the newspapers some time ago by the growing election clamour. The new fixed term Parliament Act meant, come hell or high water, the elected political party must govern for five years.

Like it or not, even if the steam had gone out of the boiler of legislation and they spent their remaining days staring idly out of the window, the government must limp on and crawl past the finish line on May 7th, the date of the next general election. That date was now just a few days away.

***

During the winter months, Jim and Summer's relationship had grown strong and close. Even so, Summer felt Jim kept her out of certain areas of his life. A remoteness, or a vagueness, when explaining what he did for a living, or what he did when they weren't together. The phone calls from friends she had yet to meet. How he went into another room or he sought privacy when certain calls came through. And others he'd simply call back later rather than talk to right then. Always apologising though, and telling her it was nothing, just business. She shouldn't worry.

Well, she did worry, not much at first, but now it was beginning to annoy her. She felt excluded and she didn't like it? Strangely, she didn't think it was another woman. No, this was something else.

She'd set her mind on having it out with Jim and soon. Not a row, she didn't want that, but an explanation. She wanted in on this other secretive life he seemed to be leading. '*How bad could it be?*' she wondered.

***

Jim enjoyed cooking, especially when Summer visited. She was suitably impressed the first time he'd invited her back for a meal. She admitted she couldn't cook toast. Give her any meal in a box and she could throw the plastic container into the microwave and have it on the table in three minutes – after stabbing the transparent film several times of course – she wasn't completely without skills.

She excused herself with the 'I live alone, so what's the point' argument. But then, so did James. That was annoying. Mr. Bloody Perfect was how she teased him. But he was a good, unpretentious cook. Simple but tasty food and tonight was no different. Italian was his speciality, but anything with herbs, spices, and sauces seemed to fly out of pans and onto plates with effortless panache. The way to a woman's heart, as they really ought to say.

Tonight, James cooked a delicious Spaghetti a la Carbonara served with an inexpensive but very quaffable Montepulciano d'Abruzzo.

By the time they'd finished their meal and retired to the sofa, most of the wine had been consumed and Summer's reticence to bring up the subject of James's 'other life' had pretty much disappeared along with it.

After a long kiss and a compliment about how delicious the meal was, she paused to gather her resolve. Then, sitting up straight, hands on her knees, she turned to look at him with a purpose filled gaze.

'James, we've known each other for a few months now. It's been good, even though the way we met was...,' she searched for the right word. 'Well, unconventional would be the only way to describe it.'

'Unconventional? Yes, I'd agree with that,' Jim said cautiously, wondering where this was going.

'How well do you know me, James?'

'In all the important ways, I think I know you very well, Summer. I know you're Canadian, you're divorced, and you worked at Metro Metals Futures but you're now – for the time being anyway – in-between work and looking for something more interesting to do. You're intelligent and have a wicked sense of humour. Oh yes, I nearly forgot, you are the most beautiful woman I have ever met.'

Summer lent in and kissed him. Then she put her hands on his shoulders and pushed him back a little so she could look directly into his eyes.

'You know a lot more than that about me, James. But what do I know about you?'

Jim started to reel off what he thought was a definitive list of things.

'Well, right up front I told you about my past life. You know I was in the army. You know I went to prison. You know I can cook and you know I'm extremely attracted to you and ...' the list petered out unexpectedly.

'Exactly, James. Yes, there are things in your earlier life, before you met me, that you've been very open about, but what do you do now? There are times when you seem very secretive. The phone calls that you won't take when I'm with you or you go into another room to take. And what do you do for a living? You seem to have time on your hands, but you're obviously not retired. I know about your friends Zero and Hollywood but you seem reluctant for me to meet them. And...'

'Ok, ok, I see what you mean,' Jim interrupted her in a calming voice. He could see that this was really bothering her. What could he say? What should he tell her?

'Look, Summer,' he said seriously. 'There are things that I'm involved in that if I tell you, might seriously risk our relationship and that is the last thing I want to do.' He paused, waiting for a reaction.

Summer said nothing and waited for him to go on.

'I do have a life that, how should I explain it? That runs alongside our life. It's not one I'm proud of, but it's coming to an end. I couldn't get back into the city because of my prison record. That also excludes me from returning to the army. Those are the two things I know.' He chose his next words carefully. 'In fact I'm excluded from most things of a financial nature, at least in the legitimate way,' he left that hanging there.

'Legitimate?' Summer caught the meaning. 'So, not legitimate. Do you mean illegal?' she said it with just a frisson of excitement in her voice.

'There's no other way to say it.'

'Here it goes," Jim thought to himself.

'I might have robbed a bank.'

Silence! But she hadn't got up and left. Not yet.

'Well, to be completely accurate, I might have robbed three.'

'What, on your own?' the penny dropped. 'Oh no, of course not. It was you and those friends of yours: Hollywood and Zero.'

Jim held his breath. Summer could be unpredictable.

'Wait a minute.' She got up and walked over to some old newspapers lying on a chair. Leafing through, she found one that was folded open to an inside page and brought it back to the couch.

'There's no way I would have connected that picture to you,' she said with a laugh showing Jim the three artist sketches staring out from the page. 'It looks nothing like you, whichever one you're supposed to be.'

Jim pointed to his alter ego.

'Not very flattering is it?' he said.

Summer got serious and leant back against the cushions away from Jim. She looked at him for a while. Jim said nothing. What could he say? The ball was in her court now.

They sat there for a long, silent moment, broken suddenly by the loud ringing of his mobile phone.

***

There were at least forty-six Charles or Charlie Dawson's in London and the six counties that surround it. Those were only the ones registered on the data base. There were probably more.

It took several days of knocking on doors and phone calls, but eventually they got it down to five addresses yet to be eliminated. Or, hopefully, four eliminated and one target found.

Charlie hadn't gone out of his way to get himself onto the register of voters, or make himself visible in any way, but when he got the council flat they did the job for him. So he and his address popped up on the police radar.

When he arrived back at his flat after a day out, just as he put the key in the lock, a neighbour popped his head out and told him about a visit from the police. They had asked the neighbours on either side what they knew about the occupant of the flat next door. They didn't know much and probably wouldn't say much if they did.

This news frightened the life out of Charlie. They would definitely be back, so this flat was old news. They were on to him. *Toni and Jim too?* he wondered?

Once inside his flat he took stock. What could he take with him? The bloody DVD collection would have to stay for the time being. Travel light. Change of clothes and the cash. He was used to roughing it, but the cash was going to be handy. Take the mobile – don't forget the charger.

A final look around and he stepped out of the front door and down the two flights into the street.

He suddenly felt very visible. They could be watching him now. He headed to the nearby tube station and took a train out of the area. The further he travelled, the safer he felt. He needed a bolt hole. A safe place.

He realised he had set off in the direction of Jim's flat without actually planning to. No mobile signal underground, he'd have to wait until he surfaced before calling him. He was sure Jim would take him in.

As the train rattled through the noisy tunnels it dawned on him that he was a fugitive, like the movie but without the one armed man as the villain. Harrison Ford knew he wasn't guilty. Charlie didn't have that luxury. He knew he was.

***

The shock of the sudden ringing of Jims mobile, in the silence after he had revealed his secret career to Summer, made them both jump.

Very few people knew this number and he wasn't expecting any calls. He picked it up and answered it warily.

'Yes?'

'They're on to me, Jim, you've gotta help me mate.'

'Calm down Charlie,' easy to say. Jim's heart started pounding too. 'Who's on to you?'

This time, Jim didn't take the phone to another room. He wasn't hiding anything from Summer now. He watched her to see how she would react to the call.

'The bloody police. Somehow they've got my name and address,' the panic and adrenaline gave Charlie's voice a higher pitch. 'They were at my place this afternoon while I was out. They even asked my neighbours about me. That's how I knew they'd been there.'

'The police may have been there for completely innocent reasons. Have you paid your TV license?' he knew that was a daft thing to say.

'Look Jim, I'm outside your place in the street right now.'

'My place!'

'I couldn't think of anything else. I need a bed for the night.'

'You can't stay here, Charlie, I've got a guest. Summer's with me,' he said as he got up to look out of the window.

'I can sleep on the couch, Jim,' Charlie pleaded.

From across the apartment, James heard the most unexpected words from Summer. She had gone over to the speaker phone by the front door.

'Come on up, Charlie.'

She pressed the door buzzer to let him in, walked back into the living room and returned to the couch.

'Let him stay here, James. He's your friend. You can't abandon him,' she said, looking up at him.

'You're welcome Charlie,' he said ironically into a phone-line that was already dead, as he sat back down next to Summer.

They both waited in silence for Charlie to arrive. They could hear his footsteps echoing in the stairwell as he ran up the stone steps. After no more than thirty seconds he burst through the door, slammed it shut, and bounded into the room.

'I knew you wouldn't let me down Jimbo,' he said, dumping his travel bag on the floor.

He went over to Summer and took her hand.

'Jim, you said she was beautiful but that word doesn't go anywhere near describing her.'

He became coy and awkward as he always did when he met a girl for the first time.

'I'm Charlie Dawson,' he stammered. 'My friends call me Hollywood. I hope you'll call me Hollywood,' all spoken in a nervous rush.

Jim completed the rest of the introduction.

'Charlie, this is Summer. Summer meet Hollywood.'

She held out her hand and smiled.

'Hello, Hollywood. Pleased to meet you at last.'

Charlie collapsed in besotted bliss onto the sofa opposite. It was as close as any man could get to being a golden retriever without actually rolling over on his back, putting all four legs in the air and hoping she'd come over and rub his tummy.

Jim went over to the drinks cabinet and poured Charlie a large whisky.

'Here, get this down you Charlie. It'll calm your nerves.'

Charlie took it gratefully and swallowed a huge mouthful.

'Look Charlie, you can stay tonight but I think it would be best if you moved in with Toni over in Clerkenwell until we see how things develop.'

'OK, but if the police have got my address, who's to say they don't have yours or Toni's?'

'Well, they haven't knocked on my door yet and Toni hasn't called, so maybe you're the only face they can put a name to at the moment,' Jim attempted a more reassuring tone. 'Perhaps they are only making enquiries. You know, to eliminate you from their investigation. A fishing expedition.'

'Well I can't think of an alibi that would stand up for long. I'm on the run Jim, a bloody fugitive,' then he added. 'That's the Goldfinger job over and done with isn't it? I mean, we can't go ahead with it now.'

'Slow down, Charlie. It's too far down the road to abandon now. Others are involved.'

Summer's ears pricked up at this new information.

'James, what Goldfinger job?'

Charlie turned back to Jim.

'I'm sorry, Jim, I didn't mean to blow it for you,' he said ruefully.

'It's OK, Charlie. Summer and I have been having a chat about things, you know, about our banking activities. I just didn't get that far yet.'

'Is anyone going to tell me what this Goldfinger job is?' Summer repeated. 'Exactly how much more do you have to tell me, James?'

'Listen Charlie, I'm not going to keep anything from Summer, so for better or worse as they say, here goes.'

James filled Summer's wine glass from a fresh bottle and calmly told her everything. Charlie butted in every now and then to claim responsibility for the idea and to explain the Goldfinger plot from the film one more time. Jim let him have his moment of glory. There was no rush. They had all night.

Summer listened in silence with little reaction to James's astonishing story. He struggled to read what she was thinking. Well, she still hadn't got up and walked out yet, so he just pushed on.

He eventually got to the part where the plot required the help of someone from within the Bank of England. He told her about Victor Avery and their nefarious history and it was at this point that Summer started to draw the strings of the whole story together.

'Did this have anything to do with that smart phone of yours, James?'

She turned to Charlie.

'Did James tell you that that was how we met, Hollywood?'

'No, this bit is all news to me.'

As he spoke Jim got up and went over to the old IKEA wall cupboard and pulled a book from the handful that lay in a small stack on one of the shelves. He brought it back to the couch and opened it. Hidden inside a hollowed compartment was the smart phone, which he took out and switched on.

'Here's why Victor Avery will do anything I want.'

He selected a file and played it on the mobile's internal speaker for both Summer and Charlie to hear. They both listened in mesmerised silence as the scale of Avery's treachery became clear.

'So you took the blame for the whole fraud, James, and Victor Avery got away with it,' Summer said when the file had finished playing. 'This is the same

Victor Avery who now runs the security at the Bank of England?'

'The very same,' Jim said. 'To put it politely, I now have two of Victor Avery's most precious possessions cupped in my hand. He has no option but to help us, or I arrange that he goes to prison for a very long time.'

What James hadn't revealed yet was the small issue of his, still to be recovered, share of the Metro Metals scam. He looked at Summer and took a deep breath.

'So there it is. That's pretty much everything.'

She didn't reply immediately, she just stared at the smart phone lying on the coffee table. Then finally,

'I don't know what to say, James. This is serious.'

'She's right, Jim. You don't want to get her involved in this business.'

Jim said nothing. He just waited.

'You'll get caught. You all will. It's just too dangerous. Who needs that amount of money anyway?'

Jim noticed she hadn't said anything about right or wrong yet.

'You're right Summer, it's crazy and dangerous and you shouldn't get involved. Go back to Greenwich tonight and wait until this whole thing is finished one way or the other.'

She gave the idea short shrift.

'But I'm not sure I want to just sit in Greenwich on my own while all the excitement's happening over on this side of the river, James.'

Jim caught the hint of playful admonishment in her voice. The whole idea had made her pulse race. So he gave her the other option.

'Or, you could sleep on it tonight and make your mind up in the morning,' he said. 'But whatever happens, I've got to make sure you're safe.'

It was late in the evening by then. Charlie grabbed the couch but struggled to sleep; the reality of coppers knocking on his door; his new life as a fugitive; the bloody lumps in the cushions – *'must be getting soft.'*

***

The early morning spring sun streamed like a laser through the tiny gap between the drawn curtains. The sunlight, the noise of traffic and the uncomfortable couch all conspired to get Charlie up and about earlier than he might otherwise have been. He found some cornflakes in a kitchen cupboard and made some instant coffee.

Next job. Call Zero to blag some couch time at his place. If he agreed, then Charlie might as well get over there ASAP. With any luck his mother would have a cooked breakfast waiting when he arrived.

Toni wasn't as up for it as Charlie had hoped. He worried that the police might come sniffing around looking for Charlie. But Charlie pointed out that there was no reason for the police to know where he was, so why would they knock on Toni's door?

Toni reluctantly agreed – a short stay only – and yes, if he came round now, breakfast would be ready. Job done as far as Charlie was concerned.

He left Jim's flat, closing the door quietly behind him.

James and Summer made a late start of the day. First thing they noticed, Charlie had gone and they were on their own again. They had breakfast without much chit-chat. Summer was subdued. She wasn't a morning person, but this was different. Last night's revelations were obviously still going through her mind.

He took her hand and sat her down on the couch.

'How are you...really?' he asked.

'Oh, you know how it is,' she said matter-of-factly. 'Your boyfriend tells you he's a serial bank robber. Then he tells you he's planning to rob the Bank of England and, oh yeah, the police have taken a mild interest in one of the gang. I can't wait to tell mum and dad.'

'Very funny. I'm serious, Summer. It might be better – safer for you if I...if we...'

Summer interrupted.

'I'll take my chances, James. It's my choice, a quiet life or adventure, remember?' she said.

'You took a chance with me from the very beginning,' James said. 'I can't ask you for more.'

'My choice, James,' she said. Her mind made up.

'Well, if you're really sure, then I want you to listen to me, Summer. I told you about the Goldfinger job last night, but I left out an important detail. What I'm going to tell you now, no one else knows. Not even Charlie. And then I'm going to ask you to do something for me. It won't be dangerous, but there could be an element of risk.'

She laughed at the intrigue.

'What have you got in mind, James Stack?'

The Master Plan

14 days

May 7th passed and the general election had gone pretty much as the pollsters had predicted. Fed up with austerity, British voters have tossed 'This Lot' out and put 'The Other Lot' back in. From now on, because 'The Other Lot' had returned to power, the fickle UK population had already disdainfully re-badged them 'This Lot.'

***

'He's just vanished into thin air, sir,' Yates said to DCI Deakins. 'Officers have been round several times. Neighbours say they haven't seen him for days.'

'OK, it sounds like this is our man and he's got wind of our interest in him. He's gone to ground, but I'll bet he's still in London,' Deakins said. 'Get a warrant and we'll go in and have a look around.'

***

'Very smart,' was Jim's first reaction when he entered the lobby of The Montgomery Hotel and Casino in Covent Garden. An intimate space of seductive extravagance. All polished brass, glass, and white marble. The stark ambience softened with the lush greenery of a miniature Hanging Gardens of Babylon planted in discreet and random openings around the high walls of the atrium. From the gold piping on the concierge's midnight blue uniform, to the silken professionalism of the exquisitely tailored receptionists, this was luxury central for privacy seeking high rollers.

A flunky had escorted him up to the penthouse office where Gerry Conners ran the London end of Franco Borriello's empire. He was on the phone when Jim walked in. From the sound of the conversation, New York was giving him grief.

The call finally ended. Conners put the phone down and looked up.

'I tell you, Jim, it gets harder to keep them happy.'

Conners leaned across his desk, offered his hand and gestured to one of two deep leather chairs.

'Take a seat,' he said. 'You like a coffee or something stronger?'

Before Jim could answer, he told the butler-flunky who had retreated a discrete distance away, to bring coffee. Then he dove straight in.

'OK, let me tell you how it is Jim. We're a very successful organisation. I think I may have mentioned that last time. This is just one of several similar hotels in London, Europe, Asia and the good ol' U S of A. They make good money for us. But other business interests earn more. Much more.' He gave Jim a chance to be impressed.

Jim just sat there.

Conners got up and walked over to the large picture windows and gazed out over the panorama of London like some great emperor assessing his domain.

'As much money as we make, an organisation like this needs a lot of money to keep it going. You have no idea the kind of overheads we have.' He turned to look at Jim.

Jim didn't know if he was expected comment on that. He had no idea what to say so he just shrugged.

195

'Anyway, Toni's conversation with Franco came at the right time, Jim. Do you believe in serendipity?'

Nothing from Jim.

'Let me put it this way. I, that is to say the organisation, have been looking for new capitalisation, Jim. Enough to provide long term security. Banking is the name of the new game. I want us to become a substantial player in the banking business. But that takes money. More than we can call upon right now. That is, until Toni had that conversation with Franco. Do you see where this is going Jim?'

Jim finally saw a reason to speak.

'You're looking for large scale and easy-to-get-your-hands-on capital.'

'That's right. And we want to get our hands on it soon.'

He walked over to the chair next to Jim and sat down.

The butler-flunky returned with the coffee, poured two cups, and left.

Conners picked up a cup but didn't drink. He leaned forward to Jim and spoke quietly, as though he was passing on a great secret.

'We need a solid plan for the Goldfinger project and quickly. No more waiting around. Once the starting-gun is fired, what happens next? If they buy it, where will they take the gold? We need to start putting things in place. Information Jim, solid, inside information. Now, is that what you've got for me or are you just wasting my time?'

'That's why I'm here, Gerry,' Jim said, pulling out two sheets of folded paper from his inside pocket. 'This is Avery's strategy. His step-by-step plan to remove the UK bullion to a place of safety.'

Avery had chosen not to use a computer or any other electronic device to write his brief. Hand writing left no digital record. Jim had transcribed it and printed off two copies. He handed one to Conners, who nodded appreciatively as he glanced swiftly through it.

'Christ Jim, he's handed us keys to the kingdom. Let me get one of my associates to sit in on this.'

He picked up the desk phone.

'Is Davis in the building?' A pause as whoever he was talking to asked someone else.

'OK, tell him I want him up here now.'

Conners got up and walked around to his fancy big boss chair behind the large rosewood and ebony desk.

He went over the document again while he waited for Davis to arrive.

'This is extremely sensitive information, you sure we can we rely on it Jim?'

'It's as solid as the ten commandments.'

Conners shook his head slowly as he read.

'What the hell is it you've got on this guy, Jim?'

Davis arrived and, with a nod to Jim, sat down. As Jim was about to discover, this was a man who said little but got things done.

Conners introduced Jim and handed Davis the document.

'Take a look into the future, Mike. It's an insider's guide to picking the Bank of England's pockets,' Conners said. 'When the game goes into play, this is how they'll respond.'

Mike Davis took his time to absorb everything on the page. A handful of single spaced paragraphs typed on an A4 sheet.

Jim reached over for his coffee and took a sip while he waited for Davis to finish. Davis turned the page over to see if there was any more on the other side.

'A barge on the River Thames,' Davis said eventually. 'That could be tricky.'

Conners turned to Jim.

'Yeah Jim, out on the river in the middle of London for everyone to see. It's very risky for us. Much too visible. Is this Avery's only option?'

'Think about it, Gerry. He's the head of security at the Bank of England. If he came up with a reckless or amateur solution they'd begin to smell a rat. He took the view that the precautions they take would, by necessity, be very short term. He'll recommend they park the UK bullion a short but safe distance from the bank and if nothing happens within twenty-four to, say, forty-eight hours to be on the safe side, they can quickly put it back in the vault.'

'That's fair enough,' Conners said. 'Whatever your problem is with this Victor Avery character, he thinks way outside the box. It's as clever as hell.'

'Yes it is and we have to be just as clever. Perhaps even more so,' Jim said. 'All Avery can do is set it up. It's up to us to find a way to take it.'

'It makes our job trickier,' Davis said. 'But it has the advantage of giving them a level of confidence that just might make them complacent.'

'OK, Mike, so how do we deal with it?' Conners said.

'I'll need a large scale map of the Thames centred on the City of London with detail down to meters on each side,' Mike Davis said.

Gerry Conners told him to get on to it and then turned to Jim.

'You've had this for a couple of days Jim, any ideas?'

'Maybe.'

Jim went on to describe an idea he'd been working on which involved his signature tactic – distraction. Keep them watching one thing while you're busy doing something else.

Davis was impressed.

'Smoke and mirrors? That just might work. I'll see what we can arrange.'

'Now, as big an operation as this might appear to be, Avery said he wants it to be as low key as possible. He's going to discourage press interest,' Jim said.

Mike Davis butted in.

'That works in our favour as well. Low key is good.'

Another business suited heavy arrived with the map of London as Gerry Conners looked at both of them in amazement.

'Low Key! You don't think a bloody great barge, which I assume will be surrounded by police launches in the middle of the busiest section of river in one of the world's biggest cities, might get noticed by someone?'

'Perhaps not. I've already asked Avery about this. It turns out rather conveniently there's a waste paper transfer-facility owned by Tower Environmental down by the river between the Cannon Street main-line bridge and Southwark Bridge.'

Jim took the map and opened it out across Conner's desk. He found what he was looking for and followed the route with his finger as he spoke.

'Here's the bank and just down here by the river is the container loading facility. The gold will be loaded into Tower Environmental containers within the Bank itself, so there's no way anyone could know that they contain anything other than waste paper.

It's a perfect camouflage. Then, it's a very easy ninety second drive south down a narrow road called Wallbrook, then across Cannon Street to Dowgate Hill. Finally across Upper Thames Street and into Cousin Lane. As I've shown you, that's where the environmental company has a container loading dock.

Once the barge has been loaded with the containers, it will simply be moored in the river around about here.' He drew an X in the middle of the river. 'As always, that's where the treasure will be.'

Conners took a sip from his coffee and leaned back in his chair. He had the air of a potentate able to conjure resources at the click of a finger.

'Mike, we have some warehousing interests down the river. What kind of connections do they have with barge companies?'

'Are you suggesting we could supply the barge?' Davis said. 'It's beautiful.'

'Well, they're going to need a barge, so we'll make sure there's one available on the day of the...er...'

Jim interrupted helpfully.

'The event?'

'Yeah, the event,' Conners redirected his attention back to Davis. 'That way we can be certain the barge will be available at short notice. It'll look highly suspicious if Avery pre books it himself, so we'll be doing them a favour,' he said with a grin. Then to Jim. 'Mike will give you the contact details to pass on to Avery.'

Jim looked at Davis. Davis just nodded.

Gerry Conners moved the meeting on.

'There's a whole lot to do. Mike, you continue to come up with a workable plan.'

'I've already got some ideas, but I need a target date for the event,' Davis said turning to Jim.

'We shouldn't delay,' Jim said. 'I'm handling Avery, but I don't want to give him time to develop a guilty conscience. We should go as soon as possible.'

'Just how much gold bullion are we talking about here?' Davis asked.

'Well, if nothing has changed, it could be as much as 350 tonnes,' Jim said. 'But to be honest, I don't see how they could move that amount in such a short time.'

'350!' Davis said. 'That will take a lot of shifting.'

Conners was spellbound by the number.

'That, Jim, is why we get the biggest slice of the cake. Storage and handling. Turning it into a liquid asset. It's what we do.'

'I agree with Jim,' Davis said. 'I don't see how they can get it onto a barge in such a short time and anyway, it could be too much to handle, even for an outfit like ours.'

'Perhaps we should be thinking in terms of a smaller prize?' Jim said.

Conners gave Jim a withering look.

'We take it all,' he said emphatically. There was something manic in Conners' eyes. No discussion. 'When will the plan be ready Mike?' Conners asked.

'I'll have something ready by the end of the week,' Davis said.

Conners looked at his diary.

'So we could be good to go before the end of May. Let's meet again in five days.' Conners said. 'Anything else?'

'Well yes, quite an important question actually,' Jim said. 'Do you have any Embassy contacts?'

Davis and Conners both looked at each other, then back to Jim.

'Embassy contacts? What do we need those for?' Conners asked.

'To kick this thing off convincingly, the message that reveals the bad news about the threat within the Bank must appear to have come from a remote outside source. Even though Avery is expecting it, and believe me, he will do everything he can to encourage the credibility of the message, we have to be very subtle about how the message reaches the Bank. This is extremely critical.'

'What have you got in mind,' Davis asked.

'Whichever unknown group planned this scheme, they will remain anonymous, not only because they don't actually exist, but because they must appear to be untraceable. No one will be claiming this on behalf of some crazed fanatics. This fictitious group will pass the message through a second or third party whose credentials should be without question. An embassy for instance. This will give the story an unimpeachable provenance.'

'I see what you mean,' Conners said. 'The embassy gets in contact with the Bank of England and tells them they have received this information from a very reliable source that is unwilling or unable to reveal its origin.'

'Muddy the waters,' Davis said

'That's right,' Jim said. 'They might think it's some kind of crazy political faction from Eastern Europe or South America with an axe to grind. Perhaps they're out to destroy a western economy as an act of revenge. However you want to sell it, they've used a known channel of communications within the initial, second party country.'

Jim noticed the conspiratorial look that flashed between Conners and Davis.

'We might be able to help there,' Conners said. 'Our organisation has some very reliable contacts at a number of foreign embassies.'

'Well, whatever you come up with,' Jim continued, 'the trail must be utterly convincing but untraceable beyond the first embassy or consulate source.'

'And of course they have such a short time frame to react,' Davis pointed out. 'The message only has to hold water for twenty four hours.'

With that agreed, Jim left the crime-syndicate boss and his lieutenant to put the finer details to their plans.

At Ronnie Scott's, Gerry Conners had made James the classic 'Godfather' offer he couldn't refuse. A verbal contract with the single clause: "The organisation will do the lion's share of the heavy lifting for a lion's share of the take."

Well, Jim thought, *time to flex those muscles big boys. Let the heavy lifting begin.*

On the tube journey back to his flat, Jim went through everything that had been discussed. Even with impeccable inside help, this whole caper had more wrinkles than a bed sheet in a bordello. It couldn't possibly work. Could it?

Passport

8 days

It was a generously sunny morning for late spring. The smell was of warm tarmac, exhaust fumes, and dust that swirled lazily around buildings and rose into the air in the thermal eddies of the city heat. A gentle, warm breeze carried it across green, open spaces – blending with the subtle aroma of cherry blossom. Distant chatter of lively Spanish conversation mixed into the busy din of traffic. And from somewhere, the occasional drift of tobacco smoke gave it a typical southern European ambience.

Not bad for Finsbury Park, Charlie thought.

Not that he was in the mood for such idle observations as he anxiously approached the tower block; a squat four storey brick and concrete seventies eye-sore, overdue for demolition, but just waiting for some heritage bureaucrat to 'save it for the nation' with an untouchable grade two listing.

He couldn't see anything suspicious as he ducked and dodged into side streets and doorways, before finally making it to the stairwell leading up to his floor. He slipped into the building and quickly ascended the two flights of stairs to the landing that lead through a door on to the second floor corridor. His flat was the fourth door along. The corridor was a long passageway open to the world on one side, allowing Charlie a chance for a quick look down to the street below to make sure it was all clear before hustling along to the entrance of his flat.

Just before he reached his door, he had to negotiate his way around an old armchair, a filthy mattress and a box of other junk that had been dumped since the last time he was there. He was determined, whatever the outcome of events, he'd definitely not be returning to this place.

***

Since lodging with Toni for the past few days, he'd been reluctant to show his face in the street because of the distinct possibility the police were looking for him. Now though, it was urgently different.

Jim had called a meeting to update Toni and Charlie on developments. It was to be at Toni's place in Clerkenwell.

He arrived by taxi with three boxes of pizzas. Toni took Jim into the small kitchen and switched the kettle on. Jim sat at the kitchen table. Charlie arrived shortly after, heralded by footsteps pounding heavily down the stairs into the hall before bursting through the door into the kitchen in his usual cheerful way.

'I thought I could smell Pizza! Top man, Jimbo.'

'Tuck in, both of you, before they get cold,' Jim said amiably. 'How's life as a hermit Charlie? Getting cabin fever yet?'

'I'm OK, thanks to Zero...and his mum. But if I go outside, I'm stuffed. I need a way out, Jim,' Charlie implored.

'I'm working on that, have faith,' Jim said. 'How about you Toni, all good?'

Toni looked at Charlie and then at Jim.

'Well, I'm OK, but Charlie can't stay here forever. You know how it is, Jim.' He changed the subject.

'You said you have news, how did the meeting go with Gerry Conners? He's a good man isn't he? You know, a real get-it-done sort of guy. I told you I had some serious connections,' Toni boasted excitedly.

Jim was concerned at how impressed Toni was by Gerry Conners. A bit too eager? He shouldn't be surprised that Toni knew such people – his past being what it was. He chose not to mention how pissed-off he was that Toni had given everything away, including the name of Jim's inside man, Victor Avery. At least, not for the moment. But it made him wonder where his loyalties really lay.

'Yes, he's a hard guy to refuse,' Jim said pointedly. 'Which brings me to the first piece of news. It's not good, I'm afraid. Bringing Gerry Conners' boys into the picture leaves us with just twenty percent of the take.'

Charlie was outraged.

'After we've come up with the plan and everything? That's bloody cheeky. The greedy bastards.'

Toni was more generous.

'Well, I suppose they will be doing all the hard work. You know, the dangerous stuff. Perhaps we shouldn't complain at twenty percent. It's still a hell of a lot of money.'

'That's what I thought,' Jim said with frank resignation. 'It's non-negotiable anyway. Take it or leave it.'

While the others stuffed their faces with pizza slices, Jim went through what had been discussed during the meeting with Conners.

'So there's to be one more meeting in a couple of days to go over the finer details of the plan and then, two days later, the show kicks off.'

Toni and Charlie had been listening carefully. When Jim had finished there was a palpable tension in the air. A sense of the remorseless ticking of a clock, counting down to a very dangerous end game.

Toni broke the silence first.

'What part are we going to be playing in this, Jim?'

'Gerry's mob will be handling the taking of the barge and its cargo. They're getting the lions share so there's no point in getting in harm's way, directly anyway,' Jim said. 'Toni, I want you at the warehouse end to keep an eye on our percentage of the take. I don't know where that will be at the moment, so don't ask.'

'And me?' Charlie asked anxiously.

'You're in danger already, Charlie. Police might be following you and we don't want you to lead them to our little party, so I want you out of the country. Have you got your passport here?'

Charlie shook his head.

'No, when I left my flat I only took my money and mobile. No passport. I was in a hell of a rush.'

'Well, you're going to have to get it. It's a risk, I know. When can you go?'

'Don't worry, Jim, I'll sort it tomorrow,' Charlie said attempting a veneer of confidence he hoped didn't expose how he really felt.

He slept fitfully that night.

***

Charlie pushed the key into the lock, twisted it, pushed the door open, and ducked inside. He took a deep breath to calm himself and looked around his flat. Everything seemed the same as he had left it. Now. Where did he put his passport?

Outside, two floors below, two cars drew up and parked with the casual disregard for parking laws only those in authority possess. One was a police cruiser, the other an unmarked car. Two uniformed officers got out of the cruiser and two plain clothed from the other car. The larger of the two, after staring up at the block of flats for a moment, seemed distinctly unhappy about the scale of the climb he was about to undertake. They chatted together for a moment and then entered the building, leaving the female uniformed cop waiting by the cars.

This was turning out to be harder than he expected. Charlie had gone straight to the place he knew for certain his passport was – but there it wasn't. He went to the next likely place. Nothing. Then, systematically through all the drawers in each room. He was starting to panic.

He stopped for a moment. When did he last use it? Benidorm, a year ago. He went to the wardrobe and opened both doors. Not that he had much in the way of clothes. What did he wear? A jacket! Nothing. His other jacket. He squeezed the cloth around the pocket areas. He could feel something. Was that it in the inside pocket? He reached in. Got it!

The three officers were making a start on the second flight of stairs, the uniform taking the lead by a few steps. The fat guy coming up breathlessly in last place.

Charlie took another final look around. If he could just take maybe one or two of his favourite movies. He went over to the shelves. So many to choose from. If he was on Desert Island Discs, what would be the two favourite movies he'd take with him? 'As Good As It Gets' with Jack Nicolson, definitely. He found it after his fingers passed it twice, and then, lying on top of a small stack, Goldfinger. Of course. Time to go.

The uniformed officer was at the door of the landing leading to the second floor corridor.

Charlie closed the door behind him pocketed the key and started walking back towards the stairs. He reached the pile of discarded junk just as the uniformed officer came through the door onto the open-sided passageway.

Charlie froze for a moment and then dropped down to squat by the box of random crap.

As the uniform got closer, Charlie gathered some loose stuff, piled it on top of the box and then hoisted it up as high as he could in front of him. Christ it was heavy! What was in this thing?

The door opposite opened and a neighbours' head popped out.

'So, you back home again, eh?' he said in a thick east European accent.

Charlie, his face hidden from the approaching uniform by the box of rubbish, nodded his head in the direction of the copper and widened his eyes conspiratorially. The Polish guy just shrugged his shoulders uncomprehendingly.

Then the uniform was there, trying to get through the narrow space between the wall and the man with the box. They did a sort of waltz as they squeezed passed each other. Charlie turned to continue but another person was coming through the door onto the open hallway. A plain clothed woman officer, he was certain. He kept moving towards the stairs and waltzed past her, his face still hidden by the stacked rubbish.

He made it to the landing and was about to reach for the door handle when it was pushed open by a large, red faced bloke, definitely another plain clothed officer. He was gasping as he held the door open for Charlie. Charlie muttered his thanks and the fat guy spluttered a breathy hissing sound that might have been, 'don't mention it'. Charlie manoeuvred his way round him, through the door and down the stairs. He dumped the rubbish on the first floor landing just as a woman resident, struggling with the weight of two bags of shopping, came up the stairs with a child.

'You're not leaving that there are you?' she complained.

Charlie didn't reply as he ran down the stairs.

'Bleeding neighbourhood!' Were her final echoing words on the subject as he raced through the exit and out onto the street, almost colliding with the woman officer standing with her back to the building.

He threw her a quick apology as he turned and walked away smartly. He didn't want to draw attention but an urgent shout from above changed his mind.

'That's him. Don't let him get away!'

The officer gave chase but he had a head start and the advantage of some familiarity with the local rat runs through the estate that, at night, become such a dangerous labyrinth for all but the local gangs.

DCI Deakins, now back in control of his breathing and his face back to its normal pallid complexion, told the uniformed officer to kick the door of Charlie's flat open and then get down to the street to join the chase.

'You go with him Yates, I'll start taking a look around.'

He put a call out to DC Robinson back at the constabulary explaining what had just happened and told him to get forensics over. He wanted the place dusted for finger prints and possible DNA samples. Anything that might give them a clue to the identity of the other gang members. He was certain they all would have been here at some point.

Down in the street, Charlie could hear the footsteps gaining on him. He knew he couldn't out-run a bunch of coppers, but he'd give it a bloody good go. He turned a corner into a long alley, but at the other end, where the alley met a main road, another uniform was standing looking up and down the road, his back to Charlie.

He was halfway down and close to a cut-through that crossed the alley at right angles. As he turned into it, the uniform spun round and spotted him. Charlie just caught a glimpse of the copper starting down towards him – calling for help on his iPlod as he ran.

The dodge into the second alleyway gave Charlie a choice of another rat run through to graffiti daubed garages or a door to a stairway up into the neighbouring tower block.

Either could result in a dead end. He had only seconds to decide.

Who Are You?

The same day

The message was as simple as it was unexpected, 'Call this number.' A mobile number followed.

James didn't recognise the voice. He tried the call-back option but the number was blocked. So, not the same number he supposed. He played the message back again and wrote the number down. He tapped it into his mobile and pressed the call button. It rang several times and then,

'Hello, Mr. Stack,' an older man's voice, educated, confident and very blue-chip. There was a hint of mild amusement at Jim's expense.

'I'm returning your call,' Jim said. It was more of a question.

'I believe you've been looking for me, Mr. Stack.' A bored cat toying with a cornered mouse.

Jim considered this. Who had he been looking for?

'Sorry, who is this?'

The voice took it's time before answering.

'We have something in common, Mr. Stack.'

'Oh? And what's that?'

A pause. The voice was obviously relishing his advantage.

'Victor Avery'

This took Jim by surprise. Had his plan been discovered?

'I don't understand,' Jim said.

'Oh, come on, you didn't strike me as a stupid man, Mr. Stack.'

'You have me at a disadvantage. You seem to know me but I don't know who the hell you are. Can we stop playing games?'

'I don't play games, Mr. Stack,' the voice said, suddenly very serious. 'You went to prison for Victor Avery and I suspect he still owes you your share of the...shall we say, 'investment'?'

Bingo! Only one other person could know the history between Jim and Avery.

'Blackstone?'

'Very few people know me by that name, Mr. Stack,' Blackstone said. 'So, what is it you think I can do for you?'

This was all so unexpected. Blackstone was strictly off limits to Jim during the Metro Metals scam. Jim had to remind himself what it was he believed Blackstone could help him with.

'You're right about Avery. He took everything,' Jim said. 'But I have good reason to believe I can persuade him to give me his half of the code. That assumes the 'investment' as you put it, is still in the same account in Luxembourg.'

'I can confirm there is an account in Luxembourg and it may still hold funds.'

Jim thought about that for a moment. Blackstone wasn't offering much information, but seemed prepared to answer questions within a limited scope. He took a different tack.

'I recently told Avery that I wanted to find you. Is that why you got in touch with me?'

'I have been watching you for a while, Mr. Stack and no, Avery didn't contact me on your behalf.'

'Watching me for a while?' Jim found himself going to the window and checking the windows of the buildings opposite and the street below, as

though Blackstone was some kind of spy lurking in the shadows. It seemed unlikely.

'As I said before, we have something in common.'

Jim waited.

'Avery has been very careless with his, how should I put it? ...shareholder loyalties,' Blackstone said. 'You aren't the only one who has yet to receive his agreed 'dividend'.'

'You mean Avery still owes you?'

'When the Serious Fraud Office brought our venture to an end, we agreed the account should remain dormant until circumstances became more favourable. Avery insists circumstances are still unfavourable, but this is just to protect his prospects at the Bank of England.'

'But I assumed you received a percentage of the transactions before it went to Luxembourg?'

'Partly,' Blackstone said. 'This wasn't the first time we had worked together. Avery was indebted to me from a previous business venture. This new arrangement gave Avery the opportunity to make good on that debt.'

'You trusted him twice?'

'Avery had to agree to a very precise measure of control. You have a password don't you Mr Stack.'

'I have part of a code, Avery has the other part. The two codes have to be used at the same time to get access to the account.'

'Actually, Mr. Stack, you have part of the code, Victor Avery has part of the code and I have a third part of the code. All three are needed.'

This was bad news for Jim. His plan depended on getting the second part of the code from Avery. Until that moment, he had been blissfully unaware that the plan had a fault in it the size of the Rift Valley.

'Assuming the venture hadn't gone pear shaped, how would we have removed money from the account if all three of us needed to put a code in at the same time? You wouldn't have been present to enter your code.'

'You have already seen how that worked.'

'What do you mean?'

'Do you remember what happened when the account was opened for the first time?'

'That was over four years ago,' Jim said. 'I remember putting my code in and so did Avery. We were both there together.'

'That's what appeared to happen. What actually happened was this. Avery used his lap-top to access a very special account. One where funds could flow in without restriction, but required codes to take funds out. Avery entered the account number. This opened an account input portal that would remain open for ninety seconds. Our three codes don't have to be entered in a specific order. You dialled the required number on your mobile phone and heard a recorded voice telling you to enter your code using the key pad. Avery did the same thing. You both ended your calls and as far as you were concerned that was that – but when your codes were entered the system automatically sent a message to me alerting me to that fact. I then simply entered the third cypher, invisible to both you and Avery.

The account was now open and it remained open until you logged out. And before you ask, I was able manage the account remotely and see what you were seeing because I supplied the software.'

'But I knew about Blackstone, so why the secrecy about the third code?'

'It was a way for me to handle Avery and I wanted to make sure nothing moved out of the account without me knowing about it.'

'But surely Avery could have paid you when his share was transferred into his own private account?'

'As you have discovered yourself, Victor Avery is a devious character,' Blackstone said. 'I didn't want to rely on his word. I wanted to see the transfer for myself. Have you any idea how many fund transfers mysteriously go missing – lost in the ether, Mr. Stack?'

'Actually, I don't.'

'Banking is my business, Mr. Stack. I can assure you, there is nothing easier than misplacing or misdirecting to be more precise, a fund transfer – if you have the right connections.'

Unexpectedly, the conversation had come round to the very thing he wanted from Blackstone.

'That, Mr Blackstone, is why I have been trying to get in touch with you.'

'So, we have a mutual interest in each other. You want to get your hands on your 'investment' and I want the very considerable sum of money that Avery still owes me, plus a little interest.'

Jim could see the beginnings of an alliance starting to evolve. Perhaps even a partnership.

'Yes, I want to get my hands on my 'investment', but then I want it transferred somewhere safe and secure. I believe you can do that for me, Mr. Blackstone. I think it's time we met don't you?'

Blackstone found that amusing.

'But we have already met, Mr. Stack.'

That stopped Jim in his tracks. He ran the possible occasions through his mind. There were none. Or so he believed.

'We have?' he said lamely.

'Oh yes. I was one of the guests at Victor Avery's recent dinner party. The one you unexpectedly found yourself at. If you don't mind me saying, Mr. Stack, you livened up a rather dull evening.'

That narrowed it down. One of twelve people. Seven or eight if you count only the men. The guests at that party were very senior movers and shakers in the banking industry. Blackstone, or whatever his real name was, mixed in the rarefied company of the seriously powerful. That kind of influence endows you with almost miraculous powers to open doors, whisper in the ears of the great and the good, and, more importantly, make funds vanish untraceably into remote accounts.

'You mean Avery invited Blackstone to his dinner party?'

'Of course not. He hasn't met Blackstone.'

'So, he didn't know you were there? It doesn't make sense.'

'But he didn't invite Blackstone.'

The penny finally dropped.

'Not even Avery knows who you are?'

'Precisely, Mr. Stack and that's the way I want to keep it.'

Jim relaxed a little. It seemed like this Blackstone character could turn out to be an ally.

'So, what do we do now?'

'Do we have confidence in each other, Mr. Stack?'

'I think we can say that, yes.' Jim replied cautiously.

'We are after the same thing, more or less,' Blackstone agreed. 'There are things that must be done first. Arrangements that only I can set in place. You will know when we are ready to make our move.'

'How long will it take, Mr. Blackstone?'

Blackstone seemed to give this some thought.

'Just have patience, Mr. Stack. In the meantime you should persuade Avery to give you his part of the account code. You will not be able to contact me again on this number.'

The line went dead.

Jim considered all that had been said. It turned out, if he understood it correctly, that Victor Avery was under assault from two directions. From the rock of Jim's blackmail and the hard place of Blackstone's justice.

That put a spring in Jim's step as he headed out to meet Summer.

The Break In

That night

They burst through the door into Jim's flat, laughing breathlessly from the exhaustion of chasing each other playfully up two flights of stairs. Then in a sudden serious moment, embracing each other as Jim pushed Summer against the wall and kissed her, kicking the door closed with his foot.

He led her down the short passageway into the lounge. They stumbled across to the sofa, their way lit only by the soft iridescent glow from the city streets and buildings that spilled through the windows into the room. Summer pushed him back into the cushions, falling on top and kissing his neck as she started to unbutton his shirt. Jim stretched behind for the table light, nearly knocking it over as he fumbled for the switch before finally managing to turn it on.

He pushed her gently back. He didn't want to rush this.

'Let me open some wine. We've been drinking red all night, stay with that?'

Summer looked into his eyes and slowly, meaningfully, nodded her beautiful head. He knew that look.

***

They had met on the Embankment earlier that evening. It was what photographers called Magic Hour – the short period of about twenty minutes after the sun has dipped below the horizon when tungsten lighting from buildings and streets appears warm and golden against the dimming blue sky.

She was standing near Cleopatra's Needle, watching the busy river traffic. Pleasure cruisers were passing up and down, each boat strung with rows of bright individual bulbs that flashed and sparkled on the choppy surface of the water. Then she turned and smiled as she saw Jim coming towards her, the last fading moments of twilight backlighting her hair in a radiant halo. The sight made Jim catch his breath.

He had originally planned to meet by the river as an excuse to get a feel for the location where, in a few days, Gerry Conners and his mob would attempt to take the barge and its cargo. But the vision of Summer caught in the fading evening light completely distracted him.

They kissed and then took a slow walk along the Embankment passing under the Golden Jubilee and Hungerford Bridges. A right turn took them up Northumberland Avenue towards Trafalgar Square before they eventually cut across Strand and up into Covent Garden.

Dining choices were abundant in the Covent Garden area, but the evening sky was fully dark before they found a restaurant that appealed to them both. The delicious spicy aromas had them from twenty yards.

Jim noticed that The Montgomery was just a street away. He wondered whether Conners or Davis enjoyed the occasional curry. That would add an extra pinch of spice to the evening if they walked through the door.

They both ordered a selection from the 'chefs specials' menu and shared the many delicious dishes between them, washed down with a red wine that really should have tasted better than the price suggested. Or, perhaps it was the curry that tainted it.

In an entirely random moment during the meal, James looked over Summer's shoulder to the large window that looked out to the street several busy tables away. It was a fleeting distraction, but through what clear glass remained in a window festooned with Indian graphics, menus, and hand written culinary enticements, he thought he caught sight of someone outside who could have passed for Toni Zeterio. Of course it wasn't. It was just an accident of light from the restaurant playing on a shadowy figure as it passed.

He shrugged it off and surrendered once again to Summer's delightful company.

Their conversation had the easy flow of two people who knew each other well, but eventually, perhaps inevitably, it came around to the subject Jim had wanted to avoid tonight of all nights.

'Do you have a date yet when you want me to fly out?'

Jim shook his head.

'I've mentioned someone called Blackstone who was part of the Metro Metals deal. Well, he got in touch with me today, out of the blue. From what he said, the business of the account codes is vastly more complicated than I thought,' Jim said. 'But it turns out he's a very big cheese in the banking world. If anyone can deal with Avery and the foreign account, he can. The thing is, I have no idea what it is Blackstone plans to do. What I do know is that whatever Blackstone comes up with, it still depends on me getting hold of Avery's code, and soon.'

Summer thought about that for a moment.

'So when will you hear from him?'

'I don't know how fast the wheels turn in his world. I just have to wait until he gets back in touch with me. I'm hoping it's going to happen very soon because show-time is only a few days away.'

Summer seemed quiet. She nodded slightly and then went back to her food.

'Are you worried?' Jim asked.

She shook her head and continued eating.

'I don't want you to get involved unless you're absolutely sure,' Jim said.

She reached for her wine glass and raised it to Jim.

'Let's wish us luck,' she said.

Jim raised his glass back to her, but he was already wishing he hadn't told her anything about anything. She said she wanted excitement but he had no right to ask her to risk so much.

***

Jim left Summer on the couch and went to the kitchen. He found the bottle opener and unwrapped the foil from a new bottle of red wine. The cork protested with a squeak as he eased it out. While he was doing this Summer slipped into the bathroom opposite and closed the door.

He took the red wine and a couple of glasses back to the living room, placed the glasses on the coffee table, and poured a generous measure into both. Then, leaning back into the cushions, he waited for Summer to return.

She was in a playful mood when she returned.

'Either you're getting some bad habits, James Stack or Charlie has been here,' she giggled as she moved closer.

'What do you mean?' he said reaching over for the wine glasses and handing one to Summer.

'There's a pee stain on the carpet in the loo.'

Jim was genuinely surprised by this.

'Well there shouldn't be. Which side?'

'Right side if you're sitting down,' she laughed. 'Left side if you're standing.'

Jim put his glass down and went to see for himself. Summer was right. The carpet had the distinctive pattern of carelessly directed pee drops – left hand side. Could only be Charlie, but he hadn't been in the flat for a while.

He came back into the living room and stood in the middle facing Summer – thinking.

'Do you think it was Charlie?' Summer asked.

'Yes, but why would he break in to my apartment?' He was deadly serious.

He turned to look at the bookshelf.

'No!'

Grabbing the book from the shelf, he carried it back to the coffee table and gave Summer a worried frown before opening it. He didn't want it to be true, but he was already certain from the weight of the book. His suspicions were confirmed as the pages fell open to the hiding place. The hollowed section was empty. The smart phone had gone!

Pulling his mobile from his pocket he dialled Toni's number. It took three or four rings and then.

'Yeah?' He didn't sound as though he'd been woken up from a peaceful sleep.

'It's me,' Jim said. 'Is Charlie there?'

'No. Why don't you call his mobile?'

That was a good question. But somehow, Jim thought he should get some idea of what Charlie might be up to from Toni first, before calling him directly.

'Something has happened, I can't say what right now, but has Charlie mentioned anything to you about any plans he may have had?' Jim pushed a bit further. 'Has he been acting differently recently?'

'Jim, Charlie acts strangely most of the time. He's a weird guy. You know that better than anyone,' Toni said. 'He's worried about the police though. He's sure they're on to him. That's making him even more skittish.'

'Toni, Charlie isn't that weird. He doesn't do things without a good reason,' Jim said. 'Did he get his passport yet?'

'He left this morning. Said that was what he was going to do. He hasn't come back. Now, don't you think that's weird?'

That news worried Jim even more.

'Why didn't you call me Toni? If it's the police, then we all might be in trouble. Something else is going on but I can't work out what it could be. Any ideas?'

'Maybe he's got some kind'a deal going on? If he's got his passport perhaps he's already left the country?' Toni said.

'Toni. That would be very risky for him. They could be looking out for him at every passport control. I was working on some private arrangements to get him out of the country,' Jim said. 'He'd need quite a bit of cash to carry that off if he tried to do it on his own.'

'Well, perhaps he's found a way to raise some cash,' Toni offered a little too helpfully Jim thought.

But it did make sense in a weird, Charlie sort of way. The smart phone would make a good bargaining chip if he knew who to sell it to. Or blackmail. Alarm bells were starting to ring.

'Look Toni,' Jim said. 'If and when Charlie does get back, call me immediately. OK?'

'Trust me Jim, I'll call you soon as I hear anything.'

Jim ended the call and turned to Summer.

'This doesn't make sense. Charlie has no reason to steal the phone, but Toni seemed to suggest he might be planning his own escape out of the country.'

'Why would he want the smart phone?' Summer asked.

'It's a wild one, but he might think he could use it to raise money to fund his escape and a decent life style in another country.'

'Who would he sell it to, Jim?'

'It wouldn't be hard to track down a number for Victor Avery. He'd pay a good sum for that phone. So would Gerry Conners and his mob. They could raise their take by twenty percent – our twenty percent – if they got their hands on the recordings and got control of Avery.'

Summer took a sip of her wine.

'Why don't you call Charlie? See what he has to say?'

'Yeah, I might just do that, but I have to be careful. If he has been arrested, the police could have his mobile. And that could mean they'd have our phone numbers. There's all kind of ways that would not be good, Summer.'

'Try. See what happens. If this is so out of character, he'll have an explanation,' she said.

Jim reached for his phone again.

'OK, here goes nothing,' he said using the speed dial number on the keypad. It rang a couple of times.

Sometimes you give the pizza of fate a spin and the whole messy cheese and tomato pie grinds to a halt on the slice labelled 'Unlucky'.

'What?' A defiant stranger's voice. Sounded more like a youth. Definitely wasn't Charlie.

I Want To Break Free

Same day

They'd had him in the cell for the last three hours or so. Gave him a cup of tea and a day old egg and tomato sandwich. He wondered if the day old sandwich infringed his human rights. He'd check it out later.

***

So, which way? The stairs up into the building, or the rat-run dodge through to the garages? He took a step forward just as a young man barged through the door of the building. Charlie instantly saw the possibilities. But it had to be quick. He took some cash out of his back pocket and peeled off a fifty.

'Hey, mate. Help me out and I'll give you this fifty quid note.'

The teenager was about Charlie's height. He took a cautious step back.

'Whad'ya want man?'

'Look, take this fifty quid and swap my jacket for your hoodie.'

'Wha' if I don' wan' your bleeding jacket?' the kid whined.

'OK,' Charlie said tearing off another fifty. 'A hundred quid, but you gotta put my jacket on and run back up the stairs. You gotta do it now mate.' He was practically hopping with nerves as he looked up and down the alley.

The kid's eyes popped out when he saw the cash. Decision made.

'Yeah, OK,' he said pulling his grey hoodie off. 'Wha's it all about man, somebody after you?'

'That's right. But don't worry mate, once they see you're not me you'll be OK,' Charlie said as he handed the kid his blue jacket. 'You can tell 'em what you like.'

'I look like a ponce in this,' the teenager said.

Charlie ignored the comment.

'Now quick, start running up the stairs for Christ sake.'

Charlie watched the young man turn back the way he had come through the door and up the stairs. Then, still pulling the hoodie down over him, he turned and took the rat-run through to the garages as fast as he could.

Coming round the corner a split second later, the copper ran the few steps to where Charlie and the kid had swapped clothes a split second earlier. The door was still closing and the sound of footsteps running up the stairs echoed down to him.

No brainer!

He pushed through and started to climb.

A flight above him, the youth in Charlie's blue bomber jacket, headed up towards the top of the building, legs cycling with the energy of an Olympic sprinter. And racing away with him, in the pockets of the jacket: the two DVD's, a passport and Charlie's mobile phone.

The hoodie was a tight fit. It barely covered his stomach, but the hood was the bit that mattered as far as Charlie's was concerned. Feeling a bit safer he eased his pace as he considered his options. The two coppers had obviously followed the kid into the building, so, the next question – stay within the estate until it was safe to leave, or try to make for the high street now and hail a cab?

The latter seemed the better choice, so he made his way through a few more narrow alley-ways and passages, being careful to check each new crossway and corner. Then a final long narrow canyon between two buildings that took him out of the shadows and into the sunlight of the main thoroughfare.

He held back a little, checking the high street in both directions, and waited for a black cab to come into view. It seemed like an eternity before one appeared but in reality it was only thirty seconds or so. He ran out across the wide pavement, arms waving.

DS Yates had lost the trail a while back and just happened to be about thirty yards down the road when she saw the grey hoodie urgently waving for a cab. Kids in hoodies don't hail cabs. It was a reasonable assumption to make. That and the fact that the other officers had radioed in that Charlie Dawson had swapped his blue jacket for a grey hoodie.

Yates picked up her pace and was very close to the cab by the time the hoodie opened the door and climbed in. She made a note of the cab's number and called for back-up.

The cruiser arrived with the two uniformed officers within a minute, Yates climbed in and the three of them tore off, lights flashing and sirens blaring.

London is awash with black cabs and if you want to get lost in a chase, a black cab is normally a pretty good bet. Yates however, had kept an eye on the cab, noticing how it had stopped at traffic lights fifty yards further on, and then turned left. They weren't far behind.

Charlie was taken completely by surprise when the police car pulled in front of the cab. The cabbie wasn't fazed by this, he even had the foresight to keep the doors locked until the police officers arrived. Charlie didn't have a chance.

***

They'd arrested him as they took him out of the cab and cautioned him in the police car during the ride to Helmsford Constabulary. Charlie heard them talk to someone called Deakins, who, from what he could tell, was in his flat rifling through his private stuff and would join them later.

Finger printed and DNA sampled, he spent three hours or so in a cell before being taken to an interview room somewhere in the station. A duty solicitor waited there for him. Shortly after that, a fat bloke, the one called Deakins turned up. He was with the woman officer who had arrested him.

Deakins switched on the recorder He spoke to time and date the moment, then asked Charlie if he had been read his rights.

Despite protestations of coincidence from the solicitor, evidence seemed to confirm he had been in the car and the truck at the first robbery. Enough, thought DCI Deakins, to charge Charlie and get him up before a magistrate the next morning.

'Good, we're making progress at last,' Eric Deakins said to Debbie Yates as they made their way back to the CID office.

'Did you find anything at the flat?' Yates asked.

'Lots of fingerprints, and we gathered some DNA samples as well. Could be from other gang members,' Deakins said. 'Not sure how we're going to match those.' His voice trailed off as he realized how much they still had to do.

'He had quite a lot of cash on him according to the Custody Sergeant,' Yates said.

'It was only a couple of hundred quid. Can we prove it comes from the robberies?'

'That might be difficult,' she said.

They walked silently for a bit, both mentally chewing on the day's events. Then, as they went through the door into the CID office, Deakins stopped and shook his head reverentially.

'What's up?' Yates asked – concerned.

'He's got a hell of a movie collection though.'

What's Going On?

9 days

Whoever answered Charlie's mobile last night wouldn't say who he was or how he'd got hold of Charlie's phone.

Jim and Summer talked it over, trying to find a reason for Charlie to break in. There was no sense to it. No matter how many times they went over it.

Eventually, as the wine did its subtle work, they ran out of things to say and found themselves succumbing to the intoxicating rush of the evening's earlier promise – just before the yellow pee stain got involved.

***

In the morning, a late breakfast, then Summer grabbed her things and headed back across the river to Greenwich.

It was almost eleven o'clock when Charlie called. Jim had phoned Toni earlier, but he had nothing new to add. He seemed vague but again hinted at how unreliable Charlie could be. Why would he say that?

'Jim, for Christ sake! It's so good to hear your voice man.'

'Charlie, we've been worried about you. What the hell have you been up to?' James tried not to sound angry. Let Charlie talk and see what he says.

'The police arrested me yesterday midday, just after I'd got my passport from my flat,' his voice, fast and anxious. 'It was a hell of a chase. The bastards picked me up as I was trying to get away in a cab. Honest to God, Jim, it was like something out of The Sweeny.'

'So where are you now, Charlie?'

'I'm in a phone box near a railway station in Helmsford. I'm catching the next train back to London.'

'I don't understand, they let you go?'

'Well, there's more to it than that. I'll meet you in the pub in an hour or so, I'll tell you about it then.'

The phone went dead.

That phone call confirmed to Jim that Charlie couldn't have been in two places at once. How could he break into Jim's apartment if he was locked up in Helmsford nick? So, if not Charlie, then who else? Someone who knew two vital things. One; the location of the smart phone, and two; Charlie's annoying toiletry habit.

Toni!

It's not difficult to see why. His loyalties were with his family. Blood connections, no matter how tenuous, to a bunch of Neapolitan New York gangsters.

Some gang bosses demand loyalty and deliver swift retribution for any perceived disrespect, no matter how slight. They are, of course, confusing respect with fear. The Borriello's and Conners of the world were surrounded by gang members who would do anything to prove their loyalty because they lived in fear of what would happen if they didn't.

Toni was no different. He thought that when he returned to Naples all those years ago he had severed his ties with the Borriello gang in New York. On hearing the Goldfinger plan, Franco must have reminded Toni that these were unbreakable bonds and gave him an opportunity to prove his loyalty. Looked like they wanted the Goldfinger scheme all for themselves, together with Jim's leverage over Avery. Well Toni had now given them both. He had proved to be a very loyal team player - for the other side.

Well, it wasn't quite as easy as that. Jim could be a devious son of a bitch as well.

He dialled Summer's mobile. The call went to messages. She must still have been traveling in the underground part of her journey back to Greenwich. He left a message telling her about Charlie and to call back as soon as she could.

***

He got to the pub early. Though Jim didn't normally do alcohol at this time of day, he bought a pint of beer anyway. He'd drunk half of it by the time Charlie ran breathlessly into the pub ten minutes later.

'What's with the hoodie, Charlie?' was Jim's first comment after returning to the corner table with Charlie's drink. Charlie took a long slug.

'The hoodie?' Charlie seemed confused, and then remembered. 'Oh yeah, I swapped jackets with a kid during the chase.' And then more urgently. 'He's got my passport and me bleeding mobile.'

'That explains the strange voice when I called you last night.'

'They're doing me for the bank robberies, Jim,' he said resignation in his voice. 'I didn't mention you guys, so don't worry. They don't seem to have any leads, so I suppose the disguises worked better than we'd hoped.'

Jim had to admit he was relieved to hear that.

'But what are you doing out if you've been nicked?'

'They took me up before the magistrate this morning. The solicitor got me out on bail. I've got to stay at my place until the court date. Don't know when that is though.'

'Who put the money up?' Jim asked.

'No money. I've got a feeling the evidence isn't as solid as they claim, and anyway, for some reason, they don't think I'm gonna sod off out of the country.'

'God bless you, Charlie. You've got a face only a mother and a magistrate could love.'

Charlie burst out laughing at this, took another gulp of beer and then told Jim about all the madness the day before. He made it into a big, over embellished joke. Better than having to face the frightening truth of the mess he was in.

Jim listened patiently, laughing in all the right places. At the same time though, he was considering the limited rescue options available.

'OK Charlie, I'm going to try to get you out of the country.

'I haven't got a passport Jim, can't be done.'

'Charlie, your passport probably won't be any good now anyway. I'll come up with something.'

They sat quietly for a moment, sipping their beers and coming to terms with the dramatic new circumstances. The volume of noise seemed to swell and pan back and forth across the saloon as lunch time regulars started to arrive – claiming their space at the bar; at tables; in small, lively groups – away from the electronic chatter of the noisy poker machine.

'Toni broke into my flat last night and stole the smart phone,' Jim said at last.

'Jesus! Why did he do that?' Charlie was clearly stunned.

'I think he's sold out to Gerry Conners' mob.'

It took a moment for Charlie to absorb this news before morphing into faithful Labrador mode, his face full of remorse.

'I'm sorry mate. That's my fault. Me and my big mouth. I was boasting about hearing the recordings on the phone and the way you'd hidden it in a book. You know, it was like some kind of spy movie. I didn't think he'd do that. What a bastard!' He said this as he got up to get another round of drinks.

'What do you fancy?'

'Small whisky, no ice.'

Hollywood, over at the bar buying drinks, gave Jim some valuable, uninterrupted thinking time.

A bastard indeed. Jim could think of other colourful adjectives to describe Toni's treachery, but right now he had an advantage. Toni tried to set Charlie up. He wanted to deflect suspicion. Could it be to delay the discovery that the phone was now in Conners hands? But why?

Jim navigated through the possibilities under the heading '*How did Toni think Jim would react?*' Yes, he might have believed, because of the clever ploy of peeing on the carpet that Charlie had taken the phone – but he wouldn't have believed Charlie would hand it to Conners. So it was probably to make Jim waste time going off in all kinds of other directions. Time which would allow Conners to establish contact with Avery to give him the good news that the James Stack problem had gone away – but a much bigger problem called Gerry Conners had arrived.

No question. Victor Avery would freak out and the whole fragile house of cards would collapse, taking every carefully laid step of Jim's plan with it.

But, Jim's advantage – knowing Toni was the thief – changed how things could play out.

It's getting dangerous and he had to admit he was worried about Summer. He'd already taken too many risks. He didn't want her anywhere near this Goldfinger madness, which meant getting her far away from him as possible.

He felt like some manic circus act. He'd got so many plates spinning on the end of very thin sticks, one or two always seemed to be about to fall unless he kept running up and down the line giving each stick a jiggle. It was exhausting. How many more spinning plates could he handle?

And now here was, one more plate placed precariously on top of a whip like stick, spun, and then added to the end of the row. This one was called 'What to do about Charlie?'

Charlie arrived back with the fresh drinks.

'There you go mate,' he said as he sat down.

Jim took the whisky and gave it a taste, then turned to Hollywood.

'Tell me Charlie, why do you think the evidence they've got against you is weak?'

'Oh, I don't know. It was something to do with the DNA they say they found on a cigarette butt. Or was it two cigarettes? They tried to big it up. You know, make it stronger than it was, but I think somehow they were fishing. Hoping I'd give them something so they didn't need the DNA stuff – but I didn't. Whenever they asked where I was on such an' such a day I'd just say I was at home watching a movie, you know, 'cos it was my hobby. They've seen my collection at my gaff. You've seen it, Jim. It must be true.' Charlie laughed, picked up the dimpled beer glass and took a gulp.

Jim didn't know what to make of this, but he knew someone who could turn evidence on its head and make Charlie look like a saint.

'OK Charlie, I know a top brief who'll sort this out. Same lawyer I had for my case. Not cheap, but we've got the money.'

'Wait a minute. Correct me if I'm wrong, Jim, but didn't you end up going down for four years? How good was that?'

'That's true. But I had to go down to bring the investigation to a stop. Remember, I didn't want to lose the money Avery and I had made.' Jim gave that statement a moment all to itself, then added. 'Of course, I hadn't planned on Avery screwing me.'

'Must have been a lot of money Jim.'

'A great deal of money.'

The conversation paused while they both took a drink.

'OK. Don't worry, Charlie, I'll get it sorted out somehow. If the police get in touch, tell them you have proper legal representation now and you can't say anything unless your lawyer's there with you.'

They sat there and let the lively ambience of the pub fill the silence while Jim finished his whisky. Staring into the empty tumbler on the table, Jim played back everything that had happened so far. The one thing Jim didn't want was for the Goldfinger scam to collapse. At this point, Mike Davis's plan to take the barge was still in play.

Davis had been in touch and explained what he had in mind, but he needed Jim's help in one particular detail. Something Jim knew was very much within Charlie's area of expertise. While Jim was trying to fix Charlie's legal problems, why not give him something to do? So he asked Charlie if he was game.

Charlie laughed when Jim explained what he wanted him to arrange.

'That is seriously weird, Jim. I love it!' Charlie said still laughing. 'Leave it to me.'

'Look, I've got to go, but don't worry about the police, I'll get it sorted somehow.'

'Thanks, Jim. I'll just finish this and I'm off.'

'Good. Go home. Watch a movie,' Jim said as he pushed his chair back and got up to leave. 'My Cousin Vinny. That'll cheer you up.'

'Hey, I wouldn't mind Jo Pesci as my lawyer.'

Jim thought he could do a lot better than Vinny Gambini.

***

'Looks like Charlie Dawson has got himself a proper lawyer, guv,' Yates said as she stuck her head around Deakins office door. 'On the phone now. Wants to speak to you.'

Eric Deakins' heart sank. He knew what this was about. Yates folded her arms and leaned against the door frame as Deakins picked up the phone.

'Detective Chief Inspector Eric Deakins, how can I help you?' He always gave himself the full job description as a kind of shield against uppity lawyers.

'Good afternoon, Chief Inspector, my name is Penelope Mason-Zhang of Harrison Baker Associates. I have been instructed to act on behalf of Mr. Charlie Dawson, who I believe came under your purview recently and is now awaiting a court date for bank robbery.' As an uppity lawyer, Penny knew how to get under the shield.

'Good afternoon, Ms. Mason-Zhang. I've heard of Harrison Baker Associates. What are such an expensive outfit like yours doing with a case like Charlie Dawson?'

Penny immediately saw what the detective was implying. Impecunious client employs an expensive brief. Where did he get the money? Therefore, must have robbed a bank – clumsy, but predictable.

'Our fee is being taken care of by a third party and is none of your concern, DCI Deakins. May we move on to the reason I called?'

'Please do.' Deakins leaned his chair back against the wall and waited. He knew what the lawyer wanted.

'Before the Public Prosecution Service wastes everybody's time and money, I would be grateful if you would supply information pertaining to the nature of the evidence against my client. In particular, any DNA forensic evidence that you have. I assume you have it in digital form and can email it to me without delay.'

Yup, that was what he was waiting for. The bloody DNA evidence. They'll get specialists in and, brick by brick, tear the labs results apart until they prove the bank robbers were in fact Micky, Donald, and Pluto.

What could he do?

'OK, Ms. Mason-Zhang, I'll get it over to you, but frankly, our evidence is water tight and Charlie Dawson is strongly implicated.'

'Strongly implicated,' Penny repeated. 'That doesn't sound water tight to me.'

'Look, Ms. Mason-Zhang, we know he's guilty,' Deakins fired back, tired resignation in his voice.

'Do your worst. We're confident of a guilty verdict when it comes to court.'

'We'll see.' Penny Zhang gave Eric Deakins her email address and said a polite goodbye.

Eric put the phone down and shook his head.

'Is the case screwed?' Debbie asked.

'Don't know, but there'll be a shit storm from Honeywell if it is.' He pushed the email address across the desk towards her. 'Send her what she wants.'

Yates took it and left Deakins to his thoughts. He really wanted one last big collar before he retired.

'Bugger!'

The Card Trick

6 days

When Toni took the smart phone, packed in a manila jiffy bag, to the Montgomery Hotel, he was expecting to hand it directly to Gerry Conners and no one else. But it was Mike Davis who came through to the hotel foyer.

Davis was dressed in a smart black lounge suit, his long black hair slicked back. He wouldn't have looked out of place in Las Vegas. Which wasn't surprising because, as one of Conners key men, he also ran the casino security at the Montgomery.

Toni had met Davis briefly before but didn't trust him. He couldn't put his finger on the problem. Perhaps it was the impression he gave when he was in Gerry Conners' company, that Conners wasn't quite as in-charge as he liked to think. Toni had seen it before in New York; the quiet, second in command, dutifully carrying out his boss's orders. But in reality, a place man, put there to keep an eye on things in case his boss started to lose the plot and put the organisation at risk. Or worse, he starts planning the retirement of an executive board member, which could result in advancement to the senior ranks – if he chose the right executive. Or second prize – a triumphal remembrance service to recognise all the commitment and loyalty he gave during his unexpectedly terminated career.

It turned out Conners was out of the country so, like him or not, he had no choice but to hand the package to Davis.

Davis thanked him, reassured him he would pass the package on, then, politely but firmly, escorted him out from the gilded embrace of The Montgomery Hotel and into the street, where Davis thought the slimy and, in his view, untrustworthy, Toni Zeterio belonged.

***

It was two days later that Gerry Conners returned from his trip to New York. A visit demanded by Franco Borriello to provide a face to face update on the 'project'. No telephones. No emails. No texts. No second hand comments or opinions. Just the two of them in total privacy as Conners delivered the plan to Borriello. The scale of investment in cost and manpower along with its probable outcome in percentage terms in clear and unambiguous language.

It was the go, no-go moment.

And now, here he was sitting at his desk in the grand, top floor office of The Montgomery Hotel. The glare of the afternoon sun shaded by half turned vertical blinds. On the desk lay the torn remains of the opened jiffy bag packaging. In his hands the smart phone which he turned over carefully, inspecting it like some marvellous curiosity – delaying the moment that would at last reveal just what it was Stack had on Victor Avery.

He smiled as he thought about the phone call from Mike Davis while he was in New York. A call confirming that Toni Zeterio had indeed delivered James Stack's smart phone as he said he would.

He'd gone through the charade of the planning briefing with Franco Borriello. Franco was impressed and ordered the 'operation', as he liked to call it, should go ahead without any further delay. Franco had no idea that a hefty twenty percent was going to be Conners own private reward – a contribution stolen from the pocket of James Stack representing the funds he needed to underwrite his own avaricious business ambitions.

So, what was it Stack had on Avery? Well, that dirty little secret was about to be revealed. Holding the phone firmly in one hand, he pressed the silver button on the side, holding it for a few seconds as the phone's software booted up.

***

Over in Soho, Jim's phone rang. It was another message from Blackstone.

'Call this number.' A different number from last time. Used once and thrown away. This was a man who played his game low-key and clever.

Jim and Summer were having lunch in a bistro near Soho Square when the message came through. They were sitting at one of the small round tables set closely together by the window, looking out onto busy Dean Street. The sun, higher in the sky now, threw its harsh light only part way into the crowded restaurant. Such was the contrast, it was as though other lunch time diners behind them were eating in darkness. No way he wanted to have a conversation with Blackstone in front of this crowd. They abandoned their food and hurried back to his flat. It was important that Summer was with him when he made the call. After all, every decision now affected her.

It was always on the cards that something like this might happen, but the wanton destruction still shook him. The apartment looked as though a bomb had gone off. The front door had been kicked in, so he was ready for the bad news. Whoever did this stayed long enough to cause chaos while they were methodically going through drawers, tearing open seat cushions, pulling pictures from walls. They'd even lifted up carpets and strewing the contents of the bathroom and kitchen cupboards across the apartment floor. This was a desperate but professional search. Rapid and very, very thorough.

'Looks like Gerry Conners has tried to switch the phone on,' Jim said.

'Some of this is just pure bloody mindedness,' Summer said. Shocked at the destruction.

'You're right. They're making a point and they want us to know they're pissed off. But they're looking for a needle in a vast haystack. They have no real chance of finding the SD card. But it's what they do next that worries me.'

'I suppose we should make a start trying to clear this mess up,' Summer suggested.

'We might just make it habitable,' Jim said just before he walked into the bedroom.

'Jesus!'

The shock in his voice drew Summer through to join him.

The bed had been turned upside down and the mattress disembowelled with several long jagged rips. Stuffing covered the entire room, lying like a field of beige snow over scattered ripped clothes. Empty drawers drooping open, their contents buried amongst the jumble of vandalised remnants that were once Jim's wardrobe and bedding.

'Habitable?' Summer said. 'You'd better stay with me tonight.'

'Yeah, I think your right.'

They walked back into what was left of the living room.

'First, I'd better call Blackstone and see what he's got to say.'

He tapped in the number and green buttoned the phone. It took just three rings before it was answered.

'Hello, Mr. Stack.' The same smooth, imperious voice that just begged to be slapped.

'Blackstone. Good to hear from you.'

In truth, Jim was rather more than pleased to hear Blackstone's voice.

'I believe we are now in a position to recover our missing funds, Mr. Stack.'

'I'm relieved to hear it.'

'It's not quite as easy as that. The special account which I set up in Luxembourg still retains the dormant fund. From what I can tell, only one attempt has been made to enter the account and that was some time ago. Naturally, he was unable to unlock the account.'

'But Avery can't get access to the account with just his code, so why would he attempt to do so?'

Blackstone gave a little laugh.

'Avery has your code, Mr. Stack. He's had it all the time. I think you may have given it to him without realising.'

Jim recalled giving the code to an associate at the Luxembourg bank at Avery's suggestion. Obviously, the associate was Avery himself, or was handed to Avery by the associate.

'What a bastard. How could I have been so stupid?'

'Don't let it worry you, Mr. Stack. We have both been duped by Avery. Eventually, the penny will drop and Avery will figure out that a third code is needed and who the owner of the third code is, so we must move quickly.'

'How much is in the account?'

'We're looking at quite a substantial figure. More than enough to cover my debt and your earnings, which I think we can agree now includes Victor Avery's share.'

'I'm very relieved to hear it, Mr. Blackstone,' Jim didn't know what else to say.

'I have a very senior connection in Luxembourg who is waiting for me to access the account. I should say, waiting for us to access the account,' he said, correcting himself. 'This person will set up the off-shore account for you and arrange the transfer.'

Jim didn't respond.

'There are some caveats, Mr. Stack.'

'Which are?'

'For politically sensitive reasons, I am unable to go to Luxembourg to attend to this matter myself. You will have to go on my behalf. You will carry a letter of authorisation. You will not open this envelope. If the letter appears to have been tampered with, my contact will disavow all knowledge of the arrangement and the fund will become inaccessible to us. This procedure must be undertaken within the next two days or once again, the window of opportunity will pass. Are we clear about this, Mr. Stack?'

'Loud and clear, but there is already a problem. I still don't have Avery's code.'

'So, get it, Mr. Stack. You've had nearly four days. I had the impression you were a resourceful man.' Blackstone sounded irritated.

'If I manage to get it within the time scale you're talking about, it's unlikely I'll be able to make it over to Luxembourg. Can someone else go on my behalf?'

Jim looked at Summer and saw an opportunity to solve a worrying problem.

'I don't like it, Mr. Stack. Do you have someone in mind? Someone you can trust?'

'Yes, to both of those questions. Someone I completely trust. She's standing next to me now.'

There was a pause.

'This would be the Canadian, Ms. Summer Peterson?'

That he knew her name and nationality shocked Jim.

'Yes,' he replied feebly. 'Yes, Summer. She would be willing to do this for me.'

'Have you been underestimating me, Mr. Stack? I have an interest in knowing everything about you. I am aware of the other game you're playing, too. It's clever, but dangerous, and I will take measures to ensure it doesn't contaminate me.'

That was two shocks in a row. Jim couldn't see how Blackstone could know about the Goldfinger plot. He tried to play it cool.

'I'm not involved in anything that can have a bearing on matters that interest us, Mr. Blackstone.'

Blackstone ignored him.

'Knowledge is power as they say, but it is also protection.' There was a pause before he continued. 'Ms. Peterson will do. Hand the phone to her.'

Summer, unaware of the nature of the conversation with Blackstone, was surprised when Jim handed her the phone. She held it tentatively to her ear with two fingers, as though it might explode.

'Yes?' she asked hesitantly.

She went on to say that tiny word two or three more times during the short conversation with Blackstone. She glanced at James a couple of times as though responding to something that had been said about him. She seemed to be receiving instructions.

He noticed, as she handed the phone back, how becoming an active part of the conspiracy changed her somehow. Gave her renewed self-confidence.

'What did you say to Summer?' he asked.

'I told her what she needed to know and no more, Mr Stack,' Blackstone said mysteriously. 'Now, get the code. No more delay,' he urged.

'If he doesn't give it to me in time?'

'That makes things more difficult, but not impossible. But he will give you the code, Mr. Stack, because he doesn't know you are aware of the third code. He knows from his last attempt that with only two of the cyphers you will remain locked out of the account, so there is no harm in giving you his code. I can assure you Avery is completely ignorant of our arrangement. And of course, you have very significant leverage over him. Our Victor Avery has a very acute sense of self preservation.'

That made sense to Jim. So Avery was back at the top of the urgent, to-do list – a plate that needed an extra spin. But he had other concerns that Blackstone just may be able to help him with.

'OK, I'll give Avery's leash a tug today.'

'One more thing, Mr. Stack. When you get the code, give it to Ms Peterson, she will know what to do with it.'

Jim turned to look at Summer. So, she was now a fully signed up member of the recovery team, Jim noted. Summer smiled and gave Jim a 'see you later' wave indicating silently that she was going to head back to Greenwich. He watched her as she left through the broken door.

'I think we're finished, unless you have anything else to tell me?' Blackstone prompted.

'There is one thing.'

Jim decided to take a chance and go out on a very risky limb.

'As you have correctly guessed, I do have another game in play, though in a way, it's very much the same target. If it stays on the rails, it could bring both of us a high level of satisfaction.'

Jim went on to reveal the plan to Blackstone.

'The adjective, Machiavellian, describes your plan perfectly,' Blackstone said with renewed respect. 'I wonder if the following information might be useful to you. I heard a whisper that in the past week, the British gold bullion inventory had changed.'

'Changed? In what way?'

'Changed is the only word that has been used.' Blackstone said. 'Whatever has happened, it has been done in great secrecy.'

Jim chewed on that news for a moment, couldn't see how it affected his plan and moved quickly on.

'Mr Blackstone, before you go, I believe you may be in a position to provide a very particular service. You, or perhaps one of your business associates.'

'I'm intrigued. What is it I can do for you?' Blackstone's initial amusement turned deadly serious as he listened to what Jim had to say.

'I think that can be arranged. Am I to assume there will be very little notice, Mr. Stack?'

'Twenty-four hours is the best I can hope for,' Jim said. 'It could be less.'

There was a pause, and then.

'Someone will be in touch.'

***

Gerry Conners was furious. Mike Davis had brought the two 'security' goons up to Conners office to explain themselves.

'So this piece of crap,' he said picking up the phone from his desk, 'is useless, just like you two sad bastards.'

The heavies stood there not showing any emotion as Conners vented his rage on them.

Davis tried to calm things down.

'We're looking for a tiny SD card that can be hidden anywhere, even in the cracks between floorboards and these guys have looked there as well.'

Conners stood there looking at Davis, head tilted forward like a bull about to charge. He said nothing.

'The only person who knows where the memory card is, is Stack. He's a tough guy but he is vulnerable. I think I know how to get him to hand the card over.' Davis said.

'So, get on with it. I want this fixed today.'

'Give me a couple of hours and then call Stack. Tell him you need him here for an urgent up-date on the plan,' Davis said.

Conners calmed a little but said nothing. He walked over to the window, his back turned dismissively to the other three. They got the message and left. Alone now, he stared through the window. The sparkle of water from the river just visible through the narrow gaps between the buildings south of the hotel. Not long now he thought. A game changer for him. And independence from that crude relic of the past, Franco Borriello. Dangerous certainly, but worth the risk.

***

The heads of department meeting had been underway for twenty minutes when Avery's phone vibrated in his pocket.

He was about to present his monthly update on current security measures, but the constant intermittent vibration distracted him. He stifled his annoyance, pulled the phone from his pocket, indicating to those around the table that it was an important call that wouldn't wait and excused himself from the room.

'Are you insane?' he hissed loudly into the phone as he searched for a quiet corner in one of the long corridors that wound themselves around the trapezoid perimeter of the enormous building. A corner that would give him an early sighting of anyone approaching from either direction. He tried hard not to look furtive.

'Two things,' Jim said hurriedly. 'The event is live and ready to go.'

He could hear Avery swallow and by the breathless 'Jesus!' just audible down the line, Jim guessed Avery's heart rate had just leapt into high triple figures.

'The other is simple. Give me your code now!'

'You bastard, Stack,' he said venomously. Then, as someone stepped out of a nearby office and headed his way he attempted an authoritative demeanour, nodding a small acknowledgment as they passed.

'I'll text it to you.'

'You've got ten minutes,' Jim said and ended the call.

Avery was left standing there, fuming at the end of a dead line, but with the minor triumph of believing the code would be useless to Stack.

Jim cast his eyes around the apartment and shook his head in despair at the damage. Despite the mess Conners men had made, he was starting to feel things were finally beginning to work out. Summer would be safely out of the country soon, just as he had hoped. But right now, he had that other tricky ball of string to unravel and its name was Charlie. He sat down on the arm of the sofa and called Penny again.

***

Penny Zhang was the petite daughter of a Hong Kong Chinese mother and Anglo European father. Smart-as-a-whip was Jim's first reaction when they met four years ago. He was very glad she was on his side at his trial.

She was only a couple of years into a career at Harrison Baker Associates then. When he got in touch the other day he wasn't surprised to find she was now a fully-fledged partner at the firm. Busy, but happy to help a friend of Jim's.

She reckoned a couple of phone calls would do it, if what Jim had told her was true. She wasn't wrong.

'So, how does it look for Charlie?' Jim asked.

'We've had the DNA results checked by our specialists and we're confident they wouldn't stand scrutiny in court.

I'll give you the short version. They have two examples from different locations. One cigarette end was found under the alleged get-away car. This had the most complete set of markers, 15 in all but probability in many of them was not high. It was close though. The other cigarette fragment was extremely contaminated. They'd taken many other examples from the scene of the abandoned truck. Most are confirmed as the main driver – the owner of the truck. Many of the others were probably other drivers or passengers. There was one that could have caused a problem for Charlie with some associated traits but cross contamination had occurred at some point.'

'So Charlie's in the clear?' Jim asked hopefully.

'Maybe. What they have is largely circumstantial with no other witnesses or firm evidence to support the DNA results, such as they are. This would be essential in a court of law. I've sent our findings and our opinion on the legal position to DCI Deakins. Let's see what happens next.'

'Thanks Penny, you're a star,' Jim said. 'Look, can you give me Deakins phone number?'

'Be careful Jim, you mustn't get involved, it could be construed as coercion.'

'Don't worry, Penny, I won't do anything to jeopardise Charlie and your efforts, but I might just be able throw Deakins an early Christmas present.'

'I'm not sure I want to know what that's all about, Jim,' Penny said. 'Anyway, from what I hear, DCI Deakins won't be around for Christmas. He's due to retire soon.'

'Hmm, that's interesting. I'll bear that in mind.'

'Just be careful.' She said her goodbyes with a promise to give Jim an update, as soon-as.

The Final Countdown

Same day

Jim was just about to leave the bomb site that used to be his home and head to Summer's apartment in Greenwich when his phone rang. It was Gerry Conners telling him to get over to the Montgomery for an urgent meeting. Couldn't wait. Had to be now. Jim pretended to be surprised. He'd been expecting this call.

'I'm on my way.'

Well this was going to be interesting and more than likely, trouble, he thought.

***

On his way over to Covent Garden, a text arrived from Avery. He glanced at it before forwarding it to Summer.

The third code – finally! Not long now and this whole bloody mess would be over and he could get on with his life and be a good deal richer – he hoped.

***

When he walked into Conners penthouse office, everything was all cosy and pleasant – at first.

'Sit down Jim, thanks for coming over. Coffee?' There were two other staff 'heavies' sitting over on the large sofas away from the desk in the far corner of the room. They were reading newspapers, and apparently taking no interest in Jim. Conners, standing at his favourite place by the large expanse of floor to ceiling window glass, was polite and friendly. Jim was on high alert. This was Conners at his most dangerous. Jim played along, He knew what Conners wanted – the SD card. So, why doesn't he just come right out and say it? Why the game?

Jim walked over and sat down, same chair as before.

'Isn't Mike Davis in on this meeting? What's so urgent Gerry?' Jim tried to sound relaxed and easy. He hoped it wasn't coming across as tense and edgy. He took a breath and waited for Conners to make the next move.

'I'm moving the 'go' date.'

Jim sat there, listening. Conners turned to face him.

'Tomorrow morning at eight, the Italian Embassy here in London will receive the message and pass it on to the Bank of England.'

Conners walked over to his desk as he spoke.

'When I say the Bank of England, Jim, I mean of course, Victor Avery, head of security.'

Jim let this information sink in before speaking. He sensed Conners was expecting him to comment.

'Eight tomorrow morning!' he couldn't hide his alarm, but he played along. 'So you want me to get in touch with Avery and warn him about this new deadline. He's not going to like it.'

'First of all, Avery has already got a plan, so he's as ready as he'll ever be and second of all, I don't give a shit what he thinks.'

Conners was getting excited, and not in a good way.

'I'm running this job and that takes me to the third of all. I'm the one who's going to talk to Avery from now on.'

Jim was aware that the big guys had moved from the sofa and were standing very close, like a wall, behind him. Obviously, they had both lost interest in the pretty pictures in the newspapers.

'I was given a present by one of your friends who, as you know, is an old friend of ours.'

Conners opened a drawer, took out Jim's old smart phone and held it up.

'Where's the card, Stack?' It was an angry command.

'What good is the card to you Conners? You have no idea what's on it,' Jim bluffed.

'I know that Victor Avery could go to jail if the recordings you made were given to the police. Avery doesn't care who's handling him, just as long as the recordings don't go public.'

Jim knew that Conners was right, but the recordings represented more than just leverage over Avery. They were an essential part of Jim's private retribution.

'You don't need to talk to Avery, I'll deal with him. That's what the paltry twenty percent deal was for. That and my original Bank of England scheme.'

Conners found that amusing.

'Twenty percent not enough? You want to renegotiate? How about you take nothing and consider yourself lucky to walk out of here?'

Jim had seen this coming. That's way he'd taken the contingency of removing the SD card from the old smart phone a few days ago. He played it tough.

'There's no way Avery will deal with you, especially without the recordings and you're not getting them, so forget it, Conners.'

'I'll ask you again.' His voice became eerily calm. 'I want the SD card, Stack. You will give it to me, believe me.' He smiled as he said it.

'What are you going to do to me Conners? Avery will freak out if you get in touch with him out of the blue.' Fateful words.

'It's not what'll happen to you that you should worry about,' Conners said with a sneer as he set his trap.

The temperature in the room dropped. He gave a nod to the heavies and then picked up the phone. Two things happened. The big guys behind Jim grabbed his arms and shoulders and pushed him hard into his seat. He couldn't move. Then he heard Conners call Mike Davis.

'Bring her in.'

A few seconds later, a door opened behind him and whoever came in, one of them seemed to be resisting. Jim's heart sank. He knew who he hoped it wasn't.

'James!' Summer's unmistakable, terrified voice.

He tried to turn and look but his view was blocked by the side of beef holding him down.

'It's OK,' Conners sneered. 'Let him see his girlfriend.'

Their grip loosened a little and Jim was able to turn to see her. Jim gave her a smile and a wink, trying to reassure her everything was OK. Despite the obvious appearance to the contrary.

'OK, take her back,' Conners ordered. 'I think he gets the message.'

Jim had to think fast. No way was he going to put Summer in danger, which meant that handing the card with the recordings over to Conners was unavoidable. But he needed to find a way to delay things so that he could put the remaining parts of his plan into play. The sudden change of timing made things even more urgent.

'You bastard,' Jim said furiously. 'I don't have the card with me. Give me an hour or so and I'll come back with it.'

Conners almost rubbed his hands with satisfaction. He got up, walked round and sat on the front edge of the desk, arms folded. He smirked arrogantly at Jim, like a man who was holding all the cards. Which of course he was – all except one.

'You should see yourself, Stack. You're pathetic,' Conners couldn't help gloating. 'I don't have time to screw around with little guys like you. This project's going ahead and you'll be lucky to hang on to your twenty percent. Everything is in place; the message from the embassy, the assault on the barge, the handling of the bullion. And now, when you give me the recordings, I'll be Avery's new pal and you'll be old news. I've got a feeling he'll be glad to be shot of you.'

Mike Davis returned to the room and gave Conners a nod.

'She's safely locked away. Grigori is keeping her company,' he said.

'And now I've got your girlfriend.' He let that threat hang in the air. He lent forward placing his hands on the wide leather armrests, pushing his face threateningly close to Jim's, searching for signs of fear in his eyes. Jim tried to turn his head away from the smell of Conners.

'Don't worry Stack, rooms in the Montgomery are all five star. She'll be quite comfortable – for a while anyway.'

After a tense moment, he sniffed, then leaned back onto the desk, folded his arms and pursed his lips. Considering his options. Finally, he glanced at his watch.

'You've got one hour.'

Jim made a move to go, but he was still being held fast by the two goons.

'Something else. You're going with Mike Davis and his crew to take the barge tomorrow night. I want you where we can keep an eye on you. I don't want you having a last minute change of mind. You know – going honest on me, Stack.'

Conners gave a slight wave of his hand.

The two heavies let go of Jim and he was off like a competitor in an iron-man triathlon event – out of the chair, out of the room, and out of the hotel into the warmth of the late spring afternoon.

He looked at his watch and considered what he should do first. Whatever happens, he had to be back in an hour. Nothing would prevent that. He was furious with himself for putting Summer in danger.

He phoned Charlie's land-line.

'Meet me at my place now.'

He hailed a cab and paid extra to find a quick way back to his flat near Brick Lane. A tough call for any cabbie, but this one did it in thirteen minutes.

Charlie arrived eight minutes later, and after '*Buzz*,' '*Click*' and two flights of stairs, he pushed through the broken door into the astonishing spectacle of the destruction in Jim's flat.

Jim was just ending a phone call.

'He'll be with you later this afternoon,' a pause as he listened – then. 'Don't blow it Deakins, I'm depending on you to do the right thing.' He red buttoned the phone.

Jim held up his hand to Charlie.

'Don't ask, there's no time to explain. Summer's in danger and I've got to get back to the Montgomery in about thirty minutes.'

In the background, on the floor next to the broken shelving, a printer whirred and served an A4 sheet onto a tray. Jim checked it quickly, folded it with another sheet and stuffed it into an envelope, sealing it firmly. He scrawled 'Deakins' in felt tip on the envelope and handed it to Charlie.

'What do you mean Summer's in danger?'

'Look at me Charlie. Do you trust me?'

Charlie gave him a sideways glance.

'Of course I do. What...?'

'According to Penny, it looks like you're more or less in the clear of the charges. She's worked her magic, OK? But I need you to go back up there again. Take this envelope, go to Helmsford and give it to DCI Deakins. He's expecting it. But be careful, I haven't given him my name. If he asks, remind him the agreement was no names. Then get back to London double quick.'

'OK, I'll go, but...?'

Jim handed Charlie a second package.

'I want you to keep this with you. It's my passport and the original hand written note from Avery. The Bank of England job is going down tomorrow morning...' he looked at his watch. 'Make that eighteen hours from now. They're taking me with them onto the barge, I don't have a choice because the bastards have got Summer.'

'Jesus, Jim. Where have they taken her?'

'She's being held at the Montgomery, but let me worry about that. I want you to stay focused.'

'This is all happening too bloody fast, Jim. What about the warehouse and divvying up the gold? We were supposed to be on dry land, not on the water playing bloody pirates. The barge was Conners' job, Jim. That's why he's getting the big slice of the cake.'

'Yeah, well it's all changed. You've got to find a way to get onto the barge, Charlie, and not just for moral support. I need you for back-up. Besides, if the escape plan is on, we stick together and get out of the country together. Keep your passport and phone handy....shit!' he just remembered, Charlie swapped his jacket while trying to escape.

'Do you think you can get your stuff back?'

'Well the kid must live in my neighbourhood. I'll try to find him. I'll probably have to buy it back.'

'Text me when you get the phone. I'll have more instructions for you.' Jim had a second thought.

'There's a pub right next to the container loading quay called The Mayor of London. Base yourself there tomorrow so you can keep an eye on what's going on. If things don't get screwed up any further, I'll see you tomorrow night. Now. Go!'

It took Jim a little longer to find a cab that was free. It was always the same when it was clocking-off time in the City. Rush hour made the journey back much slower. He called Victor Avery from the cab.

'What do you want now?' An angry head of security at the Bank of England. 'This is not a good time, Stack.'

'I don't have time for this, Avery, and neither do you.'

'For Christ sake, Stack do you know how dangerous this is for me?'

Jim ignored him.

'The show kicks off tomorrow morning.'

There was a pause and then Avery came back in a guarded whisper – must be people nearby.

'For God's sake, Stack, call it off. This is madness.' His voice tightened. Blood pressure was probably high enough to lift his hat off.

Jim looked at his watch.

Six minutes.

The taxi was stuck in traffic along Holborn near the viaduct. He'll never make it! Suddenly the taxi jerked forward and swung down New Fetter Lane towards Fleet Street.

'Keep calm, Avery. You don't have to do anything but your job. You'll be a hero.'

'It'll all point back to me.'

'Why? There are drivers and security guards you could implicate as inside men,' Jim tried to calm him. Get him thinking about self-preservation. He was good at that, Avery was.

'Yeah, that could work...'

'And don't forget your reward.'

There was more silence except for the noise of the taxi engine ticking over as it waited in a queue at a traffic light.

Four minutes.

He thought it'd be quicker if he got out and ran!

'Are you still there?'

'Yes.'

'Whatever happens, stay with the plan. Nothing matters now except the plan.'

'It's all right for you, Stack, you've got nothing to lose.' Avery was reaching the limits of self-control.

'You have nothing to worry about, Victor. This will all be over in two days and you'll be the one to discover the truth: A clever bomb hoax designed to get gold out of the bank, perpetrated by a London gang. Nothing you could plan for.'

'But how does the gang know the gold will be on a barge? It could only have come from me.'

'They don't know, do they, Victor?' Jim extemporised, his voice calm and reassuring. 'They're simply following the gold. The barge is just

263

one of a number of planned contingencies. You'll be giving lectures about it for years to come.'

Three minutes.

'Gotta go.' Jim ended the call, threw money at the driver as he got out of the cab and started running towards Covent Garden and the Montgomery Hotel.

He fought his way through the crowds of home going office workers, cutting across stationary traffic and into side roads that he hoped would get him closer – sooner.

One minute.

When he got to Covent Garden he was confronted by a wall of people, their backs to him and impossible to get around. He began pushing his way through.

On the other side, the crowd had formed a large circle. In the middle was a street magician standing by a trestle table with a small suitcase open on it. The performer had his hand in the air. A full deck of cards bowed in an arc like a coiled spring between his thumb and forefinger. He was just about to flick one card into the air and catch it with the other hand, intending to thrust it into the face of the bemused tourist pulled from the audience.

The magician had been working the crowd for fifteen minutes and this was supposed to be his big finish. All the street performer had to do now was utter that timeless question – 'is this your card?' – acknowledge the applause and then take the suitcase around the crowd for them to throw money in. That's how it was supposed to happen.

Not this time.

Jim finally pushed his way through into the open space, barged into the performer, knocking him and his trestle table to the ground. As he fell, the fingers of his outstretched hand squeezed just a little too hard and the entire pack of cards sprayed high into the air, floating back to Earth like large, coloured snowflakes.

Jim kept going through the opposite wall of on-lookers. He didn't see what happened next, but he heard about it in rich Mancunian language as the street magician hurled abuse at him.

Time ran out just as he arrived at the turning for the Montgomery. What he saw there bought him to a sudden standstill. Three fire engines, lights flashing, large numbers of fire officers in full fire-fighting rig and the entire population of the hotel, guests and work force milling around in the street.

It looked as though they'd been there for some time. Jim got a sense that they were beginning to wrap things up as he walked towards the chaos.

He looked up at the hotel windows but saw no visible sign of a fire. On the street he couldn't see Summer amongst the crowd. He was starting to panic.

'So you made it back then?'

He turned and there was Mike Davis.

'Where's Summer?'

'She's still in the room with Grigori. Don't worry. False alarm. I think they're letting us back in soon.'

Jim saw a chance to talk privately to Davis.

'It's not a good idea for Conners to talk to Victor Avery. You must see that it's pointless. It could undermine the whole deal.'

Davis didn't say anything immediately, but looked around as though checking to see who might be nearby.

'I'll tell you Mike, Avery is at the end of his tether. Conners could be the tipping point.'

'New York is watching,' was all Davis said.

265

A curious reply Jim thought. Did he detect a small crack in the chain of command? He dropped the subject when he saw Conners coming over.

'This is bullshit. Come on, let's get back inside,' Conners said, indifferent to Jim's arrival. 'Stack's got a small present for me, haven't you, Stack?'

***

Same chair, same heavies, same arrogant Conners sitting in front of him on the edge of his desk. He had his hand out expectantly, like a child waiting for a sweet.

Jim shrugged, he knew he was defeated. He reached into his pocket and brought out his mobile phone, prised opened the plastic case, removed the battery, and then flicked out the SD card, placing it in Conners outstretched hand.

Conners slowly shook his head.

'You had it on you all the time, you bastard,' he said with a sly grin. 'Why the run around?'

'I just wanted to make you wait Conners.'

Conners went round to the other side of his desk, sat down, and placed the card inside the old smart phone. He switched it on and browsed to where the audio files were.

'Plenty of them,' he said. 'Which one do you want to hear?'

'I don't give a shit, Conners.'

Conners ignored him, selected a file and pressed play. His lips pursed like a connoisseur, wondering what to make of a rather impertinent red wine. He nodded as he listened to the conversation between Jim and Avery, weighing up its value.

266

And then, with a jolly bleep that sounded like 'hello', but turned out to be 'goodbye', the battery went dead.

'What the...?' Conners didn't look happy.

'What do you expect Conners? The battery must be over five years old, it's knackered.'

Before Conners could reply, Mike Davis burst into the room.

'The girl's escaped!' he shouted from the door.

Conners forgot about the phone, got up and followed Davis out into the hallway and down to the guest room where Summer had been held. The door was open and Grigori was standing outside looking very sorry for himself, knowing what was coming.

'Get Stack,' he shouted to one of the other heavies before going into the room with Davis.

'How did she get away? That useless piece of meat Grigori was supposed to be guarding her.' Conners was apoplectic, his face red with rage. Out came the usual list of grievances: overpaid, no-brain employees – where did Davis find these gorillas' – are you completely incompetent? – Why didn't he just go back to the States and screw up Franco's life – and the inevitable: did he have to do everything himself?

Davis just stood there and waited until Conners had thrown everything out of his pram.

The heavy returned with Jim.

'Stack,' Conners fury moved away from Davis. He stabbed a finger at Jim. 'You,' he blustered. 'You're our guest until tomorrow night. Then you're going on a nice trip on the river. You can put some of your army training to good use.'

Then, turning to Davis,

'He's in your charge so no screw ups. We're taking that bloody gold and I want him right in the middle of it.'

Davis just stood there.

'Lock him in this room,' Conners said angrily, then emphasised loudly, 'And keep him here!'

Conners stormed out. Davis turned to Jim and shrugged his shoulders.

'So we're taking an ex-British army officer with us. What a joke. We need marines, or better yet, Navy SEALs.' Davis said. 'Just don't get in my way, Stack.'

He left the room, closed the door, and parked the heavy outside.

'He doesn't leave,' Davis said thumbing at the locked door, then leaning in close to his face. 'And neither do you!'

The Gift

15 Hours

'What the hell is this?'

Deakins was referring to the A4 sheet of paper with notes in the form of bullet points that he'd just extracted from the envelope Dawson had handed him five minutes ago.

There was another sheet of paper printed on cheap quality ink-jet paper like the other one. This had a printed message from the guy on the phone – whoever he was. And by the way, what was his connection to that lucky sod, Charlie Dawson?

DCI Deakins had, only a few hours earlier, received the full force of Superintendent Honeywell's wrath at allowing their one and only suspect for the three bank robberies to slip out of their grasp. An embarrassing de-arresting and charges dropped brought about through the effortless skill of some London brief. Honeywell was very clear that Deakins' imminent retirement would not be covered in glory.

And now this.

The accompanying message from Mr. Anonymous was cryptic. He called Yates in.

'What do you make of this?'

He handed her both sheets of paper and waited.

'Well, it's pretty unambiguous. A major robbery is about to happen in London within the next twenty four hours and the man responsible is someone called Victor Avery.'

Deakins agreed.

'The other sheet is a list, or a sequence of strategies for an event that is yet to happen,' Yates noted. 'It refers to the loading of items of value into containers within the building. The containers to be driven to a nearby river facility. From there the containers will be loaded onto a barge. The barge will then be moored on the river for twenty-four hours.'

'But it doesn't say what's inside the containers,' Yates said.

'Apparently, there will be security on board the barge,' Deakins read. 'It's very clear about that. It's a warning to the bad guys.'

'There's a time scale as well,' Yates added. 'Loading of the barge at approximately sixteen hundred hours.'

'Items of value,' Deakins mused. 'What do you think it could be? Antiques? Paintings? Vintage cars? How much can a container hold?'

'Notice that Mr. Anonymous is very insistent that no attempt should be made to prevent the robbery. He claims the robbery proves this chap Victor Avery is involved because he wrote these instructions before the event,' DS Yates was confused. 'I don't get it.'

'Well, if you read the message carefully it seems to imply that this Victor Avery fellow shouldn't know that the robbery will take place tomorrow. How can he have written a response to an event that hasn't happened, without having advanced knowledge?' Deakins said.

'Which puts him fully implicated in a robbery,' Yates ventured. 'But we can't prove he is implicated unless the robbery happens. We have to stand back and wait. Then go and knock on his door.'

'That's a risky strategy,' Deakins said warily. He was already in an extremely weak position because of the fruitless investigation into the recent bank robberies. And what with his retirement looming....

'We could get him on a possible conspiracy charge, boss,' Yates said.

Despite his reluctance to take any risks, the opportunity to polish his credentials before he retired was very seductive.

'What puzzles me,' Deakins said. 'Who did this Victor Avery write the schedule for? And how did Mr. Anonymous get hold of it?'

'Some kind of inside job with some outside help?' Yates offered.

DCI Deakins nodded agreement.

'Who is this Victor Avery, anyway?' Deakins queried. 'Give the name a run through on Google. See what comes up.'

Yates did just that and very quickly came back with an answer.

'I think you'd better take a look at this, sir.'

Deakins heaved himself out of his chair and wandered into the main office. He didn't understand why she couldn't just tell him.

Yates turned the monitor a little as Deakins pulled a chair up next to her. It took him a moment to absorb what the screen seemed to be telling him. Shocked, he sat back in the chair, wondering what to do next.

'See if you can find his address.'

'You want to pick him up now, boss?'

'Christ! I don't know.'

Born To Run

12 Hours

It was damn close.

They only had two seats left on the Luxair 17:10 direct flight to Luxembourg from London City Airport. How she made it was close to miraculous, what with security cranked up to eleven.

Catching a flight to Luxembourg! That wasn't even in the distant realms of possibility only an hour and a half ago.

***

They'd taken her as she arrived at her apartment building. Two big guys, one on either side. Threats to James' life if she gave them trouble. It was as sudden as a car crash. She was too shocked and frightened to give them any trouble as they pushed her into a car, a gorilla on either side, and sped through London, across the river, back to the Montgomery Hotel.

She was held in a room for a while until the door opened and she was grabbed firmly by the arm and marched along a hallway to a big office. That's where she saw James, held down in a chair by two more heavies. It shocked her to see him like that. They let him turn to see her. It was just seconds, but he managed to convey an 'I'm OK' look. She knew that was for her benefit. He didn't want her to worry.

Imagine: a girl enters a room and sees her boyfriend being manhandled by a couple of heavyweight gorillas. Can't see anything to worry about there.

They dragged her out of the office and back to the hotel guest room. They didn't say anything, just threw her in, but this time she had her very own gorilla. She decided to call him Boris.

He sat in a chair and watched her. He absentmindedly reached for a packet of cigarettes from the left hand pocket of his black leather coat and pulled out a lighter from another pocket. As a heavy smoker, he always needed to have his cigarettes nearby. He knew the rules of this stupid hotel: No Smoking. So he just flicked the lighter nervously on and off. There seemed to be a rhythm. It repeated every three seconds or so.

Eventually she sat down on the edge of the bed, her eyes never leaving Boris.

She went through her options. A short thought because there didn't seem to be any. What do they do in films? She wished Hollywood was here. He'd think of a scene from a movie. Something simple and clever – and annoyingly convenient.

Wait a minute! There just might be something. But she needed Boris out of the room and that just wasn't going to happen.

A little while passed and Boris seemed to be getting restless. It started with a movement of his right leg. Was it the need for nicotine? More time passed and he became a little more jumpy, both legs beginning to move nervously like an excited child. Something was bothering him, she could see it on his face. Finally, he placed the cigarette packet and lighter on the table next to him, got up and went over to the bathroom door, turning to her menacingly before going in.

'Stay!' he said with an east-European growl, before closing the door behind him.

Summer froze there for a moment. The menace in his voice still doing its work. She pulled herself together. Boris was peeing heavily into the toilet bowl – must have been a boozy lunch – she could hear it easily through the wall and hardwood door. There wasn't much time. She got up, walked over to the other side of the room, picked up a chair and took it to the bathroom door. This she had seen in a movie. You just jam it under the door handle, making it impossible to lever.

The chair had to be at an angle because it was a little taller than the handle, but the carpet stopped the legs from slipping. She did it as quietly as she could, though she didn't think Boris could hear above the noise he was making. The peeing seemed to go on endlessly.

Next. Fire!

He'd left his lighter on the table. She took it and tried to flick the electric igniter but her hands were shaking. She held her breath for a moment but she could hear Boris was finally approaching the end of his flash flood.

She tried again but her thumb caught it at an awkward angle and it twisted out of her hand, landed on the carpet and cartwheeled under the bed. She fell to the floor and groped for it blindly. Her fingers touched it but flicked it further away. Desperately, she extended her arm as far as it would go, moving it in short arcs across the carpet, trying not to panic. Then suddenly, there it was, just by her hand. She grabbed it, pulled it out, and held it up in front of her. Click! This time, a flame.

Keeping it burning, she took the lighter over to the bureaux table and opened the hotel welcome folder.

It was awkward but she managed to tear a long strip out of the room service menu, with one hand, using the elbow of her other arm to steady the folder. Holding the strip to the flame, she set it on fire, climbed on the bed, blew the flame out and held the smoking ember up to the smoke alarm.

An instant result. Lots of bell ringing noises from outside. And an instant reaction from inside. Boris was trying to get out, turning the handle at first, then, realising the door couldn't be opened, banging and shouting threats. Hard to hear above the noise outside.

Summer ran over to the door to the hallway but it wouldn't open. Of course. Why did she think it would be unlocked?

Keys. Her heart sank. So close. Where would Boris would put the keys? In his pocket of course. And where is Boris? In the bathroom and staying there as far as she was concerned. There was no way she was letting that animal out. Then she saw a glint on the table. Just a small bright sliver of metal poking out of Boris's cigarette packet, a foreign brand called Actpa. She grabbed it and poured the contents out of the paper pack onto the bed. Four cigarettes and the room keys.

Of course! Your average modern hotel uses those annoying plastic card keys. They'll get you into the room and then you have to stick it into a slot on the wall to get the lights working. But not if you're amongst the seriously wealthy, paying for exclusive personal service. They want nothing to do with such a crass system. Good enough for ordinary working people perhaps, but the elite of this world expect traditional room keys that you put into real locks on both sides of the door.

The banging and shouting from the bathroom got louder as Summer put the key into the lock. First attempt, which was remarkable considering how much her hands were trembling. She turned the key and pulled. The door opened onto pandemonium.

People running down the hallway. Staff running back and forth warning guests not to use the lifts but take the emergency exits. Simple enough for Summer to join the confusion and make her way down and out of the building. Apart from a fleeting look at a couple of gang members earlier, she had no idea who she should be avoiding.

Turned out she was lucky. She managed to get out onto the street already crowded with hotel guests being marshalled by hotel staff and then sped off as fast as she could, putting distance between her and the Montgomery. She could hear the sound of fire engine sirens growing louder. One rushed past her with a deafening noise and, following in its wake, a taxi displaying that simple invitation cherished by anyone who's ever tried to hail cab in a hurry – an illuminated yellow 'For Hire' sign.

Summer flagged it down and rode it to London City Airport via her apartment in Greenwich to get her passport.

The impossible had happened. She was back on schedule.

Bad Moon Rising

10 Hours

To the west, the sun hung wearily a centimetre above the London skyline in a strange turquoise coloured sky. Slithers of feeble light shone through gaps in the vertical blinds, striping the office in fading amber before finally disappearing completely. The first few stars were already making a faint appearance as the evening began to turn as dark as an anxious mood.

The smart phone lay discarded and in pieces on Conners' desk. He'd given up on the Avery strategy, it was too late now anyway. But he didn't like being without full control of everything. He put that to one side for the moment. More important now was a final look at tomorrow's action plan.

They'd moved to the sofas with the map laid over the low coffee table.

'What have we missed?' Conners asked Davis.

'As far as I can tell, nothing – if Avery sticks to his plan,' Davis couldn't resist a dig at Conners. 'Whatever you wanted to do with Avery, Jim Stack had him under control. He was managing him.'

'The guy's a crook,' Conners snapped back. 'I can handle crooks.'

'Who, Avery or Stack?'

'Both of them.'

Davis wasn't so sure. He was more concerned about the man in front of him, Gerry Conners. Jim Stack was right, Conners fixation with Victor Avery could have put the whole scheme at risk. He'd alerted Franco Borriello in New York to Conners' attempt at taking Stack out of the game and pocket his twenty percent. Turns out New York had been kept out of that decision and they were keen to know why.

Stack had come up with the ingenious plan in the first place and then added invaluable detail and planning which, combined with Davis's own efforts, were why the game was now on in the first place. He thought it was wiser, safer even, to keep Stack on board. He'd make sure Conners stayed with the original plan and if not, if there was the slightest hint of a hidden agenda, New York had given him freedom to 'handle the problem', and quickly. He knew what that meant.

All this went through Davis's mind as he sat back in the sofa listening to Conners megalomaniac rant. It was time to steer him back on to the one true path – to refocus his attention onto the only thing that mattered right then – getting their hands on the gold bullion.

They went back over the plan again...and again.

***

She couldn't sleep even though she'd enjoyed a good meal and two glasses of wine. Her nerves were still jangling like an over-strung guitar.

The Grand Hotel Cravat on Boulevard F D Roosevelt in the old quarter of Luxembourg City had been pre-booked in her name. As soon as she had checked in, the receptionist handed her an envelope.

'This has been waiting here since this morning,' she explained, in excellent English wrapped in a soft accent often mistaken for German.

'We were expecting to hand it to a gentleman but a caller advised it should now be handed to you when you arrive.'

Summer thanked her, took the keys and went up to her room to freshen up. Next, if everything went well with the bank tomorrow, she'd need a long haul flight out of Luxembourg. She enlisted the help of the hotel concierge to make arrangements that had already been seriously delayed.

It was still early, so she walked out into the warm evening and wasted a little time enjoying the genteel atmosphere of the old city with its fairy-tale castle spires, cobbled streets, and ancient buildings reminiscent of Austrian architecture. But more importantly, it gave her a chance to see where the bank was located – not far it turned out.

The old quarter of Luxembourg City was not a particularly large area. All the interesting bits could be discovered within a twenty minute walk.

Following the route she'd marked out on the street map taken from a shelf of tourist brochures back at the hotel, Summer found the bank discretely located in what had originally been the private, three story dwelling of an old aristocratic family on rue Willy Goergen.

It was almost invisible from the street. If she hadn't taken the short flight of stone steps up to the porch to get a closer look, she could have easily missed it. Its name, Banque Prive Du Grand Duchy, was engraved in fine copper-plate script on a small plaque mounted next to the large polished mahogany double doors. This was a bank that had no interest in passing trade. It was by appointment only – hers was tomorrow at ten thirty.

The walk soothed her nerves after the terrifying events earlier in London, but she also found that her appetite had returned, so she headed back to the hotel and took a table in their excellent restaurant.

The 'call this number' message came directly to her during the meal in a note handed to her discreetly by the maître d'hôtel. Blackstone wanted to be reassured that she did indeed have Avery's code. Summer confirmed this, then she told him about the events of that afternoon in London.

'So you think Mr. Stack is detained in the offices of this Conners character? This makes the favour he asked me to arrange a little tricky. Have you any way to get in touch with him.'

'Not at the moment.'

'Let's not worry about that now. Most important is for you to proceed as planned and take the envelope to the bank in the morning. My contact there will explain what you have to do. Are we clear about that? It's as important for Mr. Stack as it is for me.'

Summer reassured him.

'Are your own arrangements in place, Ms. Peterson?'

She explained that she should have confirmation later this evening. This seem satisfactory and so he said goodbye without ceremony.

And still she couldn't sleep.

***

'What's wrong with you, Victor? You've been incredibly preoccupied lately and you're even worse tonight.'

The last thing Victor Avery wanted to do was explain anything to his wife, but he couldn't just ignore her. He told her the job had been particularly stressful recently. Lots of pressure but it was OK, nothing to worry about.

If he thought he could get away with that, then he just didn't understand the concept of married life and the sixth sense wives seem to develop – given enough time. There was no escape.

'Look at you!' she doggedly pursued her line of interrogation. 'I've never seen you so on edge.'

The phone rang and he nearly jumped out of his skin. His wife answered it, her face a picture of suspicion after her husband's jittery reaction. A girlfriend of hers. Lunch tomorrow. The usual place. Yes, with Chloe. Bring her if you must – another busy day.

While she was chatting, Avery slunk into the living room and over to the drinks cabinet. This would be his third whisky tonight. He took a deep breath to bring his nerves under control, then he took a good slug of twenty year old single malt.

He sat in his favourite Georgian leather armchair by the large open space of the unlit fire and sank into a morose fug. The realisation that he was cornered – boxed in – and by that bastard Stack of all people. If he survived tomorrow, maybe he should just get the money out of Luxembourg and leave the country.

His wife made a perfunctory appearance at the oak panelled door to announce she was going to bed. He turned and looked sullenly at the empty space she had left behind. A stare he held long after the sound of the bedroom door closing upstairs echoed down to him. He despised everything about her. He wouldn't miss her. He'd be glad to see the back of her. A half smile formed on his lips as he fantasised about the endless possibilities in distant exotic lands.

He followed an hour and another whisky later. He didn't sleep much either.

***

At least they'd fed him. He'd left the bits and pieces of his phone on Conners' desk. The bedside phone had been disconnected, but he was surprised to find the fridge had a full inventory of booze. Well it's on them, Jim thought, so he opened a bottle of white wine – the good stuff.

He poured a glass and lay back on the bed. Staring at the ceiling, he noticed the slight blackening around the smoke detector. He realized immediately what Summer done – clever girl. Well, you can't do that trick twice.

As far as he could see, he was stuck in this room until they needed him for the assault on the barge. Not, of course, that they actually needed him. They just didn't want him having second thoughts and spoiling the party with uninvited guests such as the police. And of course, standing there on the deck of the barge with all the other goons implicated him directly if anything should go wrong.

So the next question: what time does the show kick off? Jim guessed it would take the Bank a couple of hours of running around in circles before it dawned on them the clock was already ticking. They'll get the message around eight am tomorrow morning, so, let's say they start loading gold at twelve noon. It couldn't be earlier because emergency arrangements have to be made with Tower Environmental. They'd have the weight of government bearing down to make that happen.

Jim did a quick calculation. If they really did attempt to move three hundred and fifty tons of gold bullion they'll need how many containers? A container might hold, let's say, twenty tons. That would mean about twenty five containers. The gold had to be moved up from the underground vaults. He had no idea how they did that, or how long it would take.

Another thought. Could you get twenty five containers onto one barge? Might they need two? This took him back to his original belief that they should probably only grab what they reasonably could manage.

The plan relied on the use of tour boat services that ply the river. Problem was they only run until about ten or eleven at night. Another critical element relied on the use of darkness. So the assault on the barge would have to happen by mid-evening, say around ten pm. Might be able to push it a bit later, which would be better. Were they going to keep him in this room until then? He'd just have to stick around to find out.

***

It was a no-brainer really, Deakins thought. He had nothing to lose by letting the robbery run its course before tapping on Victor Avery's door. There was an almighty risk in this strategy of course, and his career was at stake. But letting the robbery get underway would prove the truth of what Mr. Anonymous was claiming. With his credibility at rock bottom after the debacle of having to release Charlie Dawson, there was no way he could have presented what he had to Honeywell. The preening SOB would have just laughed him out of his expensively re-decorated top floor office.

Nonetheless, he was still a policeman and his instinct was to do his duty. It was a dilemma that kept DCI Deakins awake well into the night.

***

Charlie was relieved to find himself back at his flat without the fear of the police knocking on his door. How did that happen? Jim's ability to extricate himself and his friends from the most unpromising of circumstances seemed limitless. Whichever legal passage from the barristers' book of dark arts was invoked, the resulting magic got him out and free of charges. Result!

He'd taken a nervous trip back to Helmsford Constabulary and given the envelope to DCI Deakins. He didn't hang around for tea and a chat with old pals, he just rushed back to the station and caught the next train back to London.

The treachery of Toni Zeterio had yet to be dealt with. He wasn't going to get away with it, Charlie was certain of that. He went home via Zeterio's address in Clerkenwell. His mother was just leaving the house for her part time restaurant job. She claimed she hadn't seen her son all day. Obviously, Toni had sacrificed his share of the earlier robberies and the big job tomorrow, but what for?

As Charlie fell into a deep and untroubled sleep, his last thought was: what was more important to Toni Zeterio than money?

***

High above the Atlantic, in a crowded flight to New York, Toni Zeterio twisted and turned, trying to find a comfortable position in the cattle class cabin seat.

Every now and then, when he thought he'd found a less tortuous position that brought him some measure of comfort, he managed a smile as he thought about the new life that awaited him amongst the grateful members of Franco Borriello's organisation.

Franco, the man he'd sold his friends out to. Toni imagined the scene as he welcomed him back into the family with open arms and a grateful smile on his face – and perhaps an appropriate reward for bringing him such a profitable business venture?

And then there was his old flame, his distant cousin, who stupidly married one of Franco's nephews. Enough time had passed for her to realise her mistake. According to Toni Zeterio's twisted rationalisation, there was reason for hope.

Heroes and Villains

The next 24 hours

Most days, he didn't arrive at his office until nine am. But today of all days, with the certain knowledge that the 'Communication' would have already been delivered at eight o'clock, it was critical that Victor Avery gave the appearance of utter normality. This was going to take a level of coolness that even he, with an extra thick coating of arrogant superiority, might struggle to convey.

It was during the drive in that he received the call. Urgent! Get in ASAP. Can't explain on the phone. All key personnel will be there.

His heart raced. He took a hand from the steering wheel and looked at it. It was noticeably shaking. Deep, slow breaths. He must clear his mind of all fore knowledge. Anything said at the meeting must seem fresh to him, just as it will be to everyone else.

He slammed the brakes on. Bloody couriers! They rush up, threading themselves through the narrow spaces separating the lines of vehicles, next thing you know, they've swept in front and squeezed into the small gap that represented the safe stopping distance between you and the taxi in front. The traffic started inching forward. He couldn't bear the idea of travelling in with the common population, but traffic congestion was getting worse. Maybe, if he survived today, he'd use the train in future – first class of course.

***

Unusually, the meeting was being held in a smaller wood panelled room rather than the grander, first floor committee room. Still sizable enough though, for the handful of people sitting around the large, art deco, maple veneered table.

Avery was shocked to see the Governor already seated at the table as he entered the room – the last to arrive. The Bank of England chief had a schedule that made him a man rarely seen in ordinary circumstances. The Governor's presence underlined the gravity of the meeting and he thanked everyone for getting there as soon as they could. He quickly introduced everyone and Avery wasn't surprised to find representatives from the Home Office and MI5 as well as the Bank's Senior Manager of Custody Settlement and Liquidity, the Head of Collateral Management, and the Custody Manager. With Avery as Head of Security, they had the full panoply of relevant heads of departments.

How do you get the attention of such people? All Avery knew was that a message would arrive in London of such convincing provenance it couldn't be ignored. By the time it had been brought to this meeting room, the officials that needed to be impressed had already made sufficient enquiries that they were satisfied with its validity. Whatever action was decided now, in this meeting room, should be regarded as essential and urgent. He had no idea how James Stack had managed that.

Avery had hoped this preposterous madness would fall at the first hurdle, but apparently the game was very much on.

The Governor handed the meeting over to MI5's Deputy Director General, Clive Stafford, and then excused himself to attend other business. It was essential that the Bank of England appeared to be operating as normal, with no hint of the drama that was unfolding within its walls. At least for the time being, anyway. Eventually of course, they would have to deal with the media. Even now, some unlucky PR officer was being dragged back from vacation to prepare the strategic management of the bad news.

Stafford wasted no time. He handed around printed copies of a 'communication' to everyone and then launched into a brief outline of the problem. Around the table people listened with mouths open in slack jawed astonishment – and when he'd finished – by general murmurings of disbelief.

Avery, testing his nerve, threw the first question.

'But how can you be sure this communication,' he corrected himself. 'This threat – is real?'

'We've followed the trail as far as we can. It came via the Italian Embassy here in London. They were alerted by their own government who had been contacted by the Albanian Embassy. They'd received the message from the Consulate of Braszove: a small fly blown and corrupt republic in south eastern Europe that had a reputation for harbouring criminals, exiled dictators, heads of government, and assorted party members of corrupt governments. The kind of people who had the opportunity to get their grubby hands on their nation's wealth. Well, anyway, that's where we think this threat originated.'

The Custody Manager shook her head.

'No, there can't be a threat from Braszove, we aren't holding any bullion on their behalf. Never have done.'

'That's what's so clever and sinister about their plan,' Stafford said. 'We don't know which, or how many of the world's exiled leaders or disgraced government members are domiciled in Braszove, or simply use Braszove as a base of operations, but any and all would have had the opportunity to arrange for a sacrificial shipment of gold bullion destined for storage in the Bank of England's vaults to be tampered with while they were in power in any one of a number of countries. It would have been a country we do hold bullion for, of course. The problem is, we have no way of knowing precisely which country or countries might have unwittingly been involved. This plan could easily have been laid several years ago. What I want to know is, what level of damage could be inflicted and what can be done to prevent it?'

Avery picked up the document.

'According to this communication, they have tampered with an unknown number of gold bars. Hollowing them out and filling them with a small charge of high explosives that would propel a quantity of highly radio-active material into the air, contaminating the other gold around it.' Avery said. 'Is it just me, or isn't this a bit like the James Bond film, Goldfinger? It must be a joke.' Avery thought he was coming across well – very natural. Better not push his luck.

Others around the table nodded agreement.

'So we have no way of knowing which consignment and when?' The Custody Manager, Jane McDonald, said.

'The problem is much worse than that,' Senior Manager of Custody Settlement and Liquidity, Evan Cousins added grimly. 'The custodial gold gets traded internally. It gets moved around. If we don't know the origins of the contaminated gold, we have no way of knowing where those bars are now.'

'Well, according to this, we only have twenty-four hours before the gold bars start exploding.'

Stafford looked at his watch.

'That was an hour ago, so make that twenty three hours.'

Avery looked around the table at the gathered experts and waited. *'Any minute now'* he thought.

'Wait a minute,' Evan Cousins said. 'If I'm not mistaken, there hasn't been any trading of British bullion for quite a while, until recently that is. So we can be reasonably sure that the UK inventory is safe.'

And there it was. Avery saw his chance.

'That presents us with an opportunity. I think we may have a partial solution to the problem.'

Stafford's eyes lit up. Any kind of answer would be better than nothing.

'What do you have in mind?'

Avery spoke as though a plan was forming in his mind. He put forward his suggestion for separating the British gold from the rest and taking it somewhere safe, while a search was undertaken amongst the remaining custodial gold, for as long as time allowed.

'Give me a little while and I'll come up with a plan to ring fence the British gold,' he added finally.

The Permanent Secretary, quiet until now, took the lead.

'If I understand correctly, there's over four thousand tonnes of gold in these vaults, not much less if you remove the UK inventory. Can you really check all that gold in the time we have left?'

'We have to give it a try. I'll need every available member of staff though,' Avery said.

The Permanent Secretary nodded.

'How will they know what to look for?'

'There should be a slight difference in weight,' Jane McDonald said. 'Let's hope so anyway, because apart from that they'd look like any other bar of gold.'

The Permanent Secretary shook his head in despair, then turned to the Head of Security.

'OK Avery, you've got thirty minutes and no more. We can't afford any further delays.'

Avery took that as his cue to leave. Now all he had to do was steer his own security team in the direction he wanted them to go. Shouldn't be a problem. They were all hand-picked and grateful.

***

It was around midday when the door to Jim's luxury cell was opened. He was surprised to find Grigori still employed. There must be a shortage of east European henchmen. He was taken back down the hall to Conners' office. The goon closed the door behind him and Jim found himself alone in the empty room. He guessed Conners would turn up soon.

This however was an unexpected opportunity. On the desk, the parts of his phone still lay where he had left them after removing the SD card yesterday afternoon. He wasted no time gathering them up and putting them in his pocket. Across the desk was his old phone. Tempting! He glanced at the door, no one coming, so he quickly reached over, grabbed the phone, opened the back cover and removed the card. Outside in the hallway a muted bell and then the purr of lift doors opening signalled someone was coming. He quickly snapped the back of the case into place, threw the phone onto the desk, spun round and leaned against the front of the desk in the way Conners had done yesterday – just as the office door opened. Jim tried to look nonchalant, but worried it was coming across like the guilty whistling of the Artful Dodger in Oliver Twist.

Not Conners, but Davis.

'Have you eaten?'

Not the question he was expecting.

'I was given continental breakfast earlier, but coffee would be good.'

Davis picked up the desk phone and arranged for coffees to be delivered. Jim thought he could detect a different attitude towards him. Something had subtly changed in their relationship.

'How is it going? I assume the show is well underway now.' James surmised.

Davis walked over to the sofa and sat down. The map of London was still lying on the coffee table. He indicated for Jim to sit in the sofa opposite.

'Unbelievably, it's all going to plan – so far,' he seemed surprised. 'They've taken the bait and trucks have started arriving at the rear of the bank. I've got to be honest, Stack, I gave us fifteen percent tops to get this far.'

Jim shook his head in amazement.

'I know what you mean. I couldn't see any flaws in the plan, but the whole idea seemed so preposterous it really shouldn't have stood a chance. I mean, we're dealing with government departments here. Although, perhaps that explains it.'

A knock on the door and Conners' butler arrived with a tray of coffee.

'Put it over there,' Davis said indicating the desk. He waited for the man to leave before continuing.

'I've got men stationed near the bank and around Tower Environmental on the river. They're sending me feedback on everything as it happens.'

'Has the barge been ordered?'

'That had to be abandoned. Turns out Avery has commandeered one of Tower Environmental's own barges. They're unloading containers from it now, making it ready for the first container from the bank.'

'That shouldn't affect us too much,' Jim said. 'Any suspicious activity nearby? Police or security?'

Davis shook his head as he got up to get the coffees.

'Your Victor Avery did say he wanted it low-key and as far as we can tell there's nothing going on in the way of security, not yet anyway. And as far as anyone watching could tell, it's just another day at the office for Tower Environmental. Nothing unusual happening.'

Davis came back with the coffee cups and placed them on the map on the table.

Jim was suspicious of this new, warm, and cuddly Mike Davis. It was way out of character.

He understood from the beginning that he was the outsider, resentment and mistrust assumed in every meeting and agreement. Especially the part where he would only get twenty percent of the take. They were gangsters for heaven's sake! There might've been honour amongst thieves if you believed that old wives tale, but to them he was merely an amateur. Therefore he was as much a target for their avaricious ambitions as the gold in the Bank of England.

'Where's Conners?'

'Having lunch with clients in the hotel. Business as usual.'

'I guess he's given up on the Avery intimidation scenario,' Jim said.

'There's no point now.'

'And our twenty percent is still safe?'

'You're going to have to wait and see.'

Jim decided to go for broke.

'Something's changed, Davis. I can't put my finger on it, but there's a subtle difference.'

Davis reached for his coffee and took a sip before replying.

'You think so?' He paused as he put the cup back on the table. It was an excuse to consider what he would say next.

'I respect you, Stack. This plan. The way you handle yourself. You're not intimidated easily, and we can be very scary people. But believe me, you're going on that barge and you'll take your chances with the others because that's what Gerry Conners wants. Just remember, the people that really count are in New York and they're watching everything. They're expecting this job to go down without mistakes or someone will be held responsible.'

That was as far as Mike Davis was prepared to go. Jim felt there was a lot left unsaid, but it was all there between the lines – it wasn't that subtle.

The meeting ended and Jim was marched back to his luxury prison – they'd be back for him later.

***

Davis said he had stationed men down by the river to keep him updated. What he didn't know, so had Jim. Or to put it more accurately, Jim hoped he had. The definition of a spotter would be someone who can convey what information they garner back to people who can make use of it. You need telecommunications for that to work. A mobile phone would be ideal.

Charlie was sitting at a table nursing a pint of ale at the back of The Mayor of London pub. One that gave him a wide view through the pubs panoramic, river-facing windows, of Tower Environmental's operations next door. He'd been in the pub since noon, gradually table hopping for a better view as the lunch-time crowd thinned out, eventually grabbing the table he wanted in the first place. Right by the window.

Not a bad spot. He'd had lunch and it tasted good. He could see why the pub was popular.

The pub sat directly underneath Canon Street main-line railway bridge, a green painted steel construction that stretched south across the river. To the right, and separated by a narrow lane, was Tower Environmental's transfer facility. It consisted of a large concrete apron stacked with containers that would, on any other day, hold tonnes of compacted waste paper – the mountain of discarded scrap generated by the City of London's daily business activities. An enormous black gantry crane towered above, ready to lift the containers into the sky – its box-girder jib reaching out over the river. Below it, moored against the concrete quay, a large rusting barge, 132 feet long, 26 feet wide, wallowed lethargically.

Charlie was about to take another sip of beer when his phone rang.

'Yeah?'

'You got your phone back, then,' Jim said, stating the obvious.

'Yeah, that and my passport. Got it sorted last night. Cost me a hundred quid. Where have you been? I've been calling you.'

Jim gave Charlie the short version and told him the phone's battery was low, so he had to keep calls to a minimum.

'So you're stuck in a luxury hotel room until kick off tonight. I've had it worse.'

'Never mind that. What's happening down there?'

Charlie looked around to make sure no-one was eaves dropping. Then he lowered his voice.

'The first container was loaded twenty minutes ago. Hang on. Another one has just arrived.'

'Any sign of security?' Jim asked, and then added. 'Look closely, you may spot some of Conners' men. I have no idea what they look like. Just keep an eye out.'

'I can see two...no, make that four plain clothed men on the barge. Could be police, but I reckon they're private security. No sign of weaponry.'

'There won't be any visible weapons, Avery wants to keep it low-key. That doesn't mean other security services haven't been deployed. Just pay attention. And lay off the booze Charlie.'

'Don't worry, you can trust me.'

Jim had heard those words before. But to be fair, in a skirmish, there was no better right hand man than Charlie.

'Do you want me to stay until the barge is moored off?'

'Only if there's time. You've still got a key part of the plan to handle tonight. Is that still good to go?'

'Don't worry Jim. Like I said, everything's cool.'

'Good man Hollywood. In the meantime, don't call me unless something unexpected happens and try to not look conspicuous while you're eye-balling the activity on the barge.'

***

296

The face of the Bank of England building is well known: with its faux classical architecture featuring a colonnade of eight Corinthian columns set between a further six on either side. But the business end is in a nondescript road at the back. Two tall, iron and bronze doors crudely embellished with extruded ornaments and studs formed the first line of fortress like defences. The large gold vaults themselves lay hidden behind and far below ground on two levels.

Inside, hundreds of individual, blue painted steel racks, four pallets high are laid out in long lines, seven rows deep. Each pallet alone holding a tonne of gold bars. The rows of racks were separated by lanes wide enough for a small fork lift truck to operate in.

Avery was surprised how slow the loading process was. A gold bar weighed 13 kilos or 28 pounds. By comparison, its density was almost twice that of lead. With a maximum load of 320 gold bars, each stack of four pallets weighed four tonnes.

Fork lift trucks took the pallets to a heavy duty lift that raised them up to the ground floor service area. It was there that a Tower Environmental container had been reversed against the loading stage, the fork lifts simply had to roll in and out with their precious cargo. Although there was plenty of room inside, the weight of the gold meant they couldn't come close to filling its twenty foot length. Because of the weight, nothing moved quickly.

Avery noticed that there was enough room for a second container and urged the loading crew to redouble their efforts. They resented his interference but grudgingly pushed a little harder.

At the same time, below ground, the custodial staff where racing to find any gold bars that had been tampered with. Again, given the weight of each bar, this business proceeded slowly and they'd found no sign yet of any rogue bullion.

Eventually though, time would run out and they would have to retreat from the vaults.

***

The sun was getting low in the sky as the last container dropped into the hold. A tug fussed around the vessel, nosing it here, nudging it there. Finally, a hawser was drawn between them and secured around a bollard at the bow of the barge. Slowly the cable tightened under the pull of the tug's powerful marine engines and the vessel swung out heavily into the river to begin the shortest journey of its life – to the middle of the River Thames.

The tug crew moored it at each end to two of the many buoys anchored to the clay bottom along that part of the river. They waited long enough to ensure the barge was secure, retrieved the towing hawser and motored off to the next job.

And there it sat, the glory of Tower Bridge just a short distance downstream. River cruisers filled with excited tourists taking 'selfies' with the historic buildings and architectural wonders that lined the river, passed with complete indifference just metres away from the rusty barge holding the sum total of the nation's golden wealth.

If the Chancellor of the Exchequer knew anything about it, he'd doubtless be praying it wouldn't spring a leak!

***

Mike Davis came for him at eight p.m. He was dressed differently – more casually. Grigori, in a brightly coloured shirt and jeans, was with him to ensure Jim didn't make trouble. They marched him back to the office where Conners was waiting.

Conners threw some clothes at him.

'Here, put these on.'

'What's this, dress-down Friday?' Jim asked.

Conners noticed Jim's perplexed look.

'You're supposed to be a bloody tourist so you'd better look like one. They should fit.'

They weren't Jim's first choice of fashion for the smarter, casual traveller but he put them on anyway. Ubiquitous jeans, blue cheque shirt – not tucked in, beige jacket. Not very original. As he folded his own clothes, he palmed the contents of the pockets, over to the new outfit.

'You'd better get going, they're waiting for you.' Conners said dangerously.

'What, no encouraging words Conners? No motivational quote from Henry V before the battle of Agincourt to gird our loins?'

Conners took a step forward and grabbed Jim by the throat, pulling him close to his face.

'You're a funny man, Stack. It mightn't be just your twenty percent you lose today.'

Jim wrenched Conners' hand away. He had a strong grip and it took some effort to free himself. He stepped back and stared at Conners icily.

'What do you want, Stack? A piece of me?' Conners said with a sadistic laugh. There was a hyper-intensity about him. Drug-induced? Probably coke, Jim thought. Conners was into that business as well, so there was no shortage of supply.

Davis stepped in.

'Later! Get moving, Stack. Clock's ticking,' he said, his right hand opening his jacket a little, revealing a flash of gunmetal-blue pistol stock tucked into his belt. Jim recognised it immediately. A Browning 9mm – sixteen useful rounds in one magazine. It was starting to get serious.

Conners threw Jim a cocky sneer as they left the room.

On the street outside the hotel, a black Range Rover waited, engine running. Two other 'tourists' were already inside. They moved over to make room as Davis opened the door. He insisted Jim get in first, then squeezed in beside him.

They crossed over to the south side of the Thames via Waterloo Bridge before heading east. Twenty minutes later they had passed Tower Bridge and turned into the shabby end of Bermondsey riverside.

Between Bermondsey Wall West and East was a large abandoned area of hard standing leading to a derelict wharf fronting onto the river. They pulled in and drove over to join two other vehicles already parked at the river's edge.

Moored against the quay in the gloomy twilight was a large, double decked, river cruise boat. An old weathered board fixed to the railings on the second deck boasted the legend, 'Pride of the River', hand painted in a crude sun-bleached circus font that was flaking off badly, like much of the paintwork on the old boat. Apart from the regular river buses, only a few tourist boats ply this part of the river east of Tower Bridge so it was an unusual sight.

Someone was waving frantically for them to get on board. Davis and the others went to the back of the Range Rover and grabbed a big canvas bag and a couple of larger black moulded flight cases, all of which looked ominously heavy as the villains, bizarrely dressed for a vacation, carried them to the boat.

On board, Jim counted six men, not including the captain and crew. He wondered if the crew were part of the gang or simply luckless extras pressed into service. The six gang members all appeared to have communications head-sets as they headed up to the deck above.

Davis kept Jim on a tight leash so he was never very far away.

'I'm impressed,' Jim said. 'It's a good spot to set out from, Davis.'

Davis was adjusting his own head-set.

'There was no way we could use one of the regular piers up-stream. We'd have been screwed before we started.' Jim could hear the tension in Davis's voice. He was surprised at his own calmness. A quality that had served him well when leading a squad of men into a fight.

It was almost fully dark now. The boat was preparing to shove off, engines revving, captain shouting orders to the crew manning the ropes. The gangway though, was still stretched between the boat and the quay, a couple of crew standing by, waiting to pull it in.

'OK Stack, you're on. Where are all the others you promised? They should have been here by now.'

Before Davis could finish berating Jim, a vehicle turned off the unlit road in the distance, its headlights flashing and horn sounding as it raced towards the boat. What eventually arrived was a bus full of noisy passengers. The doors opened and out poured thirty or more assorted men and women laughing, shouting and drinking beer from cans.

They were dressed to party, already drunk, and clearly revved up for a good time on the river. This could be one they wouldn't quickly forget.

They hung around noisily on the quay, complaining that the boat didn't have any lights or a disco. Then, a man wearing a back-pack stepped out of the bus and, with lots of reassuring words, started herding them like a flock of sheep, up the gangway and on to the boat. It took a little while to get them all on board and they were still complaining as they milled around on the lower deck looking for the bar.

'Don't worry everyone,' the shepherd said. 'The lights and the disco will start as soon as we get going, OK?'

Someone asked about the bar and was joined by cheers of support from the others.

'Yeah, and that as well. It's going to be a great party.'

There was a general cheer and the crowd calmed a little.

Jim walked over to the party organiser.

'Where the hell did you find this lot, Charlie?'

'I went around a few clubs last night and passed the word that anyone who's up for a free river party and free booze should meet me outside Charring Cross station tonight. I was waiting there with that chartered bus. You didn't give me much time, Jim. Thirty assorted warm bodies. That's all that turned up.'

'They look like they've already had a few, can you keep them under control?'

'They're your average party goers, all they want is booze and sex. There's plenty of both to keep 'em occupied.'

'What's with the back-pack?'

'Nothing really. If we get away I thought I might need a change of clothes – you know – if we're on the run and...'

The rest of his reply was drowned out by the noise of the boat as it got underway, its engines revving loudly, pushing it out into the river, heading west towards Tower Bridge and the bright lights of central London.

A cheer went up from the crowd as the boat's multi-coloured party lights were switched on. One of the crew acting as a DJ turned the disco and PA system on and started playing loud dance music. The revellers who weren't queuing at the bar started dancing frantically. Everything looked just as it should. Just another brightly lit party boat cruising the river, with crowds of happy people having a good time.

Davis told Jim to follow him as he climbed the stairs to the upper deck. A notice had been strung across the stairway warning that the upper deck was out of bounds: 'Crew Only'.

The area was a hive of activity – sports bags had been zipped open and various weaponry was being checked and assembled, mostly hand guns, but Jim could make out at least two short automatic weapons. Looked like Spectre SMGs, Italian submachine guns, perfect for close-in fights. All very alarming.

Further along the deck, the black flight case had been opened and a strange spidery device was being rigged by two guys – the ones who'd travelled with them in the Range Rover. Jim was curious and watched as they worked. It didn't take long. When they'd finished an eight bladed helicopter drone was ready to be launched. One of the men was operating it from a hand held remote control system, checking the small electric motors. Whatever they planned to do with it, it looked like it was ready to go.

Davis walked over to join him as the grey stone and blue painted ironwork of Tower Bridge loomed above them, bright street illumination and floodlights casting a dark shadow over the noisy party boat as it passed beneath. The loud dance music from the deck below echoed back off the walls of the vast Portland Stone piers.

The squat prison fortress of the Tower of London lay on the immediate right. Dungeons that, in an earlier century, would have been their reward for the kind of conspiracy they were planning tonight. Ahead, not far away on the left, was HMS Belfast, permanently moored as a tourist attraction and a short way beyond that, in the centre of the river, the dark brooding shape of the barge came slowly into view.

'The crowd seem to be enjoying themselves, let's hope the booze holds out,' Davis said.

'What's the drone all about?' Jim said pointing to the whirring machine.

'Yeah, that's a clever bit of kit. You'll find out soon enough,' Davis said mysteriously.

As the Pride of the River passed HMS Belfast, the two drone operators started to get busy. Amongst their kit was a twelve inch LED monitor which they had just switched on. The ghostly picture had an inverted black and white appearance that Jim recognised immediately as thermal imaging. It had only one purpose. To see where all the warm bodies on the barge were. Very clever.

Davis kneeled down and stared intently at the screen as the drone rose from the deck. It made a buzzing hum as though someone had disturbed a wasp nest, but with all the noise coming from the party below and the ambient background sounds of the city on either side of the river, it had a stealth like silence as it flew high above the water.

The boat kept its distance north of the barge as it approached.

Davis told Jim they'd be making one surveillance pass and, if all appeared good to go, the assault would take place on the way back.

The drone rose high into the sky disappearing into darkness. The only reference for its position was the navigation data superimposed on the LED screen, and of course the picture coming back from the on-board thermal imaging camera.

Soon, the unmistakable shape of the barge came into view. It was surprisingly clear and close. Several hot spots could be seen moving along its length, another couple were stationary. One of them started moving but left behind a smaller hot spot. A coffee cup? Probably.

***

On board the heavy barge wallowing slowly against its moorings in the middle of the river, plain clothed security guards wandered idly along its length, sometimes in pairs, often alone. The containers had been loaded lengthways across the width of the barge, leaving little room for passing. They had torches but were instructed not to use them unless it was essential. Even then, only briefly and shielded.

Mr. Avery hadn't told them what was in the containers, though he was very explicit about keeping security low-key. Why would you want to guard a barge full of waste paper? So, the guards had played along and started their shift eagerly enough, but boredom soon set in as the sun went down. Now they were not much more than passengers staring out across the river, both sides offering entertaining views of the spectacular London river-scape.

They particularly enjoyed the brightly lit and often noisy river boats that passed by with their music blaring. You could hear the kids enjoying themselves. Much rather be there than here.

There was one passing just now – the Pride of the River. The DJ was playing a great track, 'Happy'. Who was it? Pharrell Williams? Yeah, roll on Saturday.

***

The drone hovered a hundred feet up, moving slowly down the vessel, but London Bridge was very close now, forcing the operator to command the drone to return before contact was lost.

'So, four men. Are we agreed?'

That was the general consensus between Davis and the two drone operators.

'I couldn't make out anything other than that, but you can't be sure what weapons they might have.' Jim said.

'I think Avery was right,' Davis said. 'A barge full of waste paper shouldn't need defending. Too much security and you raise suspicion.'

'Yeah, not a lot of security on the barge,' Jim said looking out across the water. 'But who knows what's lurking out there?'

That thought hung there as Jim started walking back towards the stairs.

His attention was caught by the sudden appearance of two heads peering above the stairwell, a man and a woman, obviously looking for some privacy away from the crowd downstairs. The man spotted Jim and started to climb up the last few steps, the woman followed. They were both very drunk. He put his arm around the woman and they both staggered towards Jim. Davis ran forward, his gun pointed at the couple.

'Hey man, whass that,' the man drawled as he saw the gun. 'Is tha' real?'

His eyes could barely focus. He was swaying as he looked around at the other men. Somewhere in his drink sodden head, a dim light went on and he began to notice that they too were armed.

'Wha' you lot doin' up here then?' he was laughing. For some reason he thought it was funny. The woman, though, had a clearer head. She was seriously alarmed.

'Come on, Steve,' she said putting her arm under his shoulder trying to support his weight. 'Let's get back down and have another drink.'

'Stay there!' Davis commanded. He and two other men had levelled their guns at them. The others were also starting to turn their attention to the unwelcome visitors.

'He's a Yank. Wass a Yank doing wiv a gun then?'

His girlfriend interrupted him.

'No, it's OK, we haven't seen nuffink,' the woman said. 'We'll just go back downstairs.'

'Wha' those guns for then?' the man said, his finger tapping Davis's gun.

Davis ignored him.

'Put them in the crew room behind the wheel house. Make sure they stay there.'

Two men grabbed the couple and pushed them roughly towards the rust-pitted white painted steel boxes that formed the crew quarters a few yards away.

'OK, you don't have to shove,' the woman said, annoyed. 'Look why don't you let us go? We won't say nuffink.' The man seemed subdued. The woman, however, turned angry and started having a go at him.

'You're bloody useless. Why don't you do somefing, Steve? Tell em to let us go.' Those were the last words before the steel door was slammed and bolted shut.

Davis spun around and confronted Jim angrily.

'Tell your man to keep those idiots downstairs under control. Don't let it happen again.' Davis showed Jim his gun to underline the threat.

'Leave it to me,' Jim was grateful for the opportunity to speak to Charlie out of earshot of Davis. He was just making his way downstairs when Davis warned him the boat was about to turn round for the final run.

'You've got sixty seconds, then I want you back up here where I can see you.'

'Still don't trust me, Davis?' Jim said.

Davis ignored him and turned back to the other gang members.

The music was even louder on the lower deck where the party was well underway. Men and women dancing with drinks in their hands, one or two couples slow dancing sexily despite the up-beat rhythm. Others had found dark corners to smooch in and the bar, as always, was busy handing out free drinks to a never ending line of thirsty revellers.

The boat had just passed under the Millennium Bridge and was already starting to make its turn in the middle of the river when Jim found Charlie.

'I haven't got long, Davis won't let me out of his sight,' Jim shouted into Charlie's ear. 'A couple found their way upstairs a moment ago. You've got to keep them down here, Charlie, for their own sake. There's a bunch of heavily armed men up there.'

'Armed?' Charlie looked worried. 'I'll do what I can Jim, but for Christ's sake, you keep that lot under control as well. 'The last thing we need is trigger happy gangsters starting a small war.'

The boat was picking up speed as it headed back towards the barge. The Millennium Bridge was already behind them and Southwark Bridge lay just ahead. Once they'd passed under the Cannon Street Railway Bridge, only London Bridge lay between them and the barge. Five minutes at the most.

'Listen to me, Charlie. When we passed the barge just now, which container was loaded first? The one at the Tower Bridge end, or the one at the other end?'

Charlie gave Jim a quizzical look and shrugged his shoulders.

'Does it matter?'

'Yes, I think it does. Which end?'

Charlie thought about it.

'The one at the Tower Bridge end.'

'You're certain?'

'I'm pretty sure. Why?'

'I want you to be near the container at the other end when this goes off.'

'Why?'

'Trust me, Charlie. I've got to go back up now.' Jim looked at his watch. 'We've got less than four minutes. When we approach the barge, Davis's men will come down here to get ready to jump across. Keep an eye out for them and remember I need you at the other end of the barge.'

Jim turned and made his way through the boozy crowd towards the stairs. As he did, a woman gyrated drunkenly over to him, grabbed his hand, trying to drag him onto the dance floor. He apologised and pushed her away. She took that as an insult and went to slap his face, missed, and spun round into the arms of another reveller, the insult already forgotten.

They were through Southwark Bridge. Next, Canon Street main line bridge.

Three minutes.

Jim stood on the upper deck where the men were still busy checking equipment and testing radio coms. He couldn't see Davis anywhere, then the wheel house door opened and Davis stepped out. He looked around and made his way over to Jim.

'I've just given the captain his instructions. We can trust him to do what's needed to be done. The rest is up to us.'

As the boat passed under Cannon Street Bridge, Davis turned to the other men and called them together for a final briefing. Jim was excluded and, because of the noise from the party below, he was unable to make out what was being said.

Two minutes.

Suddenly, the volume of the music was lowered and a hand mic switched on. After some howling of feed-back and the inevitable; '1-2, 1-2, testing' – Charlie's voice could be heard reminding the crowd to stay downstairs, the upper deck was for crew only. Thank you. The music got jacked way up again and the party roared on.

Up ahead and looming larger – London Bridge.

Davis reached into a sports bag, pulled out a walky-talky and turned it on.

'This is a test – confirm?' He was looking out across the river as he said this.

From somewhere, not on the boat, a metallic response. One word – quietly spoken.

'Confirm.'

A '*click*' ended the communication.

Davis turned to Jim.

'OK, this is it.' Then to the others.

'Stand by.'

One minute.

The Pride of the River entered London Bridge correctly to the right of centre. It was only as she came out through the other side that the iconic profile of Tower Bridge was revealed, illuminated brightly against the night sky. A small boat could be seen passing underneath the two cantilevered roadway sections. It was heading towards them. Immediately ahead, though, and getting closer, the black silhouette of the barge lying low on the water. A slumbering dark shape, rocking gently in the wake of the retreating tide.

The barge was still a little way ahead as the Pride of the River started to take a different track, veering gradually across the centre line of the river, putting the barge on its right hand side. To anyone on the barge this manoeuvre wouldn't draw much attention except that the boat would pass closer than usual.

At this time of night, there were plenty of similar tourist and party cruisers traveling up and down the river. One more made no difference.

Very close now, perhaps fifty yards. Davis brought the walky-talky back up to his lips and yelled a command to whoever was waiting across the river.

'Go, go, go.'

That was it!

***

For the men on board the barge, the assignment had turned into a trial of concentration. The soporific rocking of the vessel was making them a little drowsy. Not unpleasant on a warm evening like this, watching the world go by.

Most tourist boats do a short run: mostly from Westminster Pier, down to Tower Bridge, turn round, and back up to Westminster Pier, as regular as clockwork. A couple of guards spotted the Pride of the River coming back. Nothing unusual. Different song this time, 'I Will Survive' blaring out across the water. Who was it sang that now? Yeah, Gloria Gaynor. It was obviously the time in the evening when only classic disco hits will do. It was going to pass a bit closer than the other boats.

There was plenty of coffee. That helped. No toilet facilities as such, but peeing was a simple matter of standing on the side, balancing yourself against the rocking motion and – well – peeing!

One of them was doing just that, facing the south bank when, with an almighty series of bangs, the heavens lit up!

He just managed to save himself from falling in the river from shock.

The others were just as surprised and rushed over to join him. In the skies above them, a spectacular display of fireworks had begun, launched from behind buildings on the south bank of the river. An unexpected bonus on a boring evening.

***

As the Pride of the River glided in towards the barge, the music volume was lowered a little to allow for the closing distance. The noisy display was doing a great job of distracting the guards and smothering the sound of the engines.

Thirty feet...twenty...ten.

The squad of gang members had already gathered along the Starboard side, taking hold of railings and ironwork to steady themselves as they made ready to jump across.

The party revellers were split between those who wanted to know who these strangers were and what they were doing, and those who just wanted the music turned back up. Some strained to see the fireworks.

Jim deliberately took a place nearer the front of the boat. He knew Davis would be tagging him.

Just another five feet and then the river boat, its engines in reverse, gently kissed the side of the barge.

On the opposite side, unaware of what was happening behind them, the security guards were fully distracted, their attention focused on the free show – just as Jim had intended.

Back on the boat, as quietly as they could, the gang members jumped across and hid in the gaps between the containers.

Jim held back for a moment, watching how the men were dispersed as they leapt onto the barge. He felt Davis's gun pushing into his back.

Inside the boat, the revellers – too drunk to care – were giving Gloria Gaynor all their best moves. Jim didn't miss the irony of the title of the song.

'Hesitating, Stack? Last minute nerves?' he pushed the gun harder into Jim's ribs. There was a distinct metallic *snick-click* of a round being chambered.

'Do it Stack. Jump!' Davis was getting really pissed off.

He'd looked for Charlie but couldn't be sure if he'd made the leap across. Jim couldn't delay any longer. He jumped the short distance over to the barge. Davis followed.

They were at the Tower Bridge end. Just where he wanted Davis to be.

Davis flicked the coms switch.

'OK. Quietly, let's take them and use weapons only as a last resort. Confirm.'

A series of quiet grunts of acknowledgment came back.

***

The display didn't last long, but it was impressive. The guards had gathered in a group at the bow of the barge, enjoying the unexpected pyrotechnics show together. And then, slowly, they became aware that they weren't alone anymore. One of them had already turned round and started to raise his hands. One by one they each turned to see what it was had made him do that.

Crouching silently on either side, a bunch of aggressive looking men were staring menacingly up at them, weapons aimed squarely at their chests. The security guards stood there: hands in the air; a stupid look on their faces; and one question on their mind – where the hell did they come from?

The gang pushed the guards over to where Davis was waiting, checked them for weapons, and forced them down on to the rusty steel deck at the front of the barge, hands secured behind with plastic ties. The guard tally matched what they had seen on the thermal imaging – four men. They didn't have much to say for themselves. What could they say?

The Pride of the River had already pushed off and was heading back towards Tower Bridge, continuing its journey as though nothing had happened – music louder than ever. But heading towards them now, what had seemed from a distance to be a small boat, turned out to be a large tug with men standing-by on the bow ready to throw a hawser across to the barge.

Davis's plan was to tow the barge down river and vanish it from sight. They'd only need a few hours to strip the gold out and carry it away. A trick that would test the abilities of Las Vegas illusionists, Penn and Teller, if they pulled it off.

Davis sent two of his men to stand guard further back down the vessel, one on each side. Another two helped the tug crew with the hawser. The remainder stayed with him.

'So, let's see what a container full of gold looks like,' Davis said. 'Cut that lock off.'

One of the men reached into a bag and brought out an industrial bolt cutter. He placed the thick steel 'U' of the lock between its jaws and heaved the long handles together with all his strength. The lock eventually broke and fell to the rusty floor plate with a clang.

Davis grabbed the handle on the container door and pushed it up, releasing the pins at the top and bottom. The steel door swung open a little.

'Stand back,' Davis commanded.

There wasn't much room between the container and the side of the barge to allow the door to open fully, but it was enough of a gap for a man to slide sideways through.

'Hand me a torch.'

He squeezed through the gap and disappeared into the darkness. Jim took the opportunity to have a quick look for himself. It was a sight he'd never forget. The torch light reflected off of the bars of bullion, filling the interior with caustic ripples of golden light. He could live a thousand years and never see this much gold again.

Davis was just inside the container by the doors, playing the torchlight through the spaces between shelves, checking how many racks there were.

'Four,' he said as he stepped back out, still mesmerised by the vision. 'Four racks stacked four pallets high.'

It was clear that even unimpressible New Yorker, Mike Davis was shaken by the scale of wealth it represented.

'That's sixteen tonnes of gold,' he said in almost child-like wonder.

Jim wondered why there were only four racks when they could have put five or six inside. *It must be to do with the weight the container can hold*, he guessed. He looked down the line of boxes and counted. Why hadn't he noticed before? There were only six, nowhere near a full capacity for this barge.

They were all taking their turn to look inside now. Davis was fully distracted and eager to move on to the next container which was soon unlocked and doors swung open as far as they would go. Jim was on the other side of the door, hidden from Davis. This was his chance to find Charlie.

He slipped away down the barge towards one of the guards Davis had posted. It was that big east European bastard, Grigori. Jim started making small talk with him about how amazing it was seeing all the gold in the container. Grigori should go and see for himself.

Grigori started to push past Jim to go look, but then remembered the debacle back at the hotel. He was still in the dog-house. Better stay put.

Well, that didn't work, so Jim checked to see that he was still hidden from Davis and the others further down the barge and then took an almighty swing at the big man. It rocked him but he recovered quickly with an angry grunt and pushed Jim back into the gap between two containers. Jim stumbled but managed to stay on his feet – just.

Grigori attempted to rush him, but his muscle bound shoulders jammed in the narrow gap. Jim ran forward, head low and rammed into Grigori's stomach. That didn't do much good. The big man turned sideways and started crabbing towards him.

Jim backed away down the length of the container until he burst out into the narrow space on the other side. Not good! He might have to take on two of them now. He had time for the quickest of looks but the other heavy didn't seem to be around.

Grigori finally made it out through the gap, his momentum and height carrying him hard against the side of the barge, almost toppling over. Jim tried to help him on his way, but Grigori grabbed Jim's shirt. If Grigori went over, he was taking Jim with him. The heavy pushed his foot against the container and managed to lever himself back up enough to turn and grab Jim's throat in an iron grip. Swing at him as he may, Jim's fists couldn't make a decent contact with the gangster's massive, steroid enhanced body. He kneed him in the groin as hard as he could and although Grigori grunted, his hands stayed where they were – fastened around Jim's neck. Jim tried stamping on his feet and slammed another knee into his undercarriage. The guy must be made out of concrete, he just tightened his grip.

Jim's strength was failing him – his legs were starting to give way. Grigori looked straight into Jim's eyes, sneering triumphantly – he knew he had him. If the goon put him on the ground it would be all over. He couldn't last much longer.

Then a loud crack, like metal on bone. Grigori's grip relaxed and he leaned heavily against Jim as he slid slowly down to the deck. Behind him, still holding the iron bar, stood Charlie.

'I did the other one on me own,' he said cheerfully.

'Good man, Charlie,' Jim said breathing heavily. 'Help me get this sod over the side.'

They struggled with the dead weight, but eventually he slipped over and into the river, face up and moving sluggishly. The river current quickly carried him away towards Tower Bridge.

'Come on, let's see if I've guessed right,' Jim said in a hushed voice.

They had to step over the legs of the other guard who had fallen between two boxes. He was moaning quietly after the blow from Charlie's iron bar, but looked like he was out of the game for the time being. Moving quietly, they reached the last container and hid behind it as Davis and his crew moved on to box number three. Once again, the heavy duty lock was cut apart and the doors pulled open, providing a shield for what Jim hoped would happen next.

Invisible to Davis and his crew, Jim stepped around to stand in front of the container doors. There was no lock, a strong indicator that this container was different. He pulled the latch up and gently eased the doors open as quietly as he could. Inside there were no racks of gold, just pitch black darkness.

And then there was blinding light as torches were switched on and the dangerous end of six MP5 automatic weapons rushed forward out of the dark interior and thrust into Jim's face. A SWAT team of Specialist Firearms Officers in full black battle kit. Jim's reaction was to say one word.

'Deakins?'

There was some shoving from being the men.

'OK, let me through,' DCI Deakins said as he came forward, pushing the guns aside.

'You sent the envelope?'

'Yes,' Jim whispered. 'Come on, round the back, quietly.'

He put his finger to his lips then pointed the direction round to the side of the container, out of sight. They gathered at the back of the barge in the shadow of the container.

Two of them needed a pee urgently. Anywhere would do.

'Over there, there's no one on that side.' Jim said.

'How did you know we'd be here?' Deakins whispered.

'I figured that as you didn't arrest Avery last night you were up for my plan,' Jim said. 'And this container was your best way in.'

'So, where are we up to? We heard everything, but saw very little, even with the endoscope camera we poked through holes in the container.'

'There are six bad guys left and three of those are just down there behind those container doors. Be careful, they're armed.'

'Don't worry, I'm staying back here. This is Sergeant Bradbury, he'll take charge now.'

Bradbury and the others gathered around Jim and listened as he quickly gave them the headlines.

'Best approach is from the other side, there's only one man there and he's out cold for the time being. You could work your way between the containers or go round and up behind them. Just one thing. There's a tug at the other end tying up, getting ready to tow this thing away. That's where the other two gunmen are.'

Jim turned and snuck a quick look around the corner of the container. The door was still open down at the third box.

He motioned Bradbury to come over and check it out.

Just then, the door was pulled closed and Davis and his crew started moving up to the next box. There was only one container between them now.

Jim put a hand up to signal quiet, then pointed to his ear for them to listen. It only took a moment and there it was, the hard snap of hardened steel breaking and a noisy clang as the heavy duty lock fell to the steel decking.

Bradbury understood.

A metallic wrenching sound as the doors were pulled open. Jim checked again, so did Bradbury. Good, Davis's mob were hidden behind the door again.

Bradbury had a quick confer with his squad, then turned to Jim and Charlie.

'OK, you two stay here. Nothing for you to do now. DCI Deakins, you'd better call the others in. By the time they get here, if we haven't taken the bad guys, we should be keeping them very busy.'

Deakins buttoned his radio.

'Gold Rush is go. Repeat. Gold Rush is go,' he whispered urgently.

A brief static 'shush' and then a tiny metallic voice.

'Copy that. Gold Rush is go'

Jim remembered the security guards and asked Bradbury to watch out for them at the far end of the barge.

All but one of the squad slipped away silently. The one who remained stationed himself at the corner of the container, just out of sight, his firearm ready.

Jim didn't think this was going to take very long, he could already see the tell-tale white spray of fast boats coming out of the dark on both sides of the river.

Distraction, that's what was needed now. He told Charlie to wait.

'Why? Where are you going?'

Jim didn't reply, he just whispered to the officer to be ready, walked round the corner and down to the open container door blocking his way.

He pushed it forward so that he could squeeze past and join Davis and the two mobsters. Davis hadn't missed him.

'That's another sixteen tonnes. Sixty-four tonnes so far.'

He glanced at the remaining two containers.

'It doesn't look like there's anything like the amount you thought was in the vaults,' Davis said with a sneer to Jim.

Jim noted how quickly Davis had moved on from 'awesome!' to 'unimpressed.'

'OK, let's open the next one.'

They walked the few paces down to the fifth box. The jaws of the box cutters bit the lock off and, just as he'd done with the other four containers, Davis pulled the door open hard against the side of the barge.'

Two things happened. Davis was shocked to see not sixteen tonnes of gold as before, but a single rack. A mere four tonnes.

'What the..?'

'That's sixty-eight tonnes,' Jim said, as surprised as Davis.

'Yeah, where's the rest, Stack?' Davis said turning to Jim. 'Is that it...?

His next words were drowned by the sound of gun fire coming from the bow.

He reacted instinctively, ducking behind the steel door and reaching for his hand gun. The two heavies had already started to run down the length of the narrow gangway to see what was happening, holding their Spectre sub-machine guns forward and ready for trouble as they went. That's when Jim grabbed Davis, dragging him into the space between the containers....and into a SWAT officer's semi-automatic held at waist height. Davis turned back to face Jim.

'You bastard!'

He raised his gun, swivelled back quickly and shot the officer in the chest. The impact sent the policeman flying backwards. As he fell, his finger pulled on the trigger. A burst of fire sprayed up against the side of the container sending bullets ricocheting off the steel in all directions. The noise was deafening.

Ducking to avoid stray rounds, Davis turned back and pushed his gun hard into Jim's face.

'Where did they come from? How many are there?' He was pissed-off and desperate.

Jim pleaded ignorance. Davis wasn't buying. He turned Jim around and pushed him back out into the narrow gangway along the side of the barge, using him as a shield.

Sporadic single shots and bursts of semi-automatic fire could be heard from all around the barge. And there was another noise coming from the river and getting louder. Davis looked out over Jim's shoulder. Just fifty yards away a police RIB, rigid inflatable boat, was bearing down on the barge at high speed. On board were several heavily armed men – weapons up and ready.

Davis pushed Jim down towards the tug, checking the spaces between the boxes. If he saw something, he fired, no matter who it was. Everyone was expendable now.

Down at the bow, a small war had broken out.

The sudden sound of automatic gunfire caused the captain to put the engines into reverse in an attempt to draw the tugboat away, but the thick steel cable tied to the barge prevented anything more than a few metres of movement. One of the mob managed to leap across the widening gap and throw himself down behind the gunwale on the stern of the tug. He lay there, automatic weapon ready, firing whenever a target showed. Another gangster hid behind the bollard on the bow firing pot shots with a hand gun. The bollard didn't provide complete cover and return fire kept him pinned down on both sides.

The tug crew tried to release the towing hawser from the tug's winch, but the cable had been pulled taught around the slowly turning capstan in the panic of the firefight.

A couple of the SWAT team managed to get close enough to fire warning shots over the tug from behind a container. The whining and ricocheting of rounds caused the winch crew to drop down to the deck, leaving the powerful winch still operating and pulling the tug slowly back towards the barge. The captain was shouting hysterically out of the wheel house window to turn the bloody winch off, as several rounds hit the steel window frame, spraying him with paint fragments and sparks.

Further down the barge, a shooter, hiding between containers, was firing automatic bursts at the two officers, preventing them from moving further forward. He was finally taken out by the one of the squad on the RIB boat coming in from the north side. The RIB boat reduced speed, came alongside, and the three fully armed officers leapt onto the barge. They were immediately pinned down by bursts of Spectre SMG rounds fired by another mobster who'd climbed up onto one of the boxes.

Meanwhile, on the floor between the first container and the bow bulkhead, four terrified guards were lying as low as they could to avoid being hit by stray bullets. Lying on the deck next to them, a wounded officer was using his coms to provide Intel to the other SWAT team members. Being low on the deck behind the bulkhead, there wasn't much to see forward, but he could see the shooter on top of the container behind him.

Davis had his arm round Jim's neck and his gun planted firmly against the back of his head, pushing him forward down the alley between the boxes and the side of the barge.

Behind him, moving slowly forward with his MP5 semi raised and sighted at Davis's back was the officer Jim had left behind with Charlie. He shouted a warning, but Davis simply turned round and put Jim's body between him and the MP5. He continued walking backwards using Jim as a shield until he reached the first container at the bow end. He ducked quickly around it, pulling Jim with him.

Now, all that lay between him and freedom was a short jump over to the tug which was now pushing hard against the bow of the barge by the pull of the hawser trapped in the tug's winch. The intense strain vibrated the multi-stranded steel cable like a fat, over-tuned piano wire, sending a fine spray of water into the air, soaking everyone on the deck of the tug.

The gunman taking cover behind the bollard was getting nervous about the stress the hawser was putting on the bollard's deck mountings – he could see what was coming. The tug's engines gave another sudden heavy push against the pull of the winch, causing another powerful shudder. The noise of the solid steel bollard straining against its rust encrusted bolts freaked him out so much that he rolled away, instantly taking a round in the side – his gun sliding across the deck to drop soundlessly against the shrieking noise of the overburdened machinery, into the water.

Near the back of the barge, lying between the containers, the first guard on the receiving end of Charlie's iron bar was starting to recover. Like the other mobster, he was a big guy with a thick skull. He raised himself painfully to a standing position and checked his 9mm hand gun. Ahead of him, towards the front of the barge, he could see the dark profile of one of the SWAT officers as he leaned out from between the containers to take a shot at a forward target. The mobster started moving slowly down the gangway, gun raised, waiting for the officer's back to appear again.

Up on top of the first container the shooter fired a steady volley of shots at another RIB boat standing off on the northern side, forcing the three officers to keep their heads down. Returning fire was a problem. Stray rounds fired up from their position low on the water could arc all the way over to the opposite bank – risking collateral injuries. But the distraction allowed Davis a chance to climb over the steel barrier that formed a collar around the barge and up onto the bow bulkhead. Jim was still on the main deck a foot or so below with Davis's arm firmly gripped around his neck causing him to bend backwards awkwardly over the bulkhead.

The SWAT officer stalking Davis now appeared from behind the container, his gun aimed and ready, though with Jim still being held as a shield, there wasn't much of Davis to safely hit. Back on the tug, the other gunman shouted from behind the gunwale that he'd cover Davis as he jumped across – his voice just audible above the tortured screech of the winch.

The distance between the tug and the barge kept varying a metre or two as the tug's powerful engines vied with the winch machinery for supremacy.

Davis waited till the tug was at its closest, then shouted 'Now!' The hoodlum started firing wildly in the direction of the SWAT team as Davis leapt across, leaving Jim standing in the open, vulnerable and in the way of a clear shot. The SWAT officer motioned with his gun and shouted for Jim to get out of the way, but Jim waited for moment, turning to check where Davis was before dropped to the deck plates.

As Davis ran across the deck of the tug towards the wheelhouse, the RIB boat on the south side manoeuvred for a position thirty feet off. Officers fired several rounds, but the random bobbing of the little boat caused the shots to go wild, missing Davis, who finally made it to the protection of the tug's superstructure. He quickly climbed the steep steel stairs up to the bridge. The captain turned, but Davis was on him, gun pushed hard against his head.

'Get me to land. Anywhere. Now!' It was a loud and deadly threat, shouted above the noise of the screaming winch gear and the thundering marine engines.

'We're not going anywhere until someone turns that bloody winch off.'

'So? Tell someone to turn it off. Now'

'They've all got their heads down, out of the way of the shooting.'

'I'll shoot those bastards myself if they don't do it.'

On the barge the officers started to inch their way forward towards the bow and their fallen comrade. They pressed themselves hard against the sides of the containers, firing pot shots at the shooter above them who was now forced to stand up for a better angle.

Further back the SWAT officer started to move forward, ducking between the boxes as he went. Behind him, gun raised waiting for a clear shot, the gangster followed. The officer ducked out from between a container one more time, his whole body in clear view. This was an easy shot. The mobster raised his gun. He couldn't miss.

The tug's engines and winch were an equal match, pulling and winding against each other like a titanic tug-of-war. The friction between the jammed cable and the juddering rotation of the capstan created clouds of oily, choking smoke, but still the thick steel hawser held its grip as firmly as ever. Something had to give.

Eventually, unable to able withstand forces that went far beyond its load bearing tolerances, strands of steel threads started to snap and unwind, making the cable thinner and weaker, causing even more strands to stretch and separate, until, with the sound of a high-explosive charge, it broke apart, sending a two inch thick, fifty foot length of hi-tensile steel cable whipping in a high arc across the transom of the tug and over the barge with the speed and sound of a crack of thunder.

The barge, having been pulled hard against its mooring buoy for so long, shot back two metres, causing the shooter on the container to lose balance. The cable whipped past, narrowly missing him by a centimetre, the wind pressure blasting him the rest of the way out into the water.

The first two containers took the full force of the cable as it came down and smashed into them, slicing through the corrugated steel boxes, splitting them apart. Such was the force of the impact, several heavy gold bars were hurled high into the air, coming down to land noisily on the top of containers and the steel decking of the barge below. A couple of splashes marked a watery grave for some of the golden treasure. Lost forever in the thick mud at the bottom of the river.

The noise of the explosion and the sudden jerk of the barge caused the gangsters shot to go wide. Like the shifting ground in an earthquake, he had to steady himself against the unexpected motion. He raised the gun again, quickly, while the SWAT officer was still an easy target. He didn't understand what happened next. One minute he was arm raised and gun aimed. The next, the gun had fallen out of his hand and his arm hung limply at his side. Then he was overwhelmed by the most intense pain. The shock caused his legs to give way and he fell to the deck alongside the ingot that had dropped from the sky and taken him out.

Freed from the cable, the tug was already quickly motoring away, a RIB boat speeding after it.

On board the barge, officers rushed over to attend to their wounded colleagues, while others checked for any other remaining members of the gang. They found the officer shot by Davis lying on the deck between two containers. Although he'd taken a point-blank hit in the chest, his vest took the force of the impact, leaving him with a large and painful bruise. A gangster found slumped against a box further back, simply gave himself up. He was holding his shoulder at an awkward angle and in terrible pain after the blow by a twenty-eight pound bar of gold.

At the back of the barge, DCI Deakins received a quick 'all clear' on the radio from Bradbury, so he and Charlie moved down to the bow of the vessel for a first look at the aftermath of the firefight.

'So, that's it? All over?' Deakins asked when he saw Bradbury.

'Yeah, it got a little tricky there for a moment,' Bradbury said. 'Two got away on the tug, but our guys are on to it. They won't get far.'

Deakins turned to Jim. He had a few questions – he kept it to one.

'What should I do with you, Mr. Anonymous? On the one hand you obviously had some involvement in this. On the other, you handed it to me on a plate. I don't know whether to arrest you, or thank you.'

'There are two things you can do. One is go and arrest Victor Avery.'

'And the other?'

'Get Charlie and me off of this barge as soon as possible.'

Eric Deakins thought about it for a moment while he assessed the scene around him: the four guards were now free from their bindings; an officer was attending to a wounded colleague; another was giving first aid to the injured gangsters. From the whimpering and blood soaked arm, the one who took the blow from the gold bar was the most seriously injured. A couple of officers had started picking up the scattered bullion, stacking the heavy bars in one of the containers.

He turned back to Jim, decision made.

'Follow me.'

They walked around the busy SWAT team and eased along the narrow ledge on the north side of the barge to where an RIB boat had tied up, the driver standing by, awaiting orders.

'Officer, I need you to take these two...' he stopped as he realised Jim was on his own. 'Where's Dawson?'

As he said it, Charlie reappeared next to Jim.

'I left my back-pack back at the other end of the barge,' he said sheepishly.

Deakins continued.

'So, which side do you want to be taken to?'

'South side.'

'Take these two over to the south bank as quick as you can.'

'Just a minute,' Jim said. 'Charlie, I need that note now.'

Charlie nodded. He'd taken the back-pack off after he'd jumped onto the barge. He was carrying it by the straps now. He placed it down on the deck, rummaged for the note and handed it to Jim.

'This is the original hand written strategy from Victor Avery.'

He handed it over to Deakins.

'There's more. My name's James Stack. If Avery tries to claim his innocence, and you can be sure the slimy bastard will try everything, then you'll need this.'

Jim took his phone out of his pocket, popped the back cover off, extracted the SD card and handed it over to Deakins.

'Don't lose this. There's a set of audio recordings that implicate Avery in a crime that happened several years ago. Listen to it as soon as you get a chance. I think you'll be interested to know why.'

Jim gave Deakins a brief account of the Metro Metals scam, his part in it, and the prison sentence he served as a result. A sentence Avery had yet to receive.

'The history is all there in the records. Check with the SFO.'

A helicopter was coming in from down river. Though still a little way off, the noise of the blades was making it harder to hear.

'Is that it?' Deakins said above the noise.

'Pretty much,' Jim said as he climbed over the side of the barge and down into the RIB boat.

He leaned across and offered his hand up to Deakins who hesitated for a moment before reaching out and taking it grudgingly. He gave Jim a quick, almost imperceptible, nod of thanks.

Then Charlie boarded clumsily, his back-pack swinging heavily in his hand. The little craft lurched causing him to stumble and fall awkwardly against the driver. He apologised with a feeble joke.

'I think I'm going to need a bigger boat, mate.'

'For Christ's sake, Hollywood,' Jim groaned.

As the RIBs engines revved up and the mooring line slipped, Deakins had a final thought.

'How did you get them to take the gold out of the vaults?' he shouted above the noise, his hands cupped to his mouth. The boat began to move away as Jim shouted a reply, but Deakins struggled to hear against the noise of the RIB engines and the blades of the chopper above him.

The RIB didn't hang around. It took off at high speed across the dark water, through London Bridge towards the lights of the southern embankment. Behind them, the helicopter was coming down to hover noisily over the barge, its brilliant halogen searchlight illuminating the retreating scene.

DCI Deakins watched them go. He wasn't sure if he'd heard correctly, but it sounded like Stack had said "Goldfinger". What the hell did that mean?

He glanced up into the bright light hovering noisily above him, then pulled his mobile out of his pocket and speed dialled Sergeant Yates's number. He had to put his finger in his ear to hear, but Yates eventually answered.

'Is Avery still inside the Bank of England?' he shouted. The down draft from the chopper was blowing a gale around the deck.

Yates confirmed that he was.

'It's all over here. Wait for me there, I'll be ten minutes. Don't let Avery leave, just keep him under observation.'

This was the big arrest he'd been waiting for all his life and there was no way he was going to miss it. He sat on the side of the barge waiting for the RIB to return, a grin on his face for the first time in a long time.

How Sweet It Is

The flight was smooth and luxurious.

The Cessna Citation business jet was heading west out of Biggin Hill Executive Airport, where Jim and Charlie had boarded it, leaving London and the stress of the last forty-eight hours far behind.

***

Two hours earlier, they had been on the RIB boat moving fast and bumping hard against the wake of other boats, as they headed towards the south bank of the river Thames.

'What about the gold?' Charlie said.

'What?' Jim shouted above the roar of the twin 300 horse power Mercury engines.

'The gold, how much was there in the end? It didn't look like three hundred and sixty tonnes to me.' Charlie yelled.

Jim leaned into Charlie to make himself heard.

'You're right. There was only sixty-eight tonnes on board.'

'What happened to the rest of it then?'

'That's a very good question. Maybe they couldn't get it out of the vaults in time. We may never find out.'

Charlie shrugged indifferently as the RIBs engines slowed and the craft approached a flight of stone steps leading up to the embankment concourse above. They timed the jump across to the first dry step and made their way up. The concourse was lined with cafes, restaurants, and bars, all of them busy with tourists, even at this late hour. None of them seemed aware of the drama that had just taken place out on the river.

Being pedestrianized for most of its length, private cars aren't permitted access, but waiting nearby was a short, smartly dressed man. He nodded an acknowledgment and walked over to them. Jim and Charlie introduced themselves. The man explained that he'd been told to look out for a boat approaching from the river, but he wanted to be sure that they were who he'd been instructed to meet.

He introduced himself as Barry, a chauffeur to a business associate who had been asked to get them to Biggin Hill airport as quickly as possible, so if they wouldn't mind following him to the car. As soon as they were seated in the back of the Jaguar XJR, the chauffeur passed a mobile phone over to Jim.

'I was asked to hand this to you as soon as you were in the car. It's already set up, so just press the green button and it will dial the number, sir.'

Jim had been expecting something like this. He green buttoned the phone and waited. Three rings later.

'Hello, Mr. Stack.' It was Blackstone.

'Is Summer safe?' Jim's urgent first thought.

'As far as I am aware she is safe and on her way. Everything went as arranged. My dealings with Victor Avery are now satisfactorily concluded and you are a wealthy man.'

Jim breathed a sigh of relief, he didn't dare believe this day would finally come.

'That's very good news.'

'I'm impressed by the way you've handled yourself, Mr. Stack. I rarely involve others in my business affairs, but in your case I would like to make an exception. If you agree and something appropriate comes along, perhaps I could ask you to make your services available again? That is, you and your colleagues'?'

'*An offer of work?*' Jim thought to himself. *To hell with that. This was the last of it. No way would he get involved in this kind of madness again.*

'I'll put it to the others,' Jim said instead. 'You never know.'

'Well, perhaps you'll hear from me one day. Goodbye, Mr. Stack.'

As before, the call ended perfunctorily. And that, Jim hoped, would be the last time he heard from Blackstone.

It took thirty minutes, heading south down the A23 through Croydon before turning left along the A232. Eventually, Biggin Hill was reached through smaller roads that wind through the Kent countryside. During the journey, Jim noticed Charlie giving him a quizzical look.

'That was some distraction ploy Jim, you walked straight into Davis's arms. What was that all about?' Charlie knew that his old army boss didn't do 'stupid'.

'There's a small mess that needs to be cleaned up and Mike Davis is the man who has to do it. As much as I didn't like the guy, I had to help him get away.'

'What mess?'

'Gerry Conners,' Jim said. 'The bullion job has gone down the toilet and Conners' job as boss of the London operation will follow it down into the sewer. It was pretty obvious Davis was sent to London to keep an eye on him. The New York bosses have known for some time Conners was planning some freelance business for himself and they'd had enough.

It was going to go bad for Conners whether or not the Goldfinger heist failed. I wanted to make sure Davis got away to get that bit done. I wouldn't want to be Gerry Conners right now.

'Very complicated,' Charlie said. 'But why is what happens to Conners important?'

'He is a direct link to us. A loose end.'

'Remind me not to piss you off, Jim.'

'Sorry, Charlie, I've been making this up as I go along. But the Goldfinger plan was never meant to succeed. It was just a gold plated con. I was surprised it got as far as it did.'

'So you always intended the Goldfinger job to fail, why the hell was that? Or will I regret asking?'

'Victor Avery,' Jim said. 'I wanted to make sure that bastard goes down for a really long time. Although I had recorded evidence of his involvement in the Metro Metal scam, I was worried that he'd still manage to escape justice somehow. He's a very well connected and resourceful man. But he's also greedy. I'd blackmailed him into taking part in the Goldfinger job, that's true, but he was also going to earn big time out of it, or so he thought.'

'But I thought you'd agreed twenty percent of the take with Gerry Conners?'

'Charlie, Conners was never going to give us the twenty percent. He wanted to keep it for himself to fund a private scheme he had in mind. That's what pissed-off the New York bosses when they found out.'

'So all that effort – all that risk – was for nothing, Jim,' Charlie said despondently.

Jim turned to him.

'Yeah, well. Cheer up, Hollywood, it's not over yet.'

Charlie had worried about getting stopped by the UK Border Agency, but in the end, getting through passport control turned out to be just a formality.

Even so, it didn't make the departure at the executive airport any quicker. They had to endure a nervous hour and a half of hanging around as flight plans were lodged and approved. Both Jim and Charlie worried that despite DCI Deakins agreeing to let them go, at any moment, cops would rush into the executive lounge and arrest them.

Eventually, though, at about two a.m., they were escorted out onto the floodlit apron where the sleek jet aircraft waited, its engines already spinning up. One of the flight crew showed them to the short stair-case extending out under the small oval doorway. They climbed the four steps and entered a world of walnut and leather luxury.

Instead of the endless rows of cramped, tourist class seating they were used to, this aircraft had eight large leather executive sofas and plenty of leg room. The interior was smaller, though. So what? They had it all to themselves for the next eight hours, and Jim intended to sleep the whole way.

It was just a few minutes after they'd reached cruising altitude that Charlie reached down for his back-pack, lifted it up and dropped it heavily onto the table in front of them.

'Guess what?' he said cheerfully to Jim who was dozing next to him.

'What, Charlie? For Christ sake I'm trying to sleep'

'I said, guess what?' As he was saying it he was rummaging in the bag, pulling something that must have been pretty heavy, free of the clothes it was wrapped in.

Jim watched him through half opened eyes. What Charlie placed on the table in all its golden splendour brought him fully awake. He sat bolt upright.

'Well, it was just lying around on the deck. I couldn't just leave it there could I? You never know who might nick it.'

'Jesus, Charlie you daft sod. How are we going to get that through customs when we land?'

'Do you know what, Jim? I don't bloody well care. If they take it from me I'll be left with what I had a couple of hours ago – nothing.'

Then Charlie said the only sensible thing that could be said at a moment like that.

'Fancy a drink?'

He went off and came back with a bottle of Champagne and a couple of glasses. The alcohol helped Jim relax enough to have another attempt at some shut-eye.

There was one delicious thought that crossed his mind before he fell asleep. He wished he could have been there to see Avery's face when he was arrested. Justice – there was no other word for it.

***

It was earlier in the evening when the first rumours started coming through of something happening out on the river. Rumours first, then certainty – the impossible was happening – the barge was under attack!

Avery had made himself busy all afternoon and into the evening, urging the staff to even greater effort in the vaults, even though he knew it was, of course, all pointless.

More people started to arrive, probably MI5 or Home Office. They didn't seem to be interested in him except to see how the search was going.

'No, no rogue bars had been discovered. They'd found nothing that looked suspicious. There was still time. Yes, they would keep searching.'

'A heroic and desperate effort' he called it. In fact the search provided the distraction he needed to blank out his own corrupt involvement.

It wouldn't be long, though, before someone wondered how they, whoever *they* were, knew the gold was out there on the barge. Who told them? And then heads would start to swivel his way. 'Victor,' they'd ask. 'Do you know anything about this?'

He couldn't hide the sweat on his forehead. The perspiration on his back that his shirt clung to. The clammy palms of his hands. The shortness of breath. A lie detector would nail him in seconds.

He kept bumping into one woman whom he hadn't seen before. He'd turn a corner, walk down a hallway, past an office and there she would be. She seemed friendly enough though. Must be a coincidence.

The annex to his office was, for the first time that evening, almost empty, just one person working at their desk. Avery walked past and into his private office. He didn't want any interruptions as he opened his lap-top and entered the URL of the bank in Luxembourg. It took a moment to come up. He checked his watch: ten-fifty. Time of day shouldn't be a factor, so he entered the account number. Seconds later, the page was displayed, it was just a blank portal containing no information, just two fields with a cursor blinking – ready for the first digit of the two private cyphers. Avery found the stored number on his iPhone and dialled it. The small phone screen quickly indicated a connection to the account. He entered the extension code, and on the lap-top, the first field filled automatically. He did the same for the second field, re-dialling this time from his Blackberry: it was important to keep both lines active. Code entered and the second field filled as before. Nearly there.

The next step might be tricky, but he believed that Blackstone wanted his money, so he'd be ready to play ball. He dialled a number using his desk phone. A very particular number that he hoped, was still active. It rang three times and a familiar voice answered.

'I've been waiting for your call, Victor.'

Two things alarmed Avery straight off. The use of his first name – Blackstone was never this friendly. And the fact he'd been waiting. How could he have possibly expected his call at this time?

'I've decided that it's probably a good time to unlock the funds in the Luxembourg account, Blackstone.' His voice a little too high, a little too nervous. He tried to bring it under control.

'I'm sure you would like to see a return on your investment, wouldn't you? It must be quite a sum by now.' He was talking too much. Far too chatty.

'So you've guessed about the third code have you, Victor?'

'Two codes won't open the account, so there had to be a third.'

'Well we can discuss why you would want to open the account without telling me on another occasion can't we, Victor? But right now you want me to enter my code, yes?' Blackstone was torturing Avery and enjoying every minute of it.

'Ah, yes. It's all set up. James Stack and I have entered our codes already. It just needs your cypher,' Avery couldn't see how Blackstone would know that Stack wasn't actually there.

Any minute now, he'd have his hands on a small fortune and the means to bury himself in some remote, and luxurious sanctuary far away.

Blackstone's code didn't show as a field, the portal suddenly opened onto the account page with its columns of figures showing the entries over the two years of the scam. There were no debit figures because, of course, Avery hadn't removed any money. He scrolled down to near the bottom of the second page. His eyes settled on the enormous figure that represented the sum of all the numbers that had gone before. His eyes grew large and his heart beat faster. It was so much more than even he had expected.

Then he scrolled down just one more row, and there it was. If retribution was a number, this was what it looked like.

The figure that had been in the credit column in the row above was now showing in the debit column. The entire account had been emptied. All that remained was a very long line of zero's.

He shouted into the phone.

'Blackstone!' His voice shaking with fury.

But the phone just went click, and once again he was left holding a dead line – his eyes transfixed to the financial devastation on the screen. He was so consumed by his misery that he didn't hear the woman's voice at first.

'Mr. Victor Avery?'

Was it that bloody woman? What was she doing in his office? He forced his head away from the computer screen and turned towards her, his face crimson with anger and frustration. It was her. The one he'd kept running in to. But she wasn't alone. Behind her – over by the door – two uniformed police officers were waiting.

It was the fat older guy standing at her side who spoke next.

***

Mike Davis used his mobile to call up a car while he was on the tug. There were several stone stairways built into the wall of the south bank near Tower Bridge. He forced the captain to bring the tug hard against the steps, preventing the police RIB boat from getting near as he jumped across, stumbling slightly, as he ran up and across to the main road where the car was waiting.

He jumped in and the car took off, heading north across Tower Bridge, turning west and disappearing into the maze of roads that lead to the West End.

Ten minutes later he slipped into the Montgomery, went up to his suite and made two calls. One was to book a first class seat on the next flight to New York, the Delta red eye at 6.20, just six hours way.

The second, was to arrange a replacement for Conners' office butler. The man usually employed would call in sick tomorrow morning. His replacement had been expecting this call. He too would be on a flight out of London later in the day.

***

The Cessna Citation swooped down towards the dark blue Caribbean waters just visible below in the early morning light. Ahead was the strip of lights that marked out the runway of Owen Roberts International airport at Grand Cayman.

Thirty minutes later, they had arrived at their hotel along West Bay Road, and were checking into their own luxury ocean-view suites. Charlie, with his usual ability to get by on sheer blind luck, still had the gold bullion bar – Customs had just waved them through.

The morning was already underway at the hotel and early risers were taking a stroll along Seven Mile Beach, the stunning stretch of white sand that separated the hotel from the warm western Caribbean Sea. They agreed to give it half an hour and then meet for breakfast.

Jim used the time to visit the hotel shops to replace the garish clothes Conners had given him twenty-four hours ago.

Breakfast was excellent and the next few hours were spent relaxing on the beach. Jim was disappointed that Summer wasn't already there at the hotel. What was keeping her? She hadn't called. Could something have gone wrong despite what Blackstone had said?

It was nearly lunchtime when they retired to a couple of stools at the straw roofed beach bar. Charlie was his usual jocular self and Jim tried to match his breezy mood, but it was becoming harder to do. Still no word from Summer. He was really starting to worry now.

The bartender was cheerful and attentive and asked what they fancied on such a beautiful day. Two beers. Why make it complicated?

'Two refreshing, ice cold beers coming up sir,' the bartender said. 'And what would the lady like?'

Jim turned and there she was. He had seen more gold in the last twenty four hours than most people knew existed, but here, standing next to him, was the one person who was more precious to him than all the wealth in the world – Summer.

They embraced and kissed for a long minute. Charlie coughed for attention. Summer extracted herself from Jim's arms, turned to Hollywood and kissed him on the cheek, laughing happily. Jim turned to the barman and ordered Champagne for the three of them. The best the house had to offer. If ever there was an occasion, surely this was it.

Summer's journey had taken over twenty hours and two connecting flights via Frankfurt and Miami which explained her late arrival. As for emptying the secret account in Luxembourg and moving it off-shore, everything had gone exactly as planned, and the total amount transferred to the Cayman Island account amounted to many millions of dollars, less Blackstone's share.

Jim promised Charlie a generous pay-cheque and the rest would be shared between Jim and Summer. In return, Charlie offered a share of his own private golden stash – if he could find a way to turn it into cash. Jim was a little more wary, warning Charlie to wait a while and be careful who he talked to about it.

They spent next few days un-winding in the warm tropical sun, drinking, eating and swimming. There seemed no reason why this new life in paradise shouldn't go on forever.

The story about the attempted Bank of England heist remained on the front pages of the locally available British newspapers for a few days. Victor Avery had been arrested with his fingerprints all over the scam. There seemed little chance of escape, plus some reports of an earlier fraud had come to light. The bleaker things got for Victor Avery, the brighter the sun shone for James Stack.

There was a little by-line in one of the newspapers about the unexplained death of the manager of the Montgomery Hotel and Casino. He was found in his office, slumped back in his chair, his shirt stained with coffee, a cup lying smashed on the floor. A possible gang-land connection was suggested.

They were all back at the busy, straw roofed beach bar late one afternoon after enjoying another untroubled Caribbean chill-out day; iced white wine spritzer for Jim, beer for Charlie, Champagne for Summer – when Jim's mobile started to ring.

They looked at each other, surprised at the unexpected intrusion. Jim shrugged, took the phone out of his pocket, hit the green phone icon and listened.

If you had the choice of any three words you'd like to hear, many people might choose those three little words that bring joy, happiness and fulfilment.

As he stared out across the white sand to the gentle surf of the warm Caribbean Sea, James Stack heard three familiar words he hoped he'd never hear again.

'Call this number.'

Epilogue

A few weeks earlier, a General Election had been held in the UK. The population, cheesed-off with the endless belt-tightening of the last five years by 'This Lot', made a collective decision to take a holiday from austerity and go for austerity-light offered by 'The Other Lot'.

They had made all kinds of promises about how they'd be able to reduce the 'eye-watering debt' without borrowing, higher taxation or deep spending cuts. Just a little nip and tuck here and there was all that was needed, they assured the voters.

Once firmly in office, the 'The Other Lot' became the new 'This Lot', and the first item on the shiny new Chancellor of the Exchequer's agenda was to finesse a sneaky sleight-of-hand. This involved a call to the Bank of England asking them to sell 300 tonnes of Britain's gold reserves. Well, they had done it before, so a precedent had been established. But this time it was worth four times the value – a very handy Twelve Billion dollars.

A few days later, when the barge was moored up in the middle of the Thames, it held every last drop of Britain's gold reserves – just 68 tonnes.

Chapter and Verse: *The song titles*

Coming up with song titles for each chapter was almost as tough as writing the book. The title has to convey the essence of the chapter, but the lyrics of the songs in most cases probably don't. There are a few chapter headings that defeated me simply because I ran out of time.

Take the Money and Run	Steve Miller Band
The Boys are Back in Town	Thin Lizzy
Watching the Detectives	Elvis Costello
Won't Get Fooled Again	The Who
Turning Tables	Adele
Thick As Thieves	The Jam
Telephone Man	Mari Wilson
Hello, I Love You,...	The Doors
Police and Thieves	The Clash
Double Agent	Rush
Owner of a Lonely Heart	Yes
Taking Care of Business	Bachman Turner Overdrive
With a Little Help from my Friends	Jo Cocker
Can't Get Enough	Bad Company
Double Back	Z Z Top
Street Fighting Man	Rolling Stones
Under Pressure	Queen
Running With the Devil	Van Halen
Tell Me Sweet Little Lies	Fleetwood Mac
The Master Plan	Oasis
Who Are You	The Who
I Want To Break Free	Queen
What's Going On	Marvin Gaye
The Final Countdown	Europe
Born To Run	Bruce Springsteen
Bad Moon Rising	Creedence Clearwater Revival
Heroes and Villains	Beach Boys
How Sweet It Is	Jnr Walker

ABOUT THE AUTHOR

After a lengthy broadcasting career, which included many happy years as a DJ on Radio Luxembourg, Mark Wesley enjoyed critical acclaim as a song writer and record producer.

Jingle composition and copy writing for radio commercials followed, but his early love of film making led him to launch the production company Mark Wesley Productions.

"BanGk!" was born from an idea originally for a crime caper movie. It was in the writing of the synopsis – the brief outline of the plot – that it became obvious a longer, more thorough draft was needed. This book – the full length novel of the story – is the result.

Printed in Great Britain
by Amazon.co.uk, Ltd.,
Marston Gate.